He'd broken the news to Martha at dawn as she stood on her head on the Afghan prayer-mat. When she'd finally climbed down, all she'd say was, 'Money is a reified mode of exchange, Simon.'

Please God, he prayed, say it was a bad dream. But God wouldn't oblige. It was no dream. There, tossed over the wicker chair and still sodden from the long, wet walk back from the casino, was the mohair suit he'd donned for the kill. There, too, mocking him from the dressing-table top were the cashier's stubs.

When he'd got his strength back, he'd struggle to the chemist and buy a ton of sleeping pills.

Dear Martha, he'd write. *Sometimes life gets too much and the decent thing is to bow out. Remember your study notes on euthanasia? Keep the hi-fi and the National Geographic magazines. Please return my library books. Good luck with your life. Sorry to leave you the washing-up.*

P.S. I've fed the cats.

She'd come back, find him stiff and cold. She'd fall to her knees and weep copious tears. She'd remember her last words to him with bitter regret and blame herself for being so heartless and insensitive.

In the Bees and Honey

Bob Shilling

CORONET BOOKS
Hodder and Stoughton

Printed and bound in Great Britain
for Hodder and Stoughton
Paperbacks, a division of
Hodder and Stoughton Limited,
Mill Road, Dunton Green,
Sevenoaks, Kent TN13 2YA
(Editorial Office: 47 Bedford
Square, London WC1B 3DP)
by Richard Clay Limited,
Bungay, Suffolk. Photoset by
Rowland Phototypesetting Limited,
Bury St Edmunds, Suffolk

British Library C.I.P.

Shilling, Bob
  In the bees and honey.
  I. Title
  823'.914[F]   PS3569.T4653

  ISBN 0-340-41424-3

this is for Gina

1

Some got their bungs in the Merc. Ricky was a dab hand at peeling off the readies while doing ninety down Park Lane and steering the car with his knees.

Others got their schmeers in restaurant toilets.

Schmeering in a public place required finesse. Finesse was Simon's province. At least, in Ricky's mind it was. For Simon had been to college.

Had Ricky been present in the loo of the Peking Duck, Richmond, on the first occasion Simon attempted to pass a bloke a schmeer, he might have changed his mind about the benefits of a college education. It was not a happy performance. In truth, Simon made a right pig's ear of it. For months afterwards he'd wake up at night in a cold sweat at the memory.

He only went and dropped the wad in the urinal.

There he was, standing at one stall, working hard at relaxing. On his right, long finished and playing for time, was Chris the Crisp, the jovial marketing boss of Britain's largest junk-food conglomerate. Behind them, another man finished drying his hands and left.

For a brief moment they were alone. It was now or never.

Simon reached into his inside pocket for the plump brown envelope. He was in the very act of handing it over when it caught the edge of the metal screen, slipped out of his grasp and fell to the bottom of the trough. At that moment, all the pipes flushed in unison. Under this small Niagara, the glue came instantly unstuck and the envelope burst open like a ripe seed-pod.

Banknotes sprang out.

Within seconds, a good few hundred quid had broken free and was floating away down the length of the trough on a frothy yellow tide of coughings and cigarette butts.

The marketing boss of Britain's largest junk-food conglomerate was at the door in a flash. He glanced back at the compromising evidence and suddenly broke into a rich guffaw. Any of the other blokes they'd got straightened would have been on their knees like a shot, fishing out the readies with bare hands. But Chris had class. He and Simon spoke the same language. They'd both been to public schools, though neither had heard of the other's.

'I'll say the prawn balls disagreed with you,' offered Chris generously.

'I'll be quick.'

'Quick? You'd better bloody not be.'

The moment he'd gone, Simon jammed a chair up against the door. He retrieved the soggy, reeking notes and dunked them in a wash-basin. Then, one by one, he held them under the hot air hand-dryer. Scottish fivers, rust-marked from the mattress springs. Bank of Ireland singles, covered with Gaelic scribbles. Tenners all dog-eared, folded, crumpled, defaced. Twenties, some used as scratch-pads for totting-ups and phone-numbers, others as dart-boards. One with a dubious watermark, another without a silver filament. All smelly, greasy, germ-infested . . . but *money*!

As he stood in that small lavatory, heedless of the hammering on the door and the gangland warfare going on in the Chinese kitchen below, Simon experienced a moment of sublime enlightenment.

The alpha and omega of it all was *money*.

Money, lucre, dough, ackers, readies, spondulicks, the folding variety. The secret of a happy life was to make enough of it not to have to go after it any more.

Holding the dry notes in a tight wad close to his ear,

8

he riffled his finger along the edges. In that sweet sound he heard the distant rustle of ball-gowns, he heard the purr of soft-throated motors and the whisper of breezes through palm trees.

Yes, money was what it was all about. And today he was already learning to launder the stuff.

Ricky lived rich. Four-hundred-guinea crocodile shoes. A Mercedes stretch-saloon. A designer suit pulled shapeless by wads of bills he'd cram into the pockets.

It had to be said that these trappings cost Ricky somewhat less than they would have cost Joe Public. The crocodile shoes were a liquidator's oversight. The Merc was a fire insurance write-off, rebuilt with parts cannibalised off the streets of Golders Green and reborn with a new face and a personalised number plate to discourage interest in its year of origin. And the suit was one of a consignment impounded by a shipping company against an unpaid Nigerian letter of credit.

But Ricky was not rich. He never could be

For two reasons.

One of these he was the first to recognise

'Some people murder people,' he would say. '*I* murder money.'

He would speak of murder in the same tone as Simon would speak of supper parties or watercolours. He'd been on pet-name terms with the Krays.

Truth to tell, Ricky didn't murder money, he *mass*-murdered it. Bundles flowed through his hands every week. If anyone he knew was short of a few bob, he'd give him a few quid. If a bill in a restaurant he liked came to a few tens of pounds, he'd leave a hundred. Doormen at clubs, hat-check girls, hotel porters, all would feel the press of a folded note in their palm as he passed.

The only thing he refused to pay was tax. Flatly. When the government outlawed all unions, sent the Pakis and the Nigs back home and made petrol a tenner a gallon to clear the rush hour on the Kingston bypass, *then* he'd pay his taxes. Gladly.

The second reason Ricky never could be rich bore upon a more sensitive subject. It was, in fact, the issue that had brought him and Simon together.

The status of Ricky's assets.

The Mercedes stretch-saloon with velour interior, air-conditioning, headlamp washers and driver's seat warmer was not precisely *his*. In fact, it belonged to a finance company who'd parted with twenty-six grand, taking it for last year's model as its log book purported. The engine number tallied, should any officious spy from the company care to check. So did the chassis number. Unless the officious spy had ultra-violet sight.

Ricky stood six-one in his stockinged feet and was built like a bruiser. He had a small scar over his eyebrow and his nose was crooked after being badly re-set during his National Service. He'd recently had his teeth capped, and for a while it looked as though he was wearing a boxer's mouth-guard. He'd agreed to pay the dentist a grand in readies to do the job; while they rucked over whether this meant a grand for each set, he went around with only the upper half done. A few weeks' heavy smoking, however, soon made top and bottom indistinguishable.

Ricky lived in a detached thirties' mansion in South London. The street, according to him, was known to all the world as Millionaire's Row, Norwood. The house had two car ports in front and enough ruched net curtaining on every window to make a chorus of can-can girls feel naked.

This was Ricky's home, but it was not exactly his own house. It was Beryl, his wife's, house. He had prudently put it in her name some years before.

The crocodile shoes, however, were his own. As was the designer suit. And a range of leisure clothes that could fit into the regulation size of attaché case approved by HM Prisons. His golf clubs were a trade sample (he'd persuaded a Korean manufacturer that he knew all the

10

Top People in British golfing) and he'd won his Rolex Oyster (or what he took for a Rolex Oyster) at a game of kaluki down the club.

He had nothing else to call his own.

For Ricky was a bankrupt.

Ricky and Simon had met one fine May morning, some months earlier. The circumstances of this first meeting were rather less than comfortable.

If anyone had told Ricky then that before the day was out he'd be teaming up with this wet-eared young ponce to do a deal, he'd have laid Beryl's house on it at a thousand to one against.

For one thing, Ricky Stone didn't like partners. For another, the boy was working for the Enemy.

2

'Richard Lawrence Stone?'

'Never 'eard of him.'

The door slammed in Simon's face. He checked the number against the file. Yes, it was 31 Green Lane, Norwood. He didn't yet know it as Millionaire's Row.

He rang again. A dog barked. The fifty-year-old prize-fighter he'd just confronted appeared to kick it quiet. Simon rang once again. The house chimed like an ice-cream van.

Ricky returned to the door, his dressing gown now open to reveal deep-crotch jockey pants hanging like a full bag of shopping. His lips protruded menacingly and a cord of spittle stretched and contracted between them as he spoke.

'Got an appointment?' he demanded.

'Steinman, Fothergill, Trelawney and Co . . .'

Ricky's face blackened and his eyes narrowed as he took in an Identikit of Simon's face. Steinman *et pals* were the liquidators who'd forced him into bankruptcy and jail. Six bleeding months, for a long-firm fraud! Course, he was innocent. Only circumstantial evidence. He'd defended himself actively in court. At one point he'd swung himself bodily out of the dock and given the prosecuting counsel a smack on the ear. Inside prison, he was the only man in his block not to earn any re-mission for good behaviour.

Simon took a step back. The man had only been out two days.

Suddenly Ricky turned and bawled indoors over his shoulder.

'Beryl, any geezer got an appointment?'

'You what, pet?' came a cigarette-rasping voice.

But Ricky didn't need the answer. He mimicked Simon's middle-class accent.

'No appointment, old boy. So tootle along now.'

'Mr Stone,' Simon persisted, 'there are creditors still anxious to trace . . .'

Ricky jabbed a finger at his face.

'What are them things?' he demanded.

'What things?'

'Them pink things sticking out the side of your boat?'

'My what?'

'Boat-race. Face. Didn't you go to school, or what? I mean your *ears*, you dumb bok. You got ears, or can you hear?'

'I heard you, Mr Stone, but as I was saying . . .'

'As *I* was saying, bugger off! And you tell Alfie Steinman from me I'll be wantin' that piece of money back. He'll know what I mean.'

Simon felt the compassion of comfortable superiority. This chap was typical of his kind: they could never distinguish what belonged to them from what belonged to their companies. The same applied to everyone else. When his firm went down the tube, he'd paid over all his money – the little he had left – to Steinman, Fothergill, Trelawney and Company. For him, that was the same as handing it over to Mr Steinman himself. Of course Mr Steinman hadn't touched a penny, *personally*.

Or so Simon thought at the time.

But this was not the moment for a lecture in accountancy. He had a job to do. He couldn't report leaving another premises without having managed to gain entry.

'Now look here,' he began again, 'I must insist . . .'

Ricky turned slowly round. Simon followed his eye.

In the centre of the hall, multiplied to infinity by pink glass mirrors, stood a large and handsome middle-aged woman. She leaned forward defiantly, like a siren on a prow of a ship. From the centre of her exaggerated bow lips drooped a cigarette, now more ash than tobacco. She wore a voluminous pink and purple house coat on top of what looked like a wedding dress. Her coppery hair shot out in all directions and from their puffy sockets her jet-black eyes blazed with fury. Against her front and not entirely hidden in the net and lace folds of the house coat, she held a longish, dark metallic object.

Ricky addressed her with mock weariness.

'Beryl, the boy don't understand English. 'Ere, gimme my gun.'

The woman reached out her hand. In it she held a pistol. The barrel glinted as it passed beneath the chandelier. Ricky spun the chamber. It sounded very loaded.

'I shoot trespassers,' he said.

'Yeah,' whispered Beryl excitedly from behind, 'he *shoots* trespassers!'

The hammer drew back.

Simon stood frozen to the spot. Then, very gradually, he backed away. He edged down the porch steps, down the crazy paving path, past the Mercedes stretch-saloon, never once daring to take his eyes off the small muzzle that followed his every step.

Suddenly he bumped into the gate post and leapt out of his skin. He'd been shot in the back! Turning around and clutching his briefcase under his arm, he bolted for his life. Twenty yards down the road he heard an almighty report and slumped against a blossoming cherry tree, waiting for the kick of pain. None came. It was the front door slamming.

But his car! It stood directly outside the house. Carefully and painfully, over an interminable length of time, he crawled in a half-crouch along the flanks of the other cars parked in the row. Finally he reached it. Worming his way inside, he fired it into life and shot out into the road like a cork from a champagne bottle. Within fifteen yards he'd winged a stationary lorry and ricochetted be-

14

tween a bollard and the kerb like a ball in a pin-ball machine. But he'd come out alive.

True, he'd never make it with Starsky and Hutch. Truer still, though he didn't know it yet, he wasn't even going to make it for much longer with Messrs Steinman, Fothergill, Trelawney and Company.

'An Englishman's castle,' said Ricky, slipping the chain over the door, 'is his hovel. Goes back to the Domesday Book. That's history, Beryl.'

He eased himself stiffly into a velveteen tasselled chair in the dining boudoir. Unconsciously he began scratching himself around the shopping bag area with the point of the gun.

'They got no bloody right,' he went on.

'They got no bloody right at all,' echoed Beryl, 'if you ask me.'

'Who's asking you?'

'No, but it's 'arassment. You paid your debt to society, pet . . .'

His glare cut her dead. She retreated behind the trellis-fringed counter that served to divide the kitchen from the dining area and busied herself stewing him a two-bag mug of tea.

Ricky put a cigarette in the corner of his mouth. Raising the gun so the barrel pointed directly at Beryl, he pulled the trigger. The hammer sprang back with a rasping noise and a short tongue of flame shot upwards out of the breech. He angled his head forward and lit the cigarette, then released the trigger to shut off the flame.

'Wild horses wouldn't have stopped *me*.'

'Nor guns neither.'

'I learned the hard way. On the knocker, right? 'Ere, doll, remember the old girl I got to buy *two* vacuum cleaners?'

'Right stitched her up, you did,' Beryl cackled.

'I did *not* stitch her up. Caveat emptor.'

15

'Yeah, and that too.'

Ricky looked at her, then looked quickly away. She'd been a right peach in her time. Never so much as looked at another man. One hundred and ten percent reem. Given him two lovely children, too. The girl, Angelina, now worked in the schmutter game; made bundles, went on fancy holidays, didn't drink, knew how to look after her looks. The boy, Kevin, was the tall, gentle giant type. Lived on Social and came home to get fed and have his clothes washed. Always reading some book or other – Marx and Trotsky and all that cobblers. Bleedin' foreigners, what had they got to teach us? If the boy thought Communism was so terrific, why didn't he fuck off to Russia? Why? I'll tell you why, Kev. Because life's better in the West. Who ever heard of anyone escaping to the *East*? You think they're queuing up at the wall in *West* Berlin?

Ricky inhaled heavily to calm himself. If he thought about Kevin any more he'd have to take a pill. The two of them had this ruck every time they met. Exactly the same ruck, with exactly the same lines and always ending in exactly the same way – Ricky, outmanoeuvred by words, barely restraining himself from delivering his smug, brainy son a poke in the face.

Why couldn't he have a son he could *understand*? A boy he could teach the *real* facts of life to? Not some intellectual poofter who lived off other people's graft. Kids these days didn't know what life was about. Take that lad Alfie Steinman had just sent along. Talked posh, but couldn't tell the time of day. What was the point of all this book education? Did they teach you in school how to get your foot inside a front door?

'The youth of this country . . . I dunno.' He sighed. 'The day they stopped National Service we should've legged it to Spain.'

'What, and get mugged in Torremolinos?'

'Beryl, money speaks all languages.'

'Yeah, and whose money, I'd like to know?'

'We'd have made do, doll. Hot countries, you don't

16

need all this crap. Kev's right: we live in a materialist society with too many possessions.'

'That's why they came and took back my lovely freezer, eh?'

'You'll have five of 'em, I promise yer. Soon as I'm straight.'

'You, *straight*?' Beryl cackled again, then broke into a fit of smoker's coughing.

'Told yer, cut down or you'll peg out.'

'Can't. It's me nerves. Livin' with Ricky Stone, Dream Merchant.'

She put his tea down on an onyx mat beside him and retired behind the trellis. She perched on a bar-stool and rolled the tip of her cigarette around the ash tray.

'Dreams is all some of us have got,' she said in a wistful tone. 'Think of all them lovely beaches, big hotels, swimming pools. Dancin' in the moonlight in bare feet. Skinny-dippin'. It ain't too late, is it, Rick pet?'

But Ricky was now absorbed in filling out a pools form. He didn't look up. He hadn't heard her.

He'd report the villain. He'd throw the book at him. An ex-con in possession of a firearm? That would put him back inside for a tidy while.

Simon drove angrily over Blackfriars Bridge to the security of the City and the gentlemanly villainy he knew.

He should have rugger-tackled him. Made a citizen's arrest.

A plane goes overhead. Simon looks up. The villain's gaze follows his. It's an old trick, but it works.

Wham! He hurls his briefcase in the man's face. He darts to the side as the gun goes off. A slug smacks harmlessly into the brickwork beside him. The woman inside screams.

Simon lunges forwards, heading the man in the solar

17

plexus. Knocks him backwards into the house. The gun flies free. It scuds with a dry clatter down the steps.

Simon spins round and flings himself on it. He rolls out of the way of Ricky's boot. But he has got the gun. He aims it with both hands, like Starsky, and barks a command.

'Freeze!'

The man surrenders. In the background, the woman weeps.

A car honked loudly behind him. The lights had turned green. Simon awoke from his reverie and drove on.

Twenty minutes later he was nosing the bonnet of the car down the spiral ramp into the basement car park of the narrow, Dickensian building which was the head-quarters of Steinman, Fothergill, Trelawney and Co.

As he passed, he looked at himself in the windscreen of Mr Steinman's Roller. It made him look thinner than ever: thin face, thinning fair hair, thin shoulders. Maybe they made the glass that way, so when you were driving along everyone outside looked poorer than ever. He puffed his chest out.

Then he caught sight of the chauffeur. The man had been bent over, buffing the back bumpers. He looked from Simon to the dented wings of his car, and winced. His hand flew to his side as if he'd been stabbed. Here was another man who confused the corporate and the per-sonal. Only, in his case, it was to cherish company prop-erty as his own. That was why he'd received two gold watches, three nominations for Man of the Firm and no less than seven commendations for Outstanding Service.

His scowl told Simon that Mr Steinman would be Hearing About This.

But events were to move too quickly for that.

Simon wrote his report, making a passing reference to Ricky's threatening behaviour, and sent it for typing. In the middle of the afternoon, he received a call from Upstairs. Mr Steinman would like to see him in the Partners' Room at five.

Alfred John Steinman had come a long way.

As Simon waited in the Partners' Room, he scanned the sepia photographs on the walls recording the dawn of the profession of Receiver and Liquidator. Scrolls and charters dating steadily back into those sooty days created the impression that Alfred Steinman stood at the end of a long line of pioneers who'd passed the mantle from father to son.

Alfred Steinman's father had been a peasant farmer in the Ukraine.

Alfred himself, escaping as a youth just after the war, had started life as an articled clerk, just like Simon. Unlike Simon, though, he'd seen opportunity in the relentless collapse of British industry and gone into the receivership business. Over the years, with a little help from a top PR firm, he'd reversed the public image of the profession. Receivers were no longer the scavengers of industry, but its saviours; no longer vulturous but virtuous. If proof were needed, there, in pride of place, hung the photo of the Duke of Edinburgh presenting Alfred Steinman with an Industry Award.

Simon took a felt pen out of his pocket and scribbled a Hitler moustache on the suave figure shaking HRH's hand.

Alfred Steinman sat in his office, separated from the Partners' Room by his secretary and the barrier of an unpleasant new perfume she wore. He stroked the lunch beneath the silk stretched taut over his stomach as he re-read the Brotherton lad's memo.

I'll be wanting that piece of money back.

19

The lunch momentarily hesitated on its circuitous downward passage. So, Ricky Stone was out. And that little incident hadn't been forgotten.

Money was a funny thing. It flowed like water in his business and, once in a while, somehow or other, he couldn't help getting his fingers wet. He often received inducements, but generally he'd send them back or, at worst, feed them down the line to his retinue. Cyril, his number two and sometime bodyguard, handled that side of things.

Generally. For he was human, after all.

God damn it, why had he had to choose Ricky Stone's little twenty-five grand schmeer to be human over?

He groaned to remember that time the previous year when a two-pound box of Black Magic landed on his desk. He could still see the semi-literate writing on the card.

'Roses are red, Violets are blue, Don't forget me, Cos I won't forget you. Signed, your pal Ricky.'

If it hadn't flashed across his mind how a gift of chocolates, certainly of the unexploding variety, was so unlike the Ricky he'd known off and on for the past twenty years, and had he not been sharp enough to notice that the cellophane had been opened and re-wrapped, and rather poorly re-wrapped at that, he might have passed the box on to Loretta, his leggy secretary of that particular month, and she would doubtless have mistaken the contents as a sweetener of a very different kind and taken it to be the proper gentleman's way of saying Thank You For The Memory.

He'd opened it. Where the chocolates should have been was a thick wad of those pink plastic envelopes, like rectangular condoms, in which banks sealed ready-counted wads of notes – fifty tenners to make a monkey, fifty twenties to make a grand.

There'd been nothing he could do for Ricky. The case was open and shut. The man had done the classic long-firm fraud: set up a clean little company, crammed

20

a warehouse with gear bought on long credit, sold it off quick, spirited the money away somewhere untraceable, then declared he was very sorry but he was going belly-up and he couldn't pay the creditors. Nothing exceptional in that. Half the high street grocery chains had started that way. But Ricky's problem was his obstinacy. He wouldn't admit to a fiddle. It seemed he genuinely believed he was the innocent victim of a frame-up. No-one else did for a minute. Certainly the jury hadn't.

Alfie bit at a manicured nail. Why hadn't he handed over the bribe, untouched, to Cyril and the boys? Better still, sent it back? Why, instead, had he slipped it into his briefcase and then – oh, what a *smart* idea! – nipped around the corner for an identical box, which he then presented to the leggy Loretta? He didn't need the money! And he certainly didn't need the aggro.

What could he do now when Ricky came after him? Deny it?

'Chocolates, what chocolates? Oh, *those*. Very kind of you. Gave them to my secretary. The girl has a terrible sweet tooth.'

No. That wouldn't wash.

Why, actually, *had* he done it?

On pay day a wise serf has three hands. Old Ukrainian saying of his dad's. There lay the answer.

Greed.

Alfred Steinman was greedy about everything. He loved food, silk underwear, women's skin, certain sexual practices, hair pomade, flattery, modern art – all in indecent proportions. He would never have one girl when he could have two, or three if they were on quantity discount.

He thought back to the gluttonies in his penthouse bedroom the night before . . .

Just then the intercom buzzed.

'Mr Brotherton is waiting in the Partners' Room, sir.'

He jerked back to the present.

'Better get it over with,' he muttered.

He rose. His lunch took a step towards its fate, the

21

secondary pleasure that food afforded a middle-aged man.

Greed. Yes, that was young Brotherton's trouble. The lad *just wasn't greedy*. He was the sort who'd find a fiver on the pavement and hand it in to a copper. Worse still, if he saw someone pocketing the fiver, he'd *tell* the copper. How could you run a business with a liability like that?

Now the boy had been talking to Ricky Stone. He clearly knew too much. And that was a liability Alfie wasn't going to afford. There was only one thing to do: say goodbye to Simon Brotherton.

Alfred Steinman turned pale. His throat seemed to emit a death-rattle.

'You mean, the man has a *firearm*?'

'It's OK,' said Simon. 'I wasn't hurt.'

The chairman ignored his reply. He turned to the memo.

'What's this about wanting his "piece of money back"? I want his *exact words*.'

For the fifth time, Simon repeated the phrase Ricky had used.

Mr Steinman eyeballed him hard during the silence that followed. Then, just as Simon was about to break the stare and blink, Steinman's manner suddenly relaxed. He came around the mahogany table and put a hand on Simon's shoulder.

'Not everyone is cut out for the rough and tumble of this work, Simon,' he said in a fatherly tone. 'You're a sensitive chap. You might feel happier in some other walk of life. Didn't you say you painted?'

'A bit of oils, sir.'

'Forget oils! Acrylics are the thing of the future! Go for something *conceptual*. They can never see through you that way.' He moved towards the door. 'Oh, the matter of your outstanding service. I don't think the firm would hold you to the absolute letter of your contract. We don't like to stand in the way of creative ambition.' His hand was on the doorknob now. 'I shall consider your letter of resignation favourably.'

Simon returned to his desk, numb. Was he imagining it, or had he just been given the boot? Why? For not getting shot?

He packed his briefcase and locked his office door, wondering if he'd find a new name on it in the morning. He travelled down in the lift with Mr Steinman's secretary. She burst into tears in the lobby and said how sorry she was. He wasn't like the others, she said. The place wouldn't be the same without him.

Still dazed, he slipped down the back stairs into the garage. As he passed Mr Steinman's Roller, a twist of paper on the ground caught his eye. It was a five pound note. Without a moment's hesitation, he bent down and slipped it quickly into his pocket.

He was half way home, figuring out how he'd tell Martha, his live-in friend, when he realised how nearly he'd been tricked. If he resigned, he'd get cut off without a penny. If they fired him, however, they'd at least have to pay him up to the end of his contract.

Three thousand two hundred and forty pounds: that was what it would come to. Not enough to buy the farmhouse in Tuscany he dreamed of, but plenty for wine and bread and canvas and brushes and oil paints. He was only twenty-five. He always had his accountancy qualifications to fall back on. Destiny had thrown the opportunity of a lifetime in his path, and he *had* to seize it!

The euphoria lasted about thirty-five seconds. Then he remembered the mortgage, the Barclaycard loan, the car on HP, Martha, his parents . . . There was only one thing to do. He'd go out that night and get absolutely and irredeemably plastered.

3

'Cash with order, Ricky my son.'

Bleeding liberty! Didn't they know who they were dealing with? They were talking to Ricky. Ricky Stone.

'Sorry to hear you got done, Rick. Anything we can do to help. Gear? Got no gear, old mate. Business dead as a dodo. You'd think it was the kipper season.'

It wasn't the kipper season – it was May. In Millionaire's Row, Norwood, the blossoms hung on the trees like Bird's Eye dream topping. Summer was in the air. Skirts were inching higher. And that was another problem for a normal man made of flesh and blood who'd just spent six months inside with a load of ponces.

'I'm looking for a runner, Ricky. Fancy a spot of graft?'

A *runner*? Ricky Stone, running gear for Elijah's Import-Export Emporium? Why, he'd set up the young git in business.

Cobblers to the lot of 'em! Ricky Stone would run his own gear. He'd find a little parcel of crappo and, bingo!, he'd have a nice little coup off. Yes, he'd be back on the map before they knew it.

Trouble was, credit didn't grow on trees if you were bankrupt.

Theoretically – not that Ricky cared a stuff for theory – an undischarged bankrupt couldn't obtain credit of any kind. That meant he couldn't buy a parcel and pay for it out of what he got from selling it. Ninety percent of legitimate deals were therefore out of the question. Sure, he could run other people's gear on commission, but that was working for another boss, and he'd been his own boss too long.

You could discharge your bankruptcy by paying off your creditors. In Ricky's case, that meant finding about two hundred and fifty grand.

He sat in his front room and lit a cigarette. This was his office, now that the Official Receiver had taken over his warehouse in Wapping, cockroaches in the khazi and all. Good luck to the bastard. This was all *he* needed: a couple of phones, a good supply of Beryl's liquid tar and half a dozen ash trays, and he was back in business.

Already the room was getting the right look. A couple of jumbo teddy bears, just come in; last year's Christmas stock but pound notes if you could afford to buy them and put them aside. Cartons of toilet deodorant, with special offer flash. Air freshener, four flavours, Arabic cans. Exercise sandals, lovely quality. Bubble bath, old pack, in Pine and Regular. Kids' cricket bats, every one signed by the England eleven. Fluorescent tennis balls, sunglasses, beach towels . . .

He looked around the room with excitement mingled with outrage. Samples of *other people's* gear. They'd got him by the bollocks. How could they expect him to earn a nicker if they didn't give him a chance?

To tell the truth, it was only two hundred grand. The fifty was interest and lawyers' fees. Lovely business them lawyers got. Just sit on their fannies, clocking it up like a taxi meter.

He'd played fair. He'd tried to clear it. At the creditors' meeting, he'd made an offer to pay it off. Twenty quid a week.

It was a story he could tell all day long.

'There was Alfie Steinman, lookin' all self-righteous, at the head of the table. Each side of him, these po-faced geezers from the bank. I'll say they were gentlemen, though. Mind you, it wasn't their money. Nice gaff they had and all. The table and chairs would fetch a few bob.

'"Twenty pounds a week, gentlemen," I says.

'Alfie plays for a long time on his desk calculator and says, "The interest alone is five hundred a week."

'So I offer him a deal.

'"OK, Alfie. Fifty grand, and we're quits. Take it, before I change my mind. That's the missus' house. Can't say fairer than that, can I? And you won't have to face *her*. 20p in the pound. Better than a kick in the Niagaras."

'Then Alfie makes this show of consulting the jury. I know what they're thinking: "If this geezer's got fifty, he's got the rest. Who can do two hundred grand straight off and have nothing to show for it?"

'Ricky Stone can. Ask the bookies if he didn't.'

'Know something, doll?' said Ricky, practising his golf swing with a kiddie's cricket bat. The blade flew apart from the handle and bedded itself into the open embrace of the giant teddy-bear.

'Know what, pet?'

'Sometimes I think I've got more front than Brighton.'

Then Ricky had a brainwave. Melvyn Harris. Why hadn't he thought of him before? The geezer owed him one.

Ricky jumped in the Merc and was in Bow within twenty minutes.

Mel showed him round. Business was bad, but somehow he'd scraped enough together to buy the next-door warehouse. This was a derelict Victorian spice factory with dripping walls and rusting gantries falling from the roof. Eyes glowed out of the semi-darkness. Melvyn employed mainly Asians – cheap labour, if you didn't ask too closely about passports. He'd crammed this warehouse from floor to ceiling with Polish

26

firelighters. Then Spring came early. Too sodding early.

Ricky was ready with a suggestion.

'It's winter in Aussie-land. Flog 'em there.'

'Do me a favour.'

'I was reading they got terrible fuel problems in Ethiopia. Oxfam will take your arm off for 'em.'

'They want *food*. You can't eat a fire-lighter.'

'I know that, Mel. But they gotta cook it somehow.'

'Rick, this gear don't *make* fires, it lights 'em. Get it?'

Pennies began dropping in Ricky's mind. He sized up the palettes knowledgeably.

'Course,' he said archly, 'there are other ways. One little fag butt would do it. You don't smoke, Mel. You'll be right in the clear.'

He took the cigarette out of his mouth and ground it carefully against the side of one of the packets.

'Hey, cut it out!' cried Melvyn. He brushed off the embers and stamped them quickly into the ground. His face was white. 'Go easy! It ain't insured yet.'

Yes, business was bad, he repeated as they returned to his office. Ricky could see it wasn't. He could see this year's drop-head Rolls in the yard. He could see Melvyn's plump, tanned belly where it stretched the buttons of his shirt, and deep among the thicket on his chest he could see a heavy gold chain that would have upstaged a mayor.

What Melvyn meant was, he didn't have any business for Ricky.

In Shoreditch, business was slow. In Houndsditch, it was sticky. It was flat in Whitechapel and slack in the Angel. No-one had seen a May like it for years. And yet the street traders were pouring into the wholesalers' and filling their vans to the roofs, and in the street markets the punters were parting with money like it was going out of fashion.

For Ricky, though, it was a different story. It was an effin' conspiracy.

But he wasn't quite beat yet. There was still Eli and Abby.

If Eli and Abby gave him a blank, then he'd pack in the job-buying game and go back to the bingo halls.

The young brothers were straight out of Mister Men. Eli, the fat one with the shiny dark suits, was Mister Nasty; Abby, the lean one with the dapper pale blue casuals, was Mister Nice. Together, they ran a firm called Westminster Promotions from a modern Aladdin's cave on the M25 Orbital. If a kid sent up for a BMX badge from the back of a cornflakes packet, if a housewife wrote to exchange five tampon covers for a pair of kitchen scales, if a rep who'd beaten his quarter's sales targets was awarded a car vacuum cleaner or an Aiwa Walkman or a monogrammed briefcase or a luxury towel set or a five-function digital computing travel alarm clock, the chances were that it came to him via the warehouse of Westminster Promotions Ltd.

The brothers were playing pool when Ricky arrived. They invited him to join them. Ricky was a natural at all ball games. He won easily. He suggested a re-play, this time with money on it. He played left-handed to give them a handicap. Even so, he cleared the table in a single grand break.

This was a mistake.

'Business?' Eli shrugged his slabby shoulders. 'Terrible.'

'Never known a season like it,' chimed Abby.

But Ricky's morale was up. He wandered around the showroom, tailed by Abby, picking up one item after another and asking the price

'One pound fifty, *thirty bob*, for that?' he exclaimed, seizing on a garden hose attachment set. 'Ask me, and I'll get you better for a nicker.'

Abby didn't ask him.

It was then that he spotted a pile of cartons piled haphazardly in the far corner. Their contents were barely identifiable from the design on the outside. But already the brain cells were beginning to stir. Ideas began bubbling. Connections forming. At the time he little realised he was staring salvation in the face. Years later, he would cherish the memory of this moment and weave around it a whole heroic tale to bewitch his grandchildren.

He went over and ripped one open.

Inside was a fancy barbecue set.

Think about it.

'Doing any good with those?' he asked casually.

'Flying out,' replied Abby, unable to contain real enthusiasm. 'Can't get enough of 'em! No sooner in than out. Don't have time to unpack 'em. We got three containers at the docks right now and the punters are crying out for more.'

'Tell me,' continued Ricky carefully as the thought crystallised, 'how do they *light* the things?'

'Eli told you?' said Abby with a quick sideways glance. 'Yeah,' he admitted, 'you could say we've been having problems on that score. They come with a sachet of this stuff, see, but . . .'

Ricky put his arm around the dapper young man's shoulder.

'Abby, my son, this is your lucky day.'

'Mel? You still there?'

'I love yer, Rick, but I can't do it. My accountant says, No dodgy deals for a spell.'

'It's kosher, Mel. Straight up. You're talking to Ricky Stone.'

'Money up front, Rick. You know the form.'

'Don't tell me about form!'

'Anyone else, I'd be glad to serve 'em. That's how it is, old pal. All right?'

'Mel, wait a mo. Mel? You there? *Mel?*'

29

Raising money had never been a problem before.

Chapati Joe lived in a Mayfair penthouse with his brothers and a small saried harem. He'd put up the money at ten percent per month plus a half share of the profit. Ricky asked if he'd been drinking, but he was a teetotaller.

He found Mo, the Iranian carpet dealer, doing a year-end stocktake at his warehouse in Edgeware. Mo had a problem. He'd done too well that year and had to lose some profits.

Ricky offered to oblige.

'Leave it to Rick,' he said. 'I *guarantee* you'll do your dough on the deal.'

But apparently the Iranian meant losing money on paper, not *actual* money.

Disconsolate, Ricky returned to the Merc. Spoke a different language, them rag-heads did.

A fine drizzle was settling in with the twilight as he drove towards the West End. Billy! Why hadn't he thought of Billy? The man always travelled around with a few suitcases of banknotes in the boot of his motor. He'd probably be in a back room at Omar's club, drinking Dom Perignon and getting plated.

But Billy was out of the country. He was fitting up another little Irish fishing trawler with a cargo of canna-bis under the cod.

Ricky was at his wits' end.

The bar was smoky. Wenches in mock-Elizabethan dress served goblets of mead, addressing the customers as 'squire' and 'me old hearty'.

Ricky ordered another Scotch and looked about him. The tills were ringing. Nice little earner, this joint. They should do something about the barmaids, though. The one who served him was a right scrawny old slag. Job her out and they'd double the takings.

He leaned towards the man on the bar-stool beside him.

'Anyone who takes two looks at *her* is greedy.'

He didn't hear the reply. For there, sitting no more than ten feet away, staring into his goblet of mead, was the wet-eared young ponce Alfie Steinman had sent round that morning.

'Oh my Gawd,' he groaned. 'That's all I need.'

Simon wasn't sure why he'd gone to this dump to get pissed. Once, when a student, he'd taken a party of Americans there. Perhaps it was the memory of the girl who'd slipped him a card with her phone number (which he'd lost when Clarissa, his live-in friend at the time, sent the jacket to the cleaners), or perhaps the thought of the outrageous commission he'd earned. Perhaps, too, he was here to spite Martha. He'd left Martha at home, writing a critique of *Men, The Second Sex* for her study group. She saw a positive side to his sacking. It would help raise his consciousness. He'd told her he was thinking of taking up painting properly. She'd given him one of her pitying glances down the length of her very straight nose and said something about 'Come the revolution'.

He swallowed the sickly drink and signalled to the barmaid for another. Behind her, through the smoke, a face came into focus.

Richard Lawrence Stone!

Their eyes met.

Ricky reached slowly into his inside pocket.

'Oh Christ!' gulped Simon, turning deathly cold.

Ricky took out his wallet. He laid two coins on the bar, then hesitated.

Maybe he could use this kid. Alfie's dough would nicely cover the first daffy of firelighters.

He swapped the coins for a fiver. He'd buy the lad a drink.

31

'Cheers.'

Simon acknowledged the drink and quickly looked away. He busied himself inspecting the bubbles on the surface of the honeyed fluid. He'd meant a half; this was a pint. He'd never finish it without being sick. He had to, though. Suppose the man took offence?

He looked up, and blanched.

The space where Ricky Stone had been sitting was empty.

'How do, old son. On your own, or by yourself?'

The thump on Simon's back nearly winded him.

'Oh, hello, Mr Stone,' he choked.

'Do any better this afternoon? Beat up any little old ladies?'

'I don't normally get involved in house calls.'

'You kiddin'?' Ricky's tone was sarcastic. He sat down and leant close. 'Give Alfie my message?'

'Well, yes.'

'What did the geezer say?'

'Actually, he didn't seem too thrilled.'

Ricky pounded a fist into his palm and let out a whoop of joy.

'Thrilled? I'd say he was right narked! 'Ere, I want you to give him another message. Say . . .'

'I don't expect I'll be seeing him again. He gave me the sack this afternoon.'

'The sack? Why, what you done? Tea-leafin' the petty cash?'

'I don't know. I was just telling him what you said about coming for the dough . . .'

'Why, the dirty poxy bastard, I'll poke his face in!' Then Ricky's eyes widened with sympathy. 'What you goin' to do for a livin', then?'

'I . . . don't know. I'm thinking of taking up painting.'

'Forget it. Decoratin' don't pay.'

'I meant . . .'

'Tell you what, though, Jimmy me old son . . .'

'Simon.'

'Listen 'ere, Sime. You're a presentable lad. Sod Alfie.

32

Be your own boss. You want to cop some nice dough? Course you do. So happens I've got an idea right up your alley. Want to hear? Barmaid, same again, please.'

4

From his sickbed in the basement flat at No. 5 Poonah Mansions, East Putney, Simon squinted through the window, counting how many bricks he could see through a single pane.

The drip of an overflow pipe finally drove him to his feet. He staggered to the bathroom. A gong pounded steadily inside his head. The bath swung up to meet him as he bent to put in the plug. Alka Seltzer fizzed deafeningly in the tooth-mug. He'd never touch a drop of that Cornish poison again.

The face that met him in the mirror looked as if it were made of slymuck. His straw-fair hair was thinner and stragglier than ever. His eyes, blue on a good day, were sunken and blood-veined. The mouth that Martha had once likened to the young Gramsci's hung slack and bloodless.

From the bath he counted the pipes running down the opposite wall in the light-well. A fallen bird's nest lay caught in the fork between two soil pipes. From a loose piece of pointing, a sickly, yellow fern struggled vainly towards the light. Pigeon-shit scarred the panes in long, straight streaks, proving just how subterranean the flat was.

In the kitchen, he knocked over the Siamese cats' litter tray. They never used it. Seeing house-training as the thin end of a wedge whose thicker end was behaviour control by Big Brother, Martha would place the tray where they had last messed. This merely meant that, over time, every square inch of the apartment came to be fouled.

He took a piece of toast and a mug of soya-bean coffee into the sitting-room and stared out at the thin line of daylight that was visible through the top tenth of the window frame.

How could he paint, living in a dungeon?

In Italy, the bedroom would look out over the Chianti vineyards, the bathroom over olive terraces. In Italy, the kitchen would give onto the patio, and from the sitting room you'd be able to look right down the winding valley and watch the sun setting behind the blue hills.

Here he suffocated. There he'd breathe.

Only one thing stood between him and his dream. Money. Who ever heard of retiring on three thousand two hundred and forty quid?

Excell Services Ltd fitted him up with a company off the shelf for a hundred quid plus VAT. Primoprint Ltd ran off some letter-heading and invoice paper while he waited. By two p.m., Simon James Brotherton was Chairman and Managing Director of Transcosmos Trading Ltd, 5 Poonah Mansions, London SW15. By three-thirty, he had opened a bank account and possessed a company cheque-book.

At four-thirty precisely, briefcase in hand and sporting his old business-school tie, he presented himself at the semi-derelict warehouse of Melvyn Harris (Wholesale) Ltd in Bow, East London.

Ricky sat in the Merc, parked up an alley two streets away. He had the radio tuned to a golf tournament, but he wasn't paying attention. He was chainsmoking and dreaming of his come-back.

'Our credentials,' concluded Simon, handing over a smartly typed sheet. 'Bankers, lawyers, accountants; you'll find it all here.'

Melvyn Harris picked his nose as he read the blue-chip list.

'This your main line of business?'

'No, no,' smiled Simon easily. 'It's offshore finance.'

'I got a little place in Marbella, myself.'

Simon nodded with indifferent interest and rose to his feet.

'I'll have the first lorry sent in tomorrow, then.'

Melvyn Harris took his hand to shake it. Simon's thumb got caught round the wrong way. Melvyn's face suddenly lit up. He responded with a strange clasp. Simon had read about masonic handshakes.

'Always a pleasure to do business with a gentleman,' beamed Melvyn and saw him to the door.

'Piece of cake,' said Simon.

'I know Mel,' chuckled Ricky, 'he'll be on the blower gettin' the SP on this Transcosmos outfit.'

'The what?'

'SP. Startin' price. The form. Get me?'

'He won't hear a bad word spoken.'

Ricky clapped him on the knee.

'Sime,' he said, 'you'll do.'

Never had a plaudit felt so good.

In the days that followed, one truck after another rolled out of the Victorian warehouse in Bow. Their destination was not Eli and Abby's premises on the M25 Orbital, but a packaging firm situated in a disused railway marshalling yard behind Penge station.

This was Ricky's masterstroke.

There, in a line on either side of a continuous moving belt, working round-the-clock shifts, stood some thirty women. In one end came the WHAM-FLAM firelighters, packed 24 sticks to a box, 12 boxes to an outer carton. At once agile fingers got to work, opening the cardboard outers, ripping apart the boxes, slitting open the cellophane inners, dividing the white sticks into fours, then shrink-wrapping and finally re-packing them in smaller boxes that bore a zazzy label marked 'BAR-B-Q LITASTICKS' and a big flash proclaiming 'Recommended Retail Price £1.99'. This meant Eli and Abby could go out at 99p per pack of four and call it half price. The fact that Ricky had paid Melvyn 25p for a box of 12 and sold them to Eli and Abby for 25p for 4, thereby trebling his money, was neither here nor there. It was just good business.

In fact, very good business.

'One for you, one for me.'

Three weeks had passed and Ricky had now collected the final payment from Eli and Abby. The last rays of the sun filtered in through the ruched net curtains and worked their way past the giant teddy-bears, up the aluminium expanding garden ladders, over last year's pin-up calendar, to the point where the flock wallpaper met the plastic cornice. A cigarette guttered in its own tar on the glass top of the desk.

Ricky sat in his vest and underpants. Before him lay a vast pile of banknotes, grouped roughly into denominations. He was working on the pile of twenties.

'One for you, one for me.'

Simon's accountant's mind was totting it up as he went. He broke into a sweat when they passed the thousand pound mark. At two thousand, he felt like telling Ricky to keep the rest, he was happy with what he'd got. It was wrong to earn so much for so little time put in. Simon, like all salaried employees, related time to money. It took Ricky to show him that was crazy; six months' hard graft might not earn a penny, while a single phone-call could make sixty grand.

At some point after five thousand, they moved on to the tenners.

'One for you, one for me,' continued the incantation.

Simon was mesmerised. It had the rhythm of a maternal heartbeart.

After twenty minutes, the pile was divided in two, with only a handful of torn and foreign notes left in the middle.

'Nine thousand two hundred and thirty-three,' pronounced Simon. 'Each.'

Ricky looked at him in amazement.

'You some kind of computer brain, or what?' He swept his bundle into his briefcase as though it was a pile of trash. 'Not a bad day's work, eh? What you goin' to do with your bit?'

'Well, after putting away a bit for tax . . .'

'A bit for *what*?' A small fleck of spittle landed on Simon's cheek. He thought Ricky would notice if he wiped it away. 'There's no tax on this, old son. It's all lovely readies.'

'I, er, hadn't thought,' replied Simon, but already he was thinking. The farmhouse had suddenly gained another wall. Maybe he had the kitchen and one bedroom, too?

'What about you?' he asked in his turn.

'Turn it into fifty grand.'

'Another parcel?'

'Nah. I'm goin' up the casino, aren't I? I got a special system, see. Gabby Goldman told me it before he died. Me and no-one else. Guaranteed past the post.' He eyed Simon warmly. 'Want to come with? We'll have a night out! You, me, Beryl and your girl.'

'Martha's not really the club type.'

'She don't like fun, or what? Come on your ownsome, then. There's plenty of lovely sorts there. What d'you say?'

Gabby Goldman, said Ricky confidentially over dinner, had owned half of London's top casinos in his time. He'd seen all the systems ever invented. Roulette, blackjack, craps, chemmy – the mug punters came in with their

38

fancy systems but they never won. They might have a short run of luck, but they always ended up losing their dough. No system worked.

Except this one.

'*No* system can beat the bank,' said Simon authoritatively. 'Gambler's fallacy.'

'Gambler's fallacy,' echoed Beryl. 'That's what I say.'

'Listen,' said Ricky. 'Gabby used to nip down to the south of France. A couple of nights in Monte and, bingo, he'd paid for his holiday.'

'Died a poor man,' said Beryl. 'I wonder why?'

'There was certain people, Beryl, what called themselves his friends,' hinted Ricky darkly.

'I mean to say,' Simon broke in, already mildly high on the Niersteiner, 'are you actually going to *play* this system, or what?'

'Sure. Wanna go halves?'

'I don't think so, thanks all the same.'

With his redundancy pay, he'd have nearly twelve and a half thousand pounds! He wasn't going to risk a single brick or tile on some crackpot gambling system.

Or so he resolved at the time.

Like all simple systems, it was built for simpletons. Like all foolproof systems, it fooled disproof.

This was how it worked.

Roulette was the game. You played only colours, not numbers. You waited until the wheel threw up a run of five of either colour – five blacks or five reds in a row – and then you played the *opposite* colour. You bet in single stakes of, say, £500. You never doubled. You played on, systematically backing your colour until you were *one unit up*. Then you stopped and waited for the cycle to start again. It might go six, seven, even eight units against you, but there would always be a point at which the balance was restored and you went one ahead. It was slow work and you had to have great self-control not to break the pattern and follow an impulse.

Technically, of course, Simon was right. Every time the wheel was spun, given it had no inherent bias and allowing for the slot that went to the house, the odds were exactly evens between red and black. Theoretically, you could have a million reds in a row and the odds on black coming up next would still be 50%. But the system was cleverer than that. It relied on the fact that, on *average*, over perhaps the course of one night, a wheel would throw as many reds as blacks. All the punter had to do was to have enough capital to back his losses until the pendulum swung back in his favour.

Ricky never once went more than six units down. Each time, as Simon verified, standing at his elbow with mouth agape, the wheel would swing back in his favour just enough to allow him to win his one unit and start back in.

The smoke thickened. The lights dimmed. Waiters crept to and fro with trays of drinks. Ashtrays filled and were invisibly replaced. Time passed but no-one recorded its passing. Punters came and went. Croupiers changed. And always the slit in the baize-covered table devoured more and more notes, more and more plastic chips.

But these were not Ricky's notes or Ricky's chips. Beside Ricky's place, a steady pile was growing. As time went on, the pile became a heap, the heap a small mountain.

Beryl had fallen asleep. Simon sat bemused and numb. He looked at his watch. Outside, dawn would already be breaking. Martha would be getting up to do her yoga meditation and bake the bread. The cats would have devoured the rice and tahini dish she'd left half-eaten and found a yet undiscovered corner to mess in. The birds would be singing in Hyde Park and there would be the smell of new hope and new promise on the breath of the air. All was going to be wonderful.

They stood on the pavement outside. The city was beginning to stir. A road sweeper truck rumbled past and swerved to avoid Ricky's Merc, parked half on the kerb. The car's exhaust billowed into the crisp early morning air. Inside, Beryl lay huddled into a fur, her mascara smudged and her jaw slack, dreaming of Copacabana beaches. On the back seat, six bulging paper bags attested to the night's success.

Ricky shook his head. He couldn't make it out.

'All this paintin' cobblers, Sime. You ain't serious? Sod the Eyeties. Stay with me. We'll make a right good livin' together.'

Simon shrugged. How could he explain his call to destiny?

'I have to give it a try.'

Ricky gave him a look as if he'd unwittingly been consorting with a leper all this time.

'You got a screw loose, kid.' He shook his head, then reached out and took his hand. His big, bloodhound eyes filled with sadness. 'Well, Sime, I wish you all the best,' he said.

'Thanks. And the same to you.'

'God bless, then. Look after yourself.'

'Bye, Ricky.'

Ricky stepped into the car and wound down the window.

'We had a spot of fun, eh?'

'It was great.'

'If you change your mind, you know where to find me. So long, kid.'

Then Ricky put his foot on the gas and disappeared in a cloud of white exhaust.

5

Alfie Steinman was in excellent spirits that afternoon. At lunch at the Bank of England, the notion had been floated across his port glass that his name was being mooted in certain quarters as a candidate for Lord Mayor. At three-thirty, he'd attended a creditors' meeting which he'd wound up within fifteen minutes, to the satisfaction of all parties. From his car, he'd phoned to clinch a deal with an American firm to buy the stock and work in progress of a defunct hi-fi manufacturer in Belfast.

And he'd even found time to stop by Lucinda's place for a piece of stress therapy.

Lucinda, or Lucy as she was known in the evenings back home in Lavender Hill, ran an exclusive sex parlour in an apartment in a smart London hotel. Her speciality was a bondage and submission routine for top executives wearied by the demands of important decision-making and looking to have a few decisions taken for them. Alfred Steinman had no especial liking for a licking. There were just times when he wearied of being always in the driving seat. Loretta and the others demanded such a strenuous performance. Of course, with his wife it was a real strain. Unappetising, too. Sex with her was like eating a dog biscuit – you had to beg for it, and it was dry and stale when you got it.

He now found himself standing in his office with a full belly, empty testicles and a warm posterior, when his secretary called through.

A Mr Richard Stone was in the waiting room. He'd been there for over two hours. He refused to go away.

Alfie felt his testicles retreating. Christ, the man had a shooter! He'd got witnesses. No: no witnesses! The subject of Black Magic would come up, and he'd have a hard job making believe the man meant voodoo.

He'd tape the conversation. If he had to go this way, at least he'd leave evidence behind to convict the villain.

He pressed the switch under the table controlling the concealed tape recorder and told his secretary to send the man in.

Ricky heaved a suitcase on the table. He didn't utter a word. He snapped open the locks.

Alfie drew back. There'd be a tommy gun inside. Or maybe a black mamba.

He gasped.

Banknotes slithered out onto the table. Mountains of them, all jumbled up, uncounted, ungrouped . . .

Ricky pushed the suitcase forward.

'Right, Alfie,' he said at last. 'You're goin' to get me a discharge. There's over a hundred grand 'ere. Plus that piece of money you're owin' me, that'll settle up the creditors nicely, eh?'

Simon parked in Grosvenor Square, on a double yellow line. He could afford to risk a parking ticket. What was a few quid when he was dealing in thousands? Before the day was out, he'd be the owner of property overseas. Besides, he felt deliciously truant; he was counting his four weeks' unclaimed holiday against his notice period.

In the first agency, they brought him coffee and settled him into a comfortable chair with a ring-binder full of photographs. A girl dressed for a point-to-point and wearing a badge saying *Amanda, Negotiator*, consulted a separate sheet of paper for the prices.

Well, she said, there was this two-room villa in a

luxury development outside Naples. Terrifically handy for the airport. Construction hadn't actually started yet; they were still draining the land. Twelve thousand five hundred might just secure the deposit on a unit.

The girl in the second agency took copious particulars. When she came to filling in the box marked 'Price Range', she laid down her pen, smiled very sweetly and asked if he'd thought of Anatolia.

In the third agency, he fell in love. It was everything he'd dreamed of. It *was* Tuscany. It *was* a farmhouse. It *was* way up in the hills. It was a hectare or two of terraces, once planted with vines and olive trees, and the views certainly looked stunning. No pylons, no autostrade, no hydro-electric plants, only donkeys carrying bundles of hay and driven by smiling, walnut-faced old peasants. True, the fabric of the building was not in the best repair, but, as the girl pointed out, that was its charm. It had 'enormous scope for improvement'.

But there was one insuperable drawback.

They were inviting Offers in Excess Of Forty Thousand Pounds.

Forty thousand and one pounds secured it within five minutes. Simon handed over the deposit – four thousand pounds and 10p – in cash. The balance was payable in twenty-eight days. If he failed to come up with that, interest would be charged at four percent over base for a further period of twenty-eight days, after which the initial deposit would be forfeitable at the vendor's discretion.

'No trouble,' said Simon. 'You'll have the balance in twenty-four hours.'

He hurried away with a sheaf of photographs. Martha would be thrilled. She could keep geese, have a child out of wedlock and get to work converting the local *commune* if it wasn't already Communist. He'd have a dealer in Milan and a gallery in Florence and sell his pictures to pay for the renovation. The Italians had a true appreciation of art, not like the phillistine English. A painter had to go where his work was valued.

That evening, Martha would be out late at her Aerobics and Consciousness class. He'd slip over to the West End.

If it worked for Ricky, it would work for him. A system, after all, was a *system*.

'The dirty, double-crossing bastard! 'Ere, Beryl, cop a load of this.'

Ricky stormed into the garden with the letter. Beryl sat up in the sun-lounge chair so abruptly that the struts caved in and she sank to the ground where she flailed around like a beached whale.

'"Dear Mr Stone",' he read, putting on Alfie Steinman's accent, '"I write to confirm receipt of £105,247.00 paid on account of your outstanding debts.

'"Whilst my clients are naturally pleased to receive this contribution, they have indicated they are not prepared to write off the balance. Until the account has been cleared in full, therefore, any application for discharge of bankruptcy is unlikely to be favourably considered.

'"At the date of writing, the sum outstanding is £146,489.55p, inclusive of interest. Yours sincerely, Alfred J. Steinman."'

Ricky picked up a golf ball lying in the grass and hurled it down the garden. It struck a gnome, staring peaceably into the pond, and knocked its head off.

'No-one turns down *40p in the pound*! That schmuck Alfie fitted 'em up. I'll send the boys round.'

'Yeah,' urged Beryl, her eyes gleaming. 'Send the boys round!'

'They'll break his fingers.'

'And shove his teeth in!'

'He won't walk again in a hurry.'

'He's as good as *dead*!'

'Dead? Don't talk like that, Beryl. It ain't proper.'

'You said it yourself, we're goin' to clobber him.'

'I didn't say *do him in*.'

45

'Same difference.'

'Beryl, are you tryin' to put me back inside for keeps?'

'He deserves to die, stitchin' you up like that.'

'He did not stitch me up.'

'He nicked your lovely dough, didn't he?'

'He did not nick it. I handed it to him. What do you take me for, a right berk?'

'But I thought . . .'

'Beryl, leave off thinkin'. Gives me brain damage.'

'Only wanted to help, pet.'

'Then get up off your fanny there and make us a pot of tea.'

Course, the old girl was right. He'd been done over right proper. And it hurt.

But he'd get even. No-one stitched up Ricky Stone and got away with it. He was a fighter. He always came bouncing back. He'd pull up the dough and show the dirty little bastard who he was dealing with.

But how? He was back to square one. Still bankrupt, still unable to get credit, still schlepping around trying to pull up deals without two brass farthings to rub together.

Come back, Sime, he groaned. I need you, kid.

The moment Simon set foot in the casino, two bouncers with broken noses peeled off and shadowed him around the tables, audibly cracking their knuckles. He'd had four large brandies before coming and he wasn't going to be fazed. He took a form card, selected a table with a pretty croupier and stood marking down the reds and blacks as they came up.

Sure enough, after every five reds, within a few throws the blacks came out one ahead.

He sauntered over to the cashier, put down five grand, being the rest of his profit, and asked for fifty £100 chips. Then he made his way back to the table and waited until a seat became vacant. He piled the orange chips on the

46

baize before him. The croupier smiled a welcome. He waited for five blacks to come up in succession.

'Faites vos jeux, messieurs.'

He reached forward and placed his first chip squarely in the centre of the red. The croupier spun the wheel and flicked the ball along its race

'Rien ne va plus.'

The ball bounced in and out until finally it came to rest. Simon couldn't see where it landed, but the croupier flashed him a special smile.

'Thirty,' she said. 'Pays on even. Pays on red.'

She shovelled across an orange chip. First go, and he'd won already! This was going to be like taking sweets from a kid. He leaned forward and eagerly waited for the sequence to start again. Behind him, the knuckles cracked louder.

It was slow work. After one hour, he was only five units up. He'd gone seven down, then hovered for ages going plus one, minus one. But he was going to stick to it. He couldn't forget the sight of the brown paper bags.

Somewhere towards midnight, disaster struck.

Five blacks were followed by a sixth, then a seventh. The twelfth was a red, and Simon began to feel the run was turning his way. But the thirteenth was a black. And the fourteenth. The twentieth and twenty-first were both reds, but the wheel was not to throw another red for Simon that night. The run became a flood, the flood a tide. Time after time, the wheel threw up another black. It was incredible. Red was forgotten. It was truly a black night.

Simon's orange pile steadily diminished. He was dumb with disbelief. He stared at the baize. One moment, the red diamond would be covered with an orange chip, the next moment a scoop came and shovelled it away. Like a clockwork zombie, he pushed yet another chip forward. He had five left, then four, then two, then just one.

Then none. He'd blown the lot.

A murmur of sympathy swept the table. There was a smooth change of croupier. From behind, a cough concealed a chuckle. Simon felt he was going to be sick.

Aching to the pit of his stomach, he stumbled to the door and out into the warm, thundery night. He was cleaned out. As he clung to a lamp-post, doubled up with agony, all he could hear through the growling of the approaching storm was the deafening sound of his brain making calculations.

Five grand!

That was 200 cheap-skate dinners out, 100 decent ones.

3 years' drinking at one bottle of wine per day.

The price of a new car.

9 months' mortgage.

10 hi-fi sets, 3 summer holidays, 40 suits, 100 pairs of shoes, 25 large rolls of canvas, 500 sable-hair brushes, 1,000 tubes of Flake White, tankfuls of turpentine, vats of varnish . . .

No more Tuscan farmhouse. Goodbye deposit. He'd lost his dream. He'd lost everything. He might as well end it all.

He lay in bed, too sick in the heart to move, let alone to think of practical ways of ending it all.

He'd broken the news to Martha at dawn as she stood on her head on the Afghan prayer-mat laid out before the window. When she'd finally climbed down, all she'd said was, 'Money is a reified mode of exchange, Simon.'

Reified mode of exchange or not, I want it *back*!

Please God, he prayed, say it was a bad dream.

But God wouldn't oblige. It was no dream. There, tossed over the wicker chair and still sodden from the long, wet walk back home, was the mohair suit he'd worn for the occasion. There, mocking him from the dressing-table top, were the cashier's stubs. There, by

48

the door, with their soles not peeling off, were the lightweight dress shoes he'd donned for the kill.

When he'd got his strength back, he'd struggle out to the chemist and buy a ton of sleeping pills.

Dear Martha, he'd write. *Sometimes life gets too much and the decent thing is to bow out. Remember your study notes on euthanasia? Keep the hi-fi and the National Geographic magazines. Please return my library books. Good luck with your life. Sorry to leave you with the washing-up.*

P.S. I've fed the cats.

She'd come back, find him stiff and cold. She'd fall to her knees and weep copious tears. She'd remember her last words to him with bitter regret and blame herself for being so heartless and insensitive. Why hadn't she climbed down from her hand-stand right there and then and folded her arms around him and told him he was her hero, her man and lover, and she'd stick by him through thick and thin and they'd live off bread and tahini (as if they didn't already) until he'd got back every penny, and more . . . ?

Like hell she would. No, she'd sit down that night and write in her diary, 'Today, Simon made an important existential decision . . .'

No point in dying just to give Martha something else to intellectualise over. No, he'd bloody well earn it all back. By himself. He didn't need Martha's or anyone else's sympathy.

As he lay back, exhausted by this conclusion and daunted by the vistas of unremitting hard slog lying ahead, Ricky's parting words echoed in his ears.

'If you change your mind, you know where to find me.'

6

Ricky prowled restlessly about the house. He'd pulled up another deal – this time a right tasty one – but they'd still got him snookered. It was the same story: thirty days terms for the hoi polloi but cash on the nail for Ricky Stone.

There was no way in this world he was letting this one go.

He'd had a visit from Spaghetti Jim. Jim, whose real name was Italian and unpronouncable, was the UK sales director for Seventh Heaven, a giant multinational cosmetics firm. He'd jobbed out clearance lines to Ricky in the past and earned himself a few quid on the side.

They were both betting men, too. Once a week, Jim called Ricky for a tip. Through his pal Billy, Ricky had an inside track to stable talk. Not that it often did him any good. Nearly always the horse he backed was pulled, failed a dope test or was short by a nostril at a photo-finish. The floor of the Merc was carpeted with crumpled-up betting-slips. Spaghetti Jim followed his advice sheepishly, but being a true gambler, he bore his losses gladly and always came back for more.

Like a true gambler, too, he was forever hungry. It was hard to support both a family and a habit on a salary, even a sales director's. Besides, he'd had a bad start to the season that year.

Enter Ricky Stone, Job-Buyer and Clearance Specialist.

Today, however, Jim had a problem that was too big even for Ricky to solve. To Ricky, such a problem was unheard of, and within minutes he had Jim pouring his heart out.

Seventh Heaven Ltd had just spent ten million pounds launching a new fragrance called *Passion*. It had a hint of bubblegum and a tinge of cocaine, and within a matter of days it had leapt to brand leader in the 18 to 25-year-old, high-disposable-income market.

Passion was expensive, intentionally so. A half-ounce perfume spray sold for £29.95, and could only be bought in the classier retail outlets.

Here, the economics of the business became important.

The actual liquid in the bottle cost somewhat less than 40p to manufacture. The real cost was in the packaging – the frosted glass bottle, shaped like a pair of praying hands and set on a throne of satin and lace, and the five-colour, gold-foil embossed carton, tied with a velvet ribbon and stuck down by a large heart-shaped blob of bright red sealing wax. The packaging came to £2.50, bringing the total product cost to less than ten percent of what it retailed for. Perfectly in line with the industry norm.

Sales were incredible, said Jim. Every week they had to revise their targets and budgets upwards. It was a bonanza.

Then disaster struck. The factory was gearing up for three-shift production when reports started pouring in from up and down the country that the *sealing wax was turning black*! Black hearts? It was unthinkable! Immediately all product was recalled from the shops. A million pieces had already been sent back and there was as much again to come. A senior vice-president had flown in from Houston, fired the whole production department, sued the sealing wax manufacturers and ordered every piece of defective stock to be burned.

'Burned?' gulped Ricky. He clutched his head. Suddenly he had a migraine.

Jim nodded miserably.

'First load went into the incinerator this morning. You'd have wept.'

Ricky pushed the phone forward.

'Right! Get on the trumpet and tell 'em to turn off the burners. Ricky Stone to the rescue! I'll clear the lot so you never knew it existed. And no screams from Boots or Debenhams or no-one. Guaranteed.'

Jim shook his head.

'No jobbing out,' he said. 'Chief's orders.'

'And burn pound notes? Jimmy, a hand in the bird is worth two in the bush.'

'Listen, Ricky . . .'

'No, you listen to me . . .'

'Look, I'm telling you . . .'

'Jimmy, are you *listenin'*? Right. Fifteen percent of retail to clear the lot.'

'It's not on.'

'Since we're old pals, Jimmy, seventeen and a half.'

'Ricky, you can't *control* where it'll end up. One of your wholesalers has only got to serve a feller who nips round the corner to the local Superdrug and . . .'

'And the shit is in the fire. Don't teach me the business.'

Yes, Ricky knew the business. This was a company's worst nightmare when clearing a parcel.

It wasn't hard to see why.

Imagine Ricky buys the parcel at fifteen percent of retail. The perfume, then, stands him in £4.50 plus VAT. He punts it to the wholesalers up and down the country for, let's say, £7.50 a lump. They go out £10.00 to the boys working the street markets, and in ten minutes Seventh Heaven Ltd's pride and joy is on the stalls at £14.95, with a bloody great flash: HALF PRICE PASSION!

Then the screams start. Boots and Debenhams are *paying* more than that to buy the stuff. They threaten to send back their stock of all Seventh Heaven Ltd products. The panic in Seventh Heaven Ltd's sales department is bad enough, but in Marketing they're jumping out of windows. Why? Because the product *image*, created by an extravagantly high retail price and backed by lavish advertising such as only obscene margins can afford, is completely and irrevocably screwed up. *Passion* is a fallen woman, and Seventh Heaven Ltd has kissed goodbye to ten million quid.

Involuntarily, Ricky began to salivate. One man's nightmare was another man's dream come true.

But how to turn the one into the other was the question. Ultimately, the answer was always *money*. Everything and everyone had their price.

He came back in, fighting.

'You're a tough bastard, Jimmy,' he said with a gesture of surrender. 'OK, take my arm off. Twenty percent, you've got it.'

Jim shook his head glumly.

'And there's five of the profit for you,' added Ricky.

Jim shrugged even more helplessly.

But Ricky was still only warming up. This was the best bit. It almost didn't matter what you ended up paying so long as you got the deal.

'You heard five? I'm sayin' ten. Paid anywhere you like. Switzerland, Bermuda, the Caymans . . .'

The man winced. He was cracking.

Here we go pop, thought Ricky. He stood up and put out his hand.

'Have we got a deal, Jimmy?'

Jim worried at his knuckles and shook his head.

'It really can't be done.'

Ricky stabbed him in the shoulder with the point of his finger.

'Know what you are, Jimmy? You're a fuckin' nonentity! You'll get nowhere in life. All you know is lickin' the boss's arse.'

'I got a job, Ricky,' pleaded the man. 'A wife and kids.'

'Cobblers! After this coup you won't need a job. You'll be puttin' your feet up in the South of France.'

'If I could find a way, believe me I would.'

Ricky sat down and lit another cigarette. He watched

the match burn until the flame met his fingers. All that lovely money going up in smoke! It was a crime. And all because some bleedin' lump of sealing wax was turning black.

Turning *black*?

The answer hit him smack between the eyes. Of course!

Suddenly he crashed the palm of his hand down on the glass table top. A half-empty sample of orange drink leapt in the air and overturned, spilling its fizzy liquid over the desk diary.

He spoke slowly, taking his time. He was going to enjoy this.

'Jimmy,' he began, 'how good is your geography?'

Spaghetti Jim was back on the trumpet the following morning. He had his managerial voice on, as if he was afraid of being overheard, but Ricky could tell he'd bitten the bait.

Black Africa sounded as far away from home as anyone could get.

Jim had put the proposition to the chief and the chief had shut down the incinerators while they weighed it up. By dumping the product in Nigeria, they would at least recover the product cost, and already that was getting into big figures. But they'd been stung before. Gear destined for remote third-world dumping-grounds had been turned around on the high seas and shipped right back into the home market. This time they'd need cast-iron assurances that the product *actually went into Africa*. If a single item found its way back, the shit would hit the fan, and Jim's balls with it.

Ricky was on home ground here.

'You're talking to Ricky Stone!' he protested.

'Quite so,' groaned Jim and went on quickly. 'That's why the deal has got to be c.i.f. Benin.'

'*C.i.f. Benin?*'

Ricky broke into a sweat. Whose side was this schmuck

on? Was he serious that the gear had to go *all the way to Nigeria*? He'd have ten percent of fuck all if it had to be backed from there! He couldn't be so dumb as to think Ricky Stone actually ran a network of mammas in the bazaars of Lagos.

'Very generous of you, Jimmy, very generous. But I thought the transport was down to me.'

'Oh, you'll pay for the transport. We'll just supervise it.'

This could spell instant disaster.

Ricky thought fast. He knew a young geezer who worked for a big container firm. He'd used him before. There was nothing he couldn't do with documentation. It'd cost five grand, ten at top weight, but worth every penny.

'Tell you what, send the gear into London docks and I'll give you full shippin' documents.'

'Delivery *abroad*, Ricky. Benin or Bangkok, I don't care, so long as it's outside this country.'

What about a handy little Channel port?

'C.i.f. Rotterdam, then.'

'For anyone else, OK. But not for you, with your form.'

Ricky was gearing up for a pitch in self-defence when he stopped. The obvious idea struck him.

'Anyone else, eh? Now listen! You know of Transcosmos Tradin'? Very big outfit. Goin' public any day. Bloke who runs it is my pal. Let *him* do the deal with your firm. You send the gear into Rotterdam and he'll give you bills of ladin' to Nigeria.'

Jim hesitated. It was clear what he was weighing up. When he spoke, his tone showed he'd capitulated.

'Just see the gear *stays* out, OK? Please, Ricky?'

'My bond, Jimmy, is my word.'

Ricky unbuttoned his shirt and slurped after-shave around his arm-pits. He tested his breath and dabbed a drop of Gold Spot on his tongue. Letting out a small belch with a muttered 'Pardon, vicar', he reached for a spotted yellow silk tie and tied it carefully into a large triangular knot.

He turned. Beryl was standing in the doorway, hands on her hips. He knew that look.

The door, made of thin hardboard, still bore the savage gashes where she'd tried to stab him through it with the kitchen knife. That was the day she'd caught him out with Sonia. Lipstick on the collar hadn't been too clever of him. She'd chased him upstairs with the knife, hell bent on murder. He'd nipped into the bathroom but he couldn't get the door shut, and he'd stood there like a lemon, his foot jammed against the bottom while the knife jabbed in and out, missing him by inches. It was a miracle he'd come out alive.

'Tartin' up for your 'ore?' she demanded.

The fact was, he was going off to find young Sime. But he wasn't going to admit to her he needed a favour from that wet-eared ponce.

'Ask no questions, Beryl, and I'll tell no lies.'

He pushed past her and started down the stairs. She grabbed the underpants he'd dropped on the bathroom floor and threw them after him. Dirty socks and shirts followed.

'She can wash your rotten old pants! And your stinky old socks! Yuk!'

'Beryl, this is business.'

'Havin' the backside off of Lady Muck, call that business? All that posh, lah-di-dah talk, it's all put on. She's conned you, Rick. Says she's thirty-seven, does she? Liar! She's forty-six, I know for a fact. You think I'm the little woman who stops back home and don't know nothin'? I know where she lives. I know where the both of you go, the hotels and the clubs . . .'

Ricky opened the front door with a sigh.

'God put me back inside for some peace and quiet.'

'Inside? Did *she* visit you in the nick? Bring you your salt-beef and lox and do your pools?'

'Drop it out, doll.'

56

'Go on, then, off you go! Don't keep a lady waitin'. Six months without, she'll be hot as a potato.'

'Beryl, would you just get off my fuckin' back?'

Ricky slammed the door hard and stomped down the path. As he stepped into the Merc, he glanced back and saw the ruched curtains parted at the edge and Beryl's face looking out, sad and abandoned.

How could he do it to her? Of course he loved her. They were a team, weren't they? She'd stuck by him in the bad days. Never looked at another man. Never would, either.

But he also loved Sonia. Well, he told her he did. With a slight intermission for bad behaviour, they'd been going for almost a year now.

Sonia ran a small, classy dress shop called The Pin Cushion in Roehampton High Street. She smelled of Old English Lavender and she never said a crude word. She went to West End fashion shows and had a bridge night once a week, but really she was a homely woman and liked to be in bed by ten. She talked nicely and expressed herself well. She was always reading some book or other. She'd given him a Georgette Heyer novel; it was a load of old bollocks but he was persevering with it, doing a page a night when Beryl was asleep, because he wanted to be able to express himself well, too.

Sonia couldn't understand why he didn't leave Beryl. He had tried, several times. Twice he'd actually packed a case. But he'd never quite made the break. He couldn't bear to think of Beryl left alone.

How much longer could he go on dipping the wick at both ends? After fifty, a man had to look after himself. The mental aggro, on top of the physical strain, was putting years on him. His six months' break had felt like a rest cure.

Women! If he had his time again, he'd have the odd bit now and then but he'd never ever get involved.

As he put his foot down on the accelerator, he frowned. Was Sonia *really* forty-six?

'This sex caper, son,' said Ricky aloud, addressing Simon wherever he was, 'it's all cobblers. Knocks you bandy. Tell you what I'd do in your shoes. Sort yourself out a nice little bird. Set her up in a pad with all mod cons. Slip her a few quid here and there to keep herself presentable. And give her a right good seeing-to, maximum twice a week. That's the secret of a long and happy life.'

On the third day Simon rose at last from the dead. He showered and shaved meticulously for the sake of morale. He sprayed his armpits with antiperspirant of a fragrance that matched his aftershave and, checking his breath, he dabbed a drop of Gold Spot on his tongue. He selected a spotted yellow silk tie and tied it carefully into a neat triangular knot.

Martha sat in her kaftan housecoat beside the gas fire. All London could be sweltering in a heatwave outside but it was permafrost in that basement flat. As she looked up over her granny glasses, the kaftan parted slightly to reveal the outline of her breasts. He tried not to look. The ground here was treacherous. One day it was OK to fancy Martha, the next it was sexist. He mostly left it to her to decide which, what and when.

At the sight of his suit and tie, she gave a small, ironic smile.

'You recidivist, Simon. Can't you cope with being out of the cage?'

She always used his whole name, never a diminutive or a pet name.

'I'm not a whatsit-ist, Martha. I'm just going to try and earn the family bread. Until Utopia dawns, someone has to.'

He liked that. Until Utopia dawns . . .

She considered him seriously. She put down the psychotherapy manual she was studying.

'Sign on.'

'What, join the *Army*?'

'Sign on the dole, fool. You'd get benefit, too.'

'Martha, I'm not scrounging off the state! Anyway, have you any idea what I'd get? It's derisory. Wouldn't keep the cats fed.'

'Did you know there are families of six living off less?'

'That's different. They live in council houses and have their bills paid. They're happy. They don't know any better.'

Whoops, a snake.

Life with Martha was all snakes and ladders. You sat with her friends who'd dropped in just as you were going to bed, you listened into the early hours as they exchanged activist gossip, you drank interminable cups of coffee (Jamaica OK, Chile bad) or glasses of cheap wine (Bulgaria OK, South Africa bad), and if you said the right things you got a few rungs up a ladder. Then, in a loose moment, you said something glib and down you slithered, back to square one.

'Don't say it!' he hurried on. 'Just testing.'

Her expression softened.

'Simon, there *is* another way.'

'Well, let's say I'm too bourgeois or too reactionary or too downright thick to see it. I shall do *my* thing in *my* way.'

A look close to admiration spread over her face. She stood up and came towards him. She drew him to her and kissed him full on the lips. The smell of henna in her hair began to arouse him. He pulled away quickly. He mustn't forget he was being *himself* – angry and independent.

He picked up his car keys and went to the door.

'See you when I see you.'

'Good luck,' she said, and he thought she meant it.

'Women!' muttered Simon aloud, addressing Ricky wherever he was. 'You can never get it right with them. If I had my time again, I'd import a nice little Polynesian girl who

59

couldn't speak English and only wanted to please her
man . . .'

'You must be Martha,' said Ricky affably to the girl standing at the door. 'I'm Rick.'
    'Ah, the Man with the Unbeatable System.'
    'That's me, darlin'. Sime in?'
    'He's out. Job-hunting.'
    'Learnin' the trade, is he? I told him, he's wastin' his
talent with that decoratin' caper. Stick with me, I said. Get
yourself some bees.'
    'Bees? He'd better not bring any in here!'
    'Nah, *bees*! Bees and honey. Money.'
    A smile broke across the girl's face and she let out a low,
silvery chortle.
    'Fancy a cup of Rosy?' she said.
    Ricky laughed.
    'You out for a lark, or what?'
    As he followed her indoors, down the dark corridor, he
sized up her legs. Too skinny. He'd seen more
fat on a chip. Still, when she took her glasses off in the
kitchen and poured him a double-strong cup of tea, he
could see she had something. Fatten her up, stick a bit
of make-up on her, get rid of that tatty bit of carpet
she was wearing . . . Sonia could sort her out a nice little
suit . . . Angelina could tell her where to get a decent
hair-do . . .
    He looked around the small sitting-room. Old-
fashioned table lamps, sofa and chairs like the ones his
parents threw out, rugs and bedspreads hanging on the
walls . . .
    'Sime could start by paintin' this joint,' he said.
    'We don't all live in Millionaire's Row, Norwood.'
    'Nor do no millionaires neither.'
    They looked at one another and burst out laughing.
Ricky knew he was going to like this girl.

'Hello, Beryl,' said Simon affably as she stood at the door. 'Just passing and thought I'd look in. Ricky about?'

Beryl clutched the folds of her housecoat in the region of her heart and her handsome dark eyes filled with pain and rage. An inch of ash from the cigarette in the corner of her mouth fell silently to the carpet.

'Ricky's in bed with that filthy old 'ore of his!'

Simon backed away.

'Oh, ah. Yes, I thought I didn't see the car.'

'She don't know who she's dealin' with! I'm the Female Clouseau. I've spent fortunes, Sime, runnin' about in cabs. I know their every move. One time I caught them in this hotel. I said to the manager, "She's a convicted prostitute and he's my husband, and did you know you're runnin' a disorderly house?"' She took her cigarette out so she could laugh better. 'Stop inside a minute, Sime.'

'Well, actually . . .'

'There's a cup in the pot.'

'Just a moment, then.'

As he followed Beryl down the corridor, ankle-deep in rugs and carpets, past the infinite-regression mirrors and through the whorled glass door into the velvet and tass-elled dining area, he sized up her exaggerated hourglass figure. Ricky always said he liked a woman with some-thing to grip onto. Of course, the poorer classes always measured prosperity by girth. It was the affluent middle-classes who created the ideal of slimness. (Martha, you're middle-class. How do you like that?) And then he remem-bered it was Ricky who belonged to the affluent classes and he was among the poorest of the poor.

'The things I could tell you!' crowed Beryl as she poured him a cup of tea as thick as molasses. 'I could write a book.'

'Why don't you?'

'No, but someone's taken my title. *Sweet an' Sour*. But I will, one day. It's all in there.'

She tapped her coppery hair and let out a cackle that dissolved into a rasping smoker's cough. She grabbed Simon's arm for support and coughed until her eyes watered. Then she gave him a look of such impish defiance that he broke into a grin. The grin flowered into a chuckle, the chuckle into a laugh, and gradually they cracked up together until they were both too weak to stand.

'Workin'-class Tory,' said Ricky. 'That's what my Kev calls me. I call him a skivin'-class Red. Why shouldn't a man work to better himself?'

'If he can get the work,' replied Martha.

'What you mean? There's plenty of work. The roads are a national disgrace. There's little old ladies dyin' because there ain't no beds in the hospitals. Schools closin' down 'cos there ain't enough teachers. Young girls gettin' mugged because the coppers are on strike duty. Why pay a geezer dole money to do nothin'? Better pay him for a job of work.'

'You're no Tory, Ricky!'

'Lady Muck don't know what she's lettin' herself in for! She thinks it's going to be all nice in bed and lovey-dovey. He'll soon get bored with that. He'll want to be back with the boys, playin' cards and effin' and blindin'. He's two people. He comes back from seein' her and he's talkin' all posh. "Speak slowly, Beryl, speak quietly, speak nicely." I don't know that man! I'm used to a loud Cockney voice. I say to him, "Ricky, be yourself, don't be someone you're not." That's not my Ricky there! He used to fight for me, protect me, run for me. I know. It's a personality change. I think he's on pot. I'm positive he's doped. Smokin' pot in bed.'

'I have seen him taking tranquillisers.'

'Yeah, he eats *handfuls* of 'em!' She pushed a plate of chocolate biscuits closer to Simon. 'Ah, well. Life is never dull.'

'Yours certainly isn't.'

'You jokin'? This has been going on year in, year out. You pick yourself up and start again. Wait for the next traumatic affair. Who will Ricky Stone fall madly in love with next? I'll have to get the record, *I Fall In Love Too Easily*. Then he comes cryin' back to me, says she's an old 'ore, she tempted me, I'm sorry. Then I get the old sob story.'

'You are quite a pair, you two.'

'Yeah, but I love him. You love your girl, Simon?'

'Well, yes, I suppose so.'

'Then you stick to her. Treat her right. Know what I mean?'

'I'll do my best.'

'You do. Listen, any detective work, I charge 50p an hour. Anything you want to know! There's a brain up there, Sime.'

'Come over one night,' said Ricky, 'and we'll go out for a Chinese. You'll love my Kev. He reads all them politics books, same as you.'

'I'd like that. Are you near a Tube?'

'What, the motor broken?'

'It's going. We can't afford it. Not after the other night.'

'But we cut up nearly twenty grand! If Simon's holdin' out on you, darlin' . . .'

'Didn't he tell you? He went back and tried your unbeatable system. That's why he's out looking for a job now.'

Ricky's eyes widened and he let out a howl of pain.

'Sime, me old china, how *could* you?'

'Don't think bad of Ricky,' said Beryl on the doorstep. 'He's not such a bad sort. Not easy bein' Ricky Stone when you're 'arts.'

'You're what?'

''Arts of oak. Broke. Your Alfie Steinman ripped him off, didn't he?'

'He did *what*?'

'Took all the lovely dough and said, "Ta very much, and now where's the rest?"'

'You mean, Ricky handed over all that money without getting the creditors to agree to discharge him?'

'That Alfie's a right evil bastard.'

Simon let out a howl of pain.

'Ricky, old pal, how *could* you?'

Ricky left East Putney and sat in the Merc for a while, drumming his fingers on the steering wheel. The poor young sap. He was a right unlucky face. Still, he'd be good and hungry now. But where was he?

He pulled away slowly into the traffic. A touch of arthritis was affecting his golf swing and he couldn't sit for long without needing exercise. He wasn't in the mood for seeing Sonia. Normally, he'd have walked the dog in Norwood Park, but that meant facing Beryl. No, he'd stop off on the way and take a stroll on Clapham Common.

Simon left Norwood and drove slowly back in the direction of home. The day was bright and sunny. Office girls were coming out for their lunch hours, the trees were almost in full bloom and everyone's face wore a smile. He couldn't go back to the dungeon yet.

He'd buy a sandwich and lie in the sun on Clapham Common and plan his come-back.

They met at the intersection of two narrow paths.

A gentle breeze stirred the burgeoning chestnuts and wafted on its back the cooing of courting doves. Mothers sauntered over the fresh, green grass with their baby strollers, and here and there early sun-worshippers were laying out their mats and creams.

The first thing each saw was the other's tie. They pulled out their own to check. They were almost identical.

'Not a bad bit of schmutter, eh?' said Ricky. 'Couple of quid from my mate in the Petticoat Lane.'

'Twenty pounds,' retorted Simon. 'From Turnbull and Asser.'

There was a moment's uneasy silence.

'Got a job yet?' asked Ricky.

'Oh, one or two possibilities in the pipeline,' said Simon.

'No Italy?'

'I'm sticking to UK property. Better long-term investment.'

Ricky cast Simon a long, thoughtful look.

'You don't say.'

'And you, Ricky? Back to the drawing-board, is it?'

'Nah. Got a bit of fat to live off, haven't I?'

Simon cast Ricky a long, thoughtful look.

'Good for you.'

Ricky kicked at the turf.

'Course, fat don't last for ever. Besides, you've got to keep active. I wouldn't go out of my way, mind you, but if a tasty little deal came along I might be tempted.'

'It's a question of relative returns. Sticking it in the bank at ten percent is hard to beat.'

'Yeah, on a deal, you have to reckon on doublin' your money.'

'Oh, at the very least. Taking into account the risk.'

Ricky took a golf swing at the air. He began to walk. Simon fell in step beside him.

'They do come up,' said Ricky nonchalantly. 'From time to time.'

'One's got to keep an open mind.'

'Never look a gift horse in the mouth.'

'You can always turn a proposition *down*.'

'I always say it pays to take a butchers.'

Simon opened his bag of sandwiches.

'Hungry?'

'I could eat a horse. Right horrible flap-jacks your Martha makes. I'd have paid a tenner not to eat 'em.'

'Oh? You saw Martha?'

'I was in your manor. Thought I'd drop by. Just for a social, like.'

'That's a coincidence! I had a meeting down your way. Took me right past your front door, so I thought I'd look in, too.' Simon offered him another sandwich. 'If I were you, I'd stick with what you've got at home.'

Ricky gave him a sharp glance. Simon managed a smile.

'I mean, Beryl and her chocolate biscuits.'

Ricky sighed.

'Beryl's the salt of the earth.'

Simon sighed, too.

'Where would we be without the ladies?'

'Where indeed, old pal?'

They caught each other's eye and grinned.

'A fuck sight better off, that's where!' said Ricky.

'You can say that again,' agreed Simon.

'Money? They *eat* money. Bleedin' piranhas!'

'They don't appreciate that someone's got to *work* for it.'

'With a missus and kids, you gotta work till you turn up your toes. Like I was sayin', if a feller comes up to me with a nice little earner, how can I afford to turn it down?'

'You think it's cheaper living as a bachelor? I get no tax relief on Martha, you know.'

Ricky shook his head with the weight of worldly wisdom.

'Funny,' he said. 'Just the other day a pal of mine stopped by my place. He was full of this amazin' deal. Course, I had to tell him I wasn't in the game no more. Mind you, the proposition did sound tasty.'

'Oh?'

'You've heard of this new perfume, *Passion* . . .'

7

'This is Mr Brotherton,' said Ricky. 'My associate.'

Simon shook hands and the four men sat down.

Terry, Deputy Cosmetics Buyer at Peabody's, the country's largest chain of department stores, sat opposite Simon. He was about thirty, with prematurely grey hair and a baby face. He wore a collar pin and gave off a heavy scent of male toiletries. Walter, his boss, looked tired and harrassed. He had the lined face and droopy eyes of a beagle after a cigarette experiment. He bit his fingers and chewed Nicorettes throughout the meeting.

The small office overlooking the art galleries and couture shops of New Bond Street was stacked to the ceiling with suppliers' samples – hairsprays, deodorants, lipsticks, shaving foams, shampoos, gift sets. Some were in discontinued packs, others were offer-flashed or trial size. All were special purchase items. Buying for the grand summer sale was in full swing.

Simon pushed his business card across the glass topped table.

'Bit quiet,' queried Terry, reading the address, 'for offices?'

Ricky chipped in quickly.

'He's got to keep a low profile in his game, Tel.'

'What game is that?' asked Walter, signing a chit someone had just brought in.

'Offshore finance,' responded Simon promptly.

'Head office in Panama,' added Ricky.

'Minimum overheads in the UK,' said Simon.

'Perfectly legit.' Ricky spread his hands. 'Just normal tax evasion.'

'Avoidance,' murmured Simon.

'Tax!' snorted Ricky, responding to the trigger-word. 'What gives the taxman the right to tell *me* how to run *my* business? There's too many bureaucrats in this country. Too many spongers, not enough earners. Am I right, Walt?'

Walter leaned towards Terry.

'Those sponges. Do we have a delivery date yet?'

A brief conversation ensued. The phone rang. Someone else came in with a message slip to be signed. The phone rang again.

Ricky laid out a complete set of *Passion* samples. There was perfume, in three sizes; eau de toilette spray, with refill; deodorant in spray and stick; body lotion and talc; bath foam, shower gel and soap. He spread out a list of the quantities and opened the *Chemist and Druggist* to where Seventh Heaven Ltd's trade and retail prices were marked.

Then he went to the door, turned the key in the lock and took the phone off the hook.

'I came here for a deal, boys,' he said, 'not a two-man comedy act.'

'Thirty-three and a third of retail.' Ricky spread his hands helplessly. 'Can't do less. I'm payin' thirty.'

Simon winced at the barefaced lie. They were paying only twenty.

Terry was punching figures into the calculator. He was obviously working out what Ricky and Simon's profit was going to be. He frowned.

'The transport's costin' an arm and a leg,' added Ricky. 'Plus I've got the geezer in the firm to take care of.'

Walter studiously kept his eyes on his jotting pad. Ricky had marked Simon's card before they'd gone in. Of course, Walter would expect a backhander, too. And Terry? Simon had asked. Walter would sort it out later with Terry. Lesson one in schmeering: Only Bung The Boss.

Simon scribbled down some figures. The parcel came to about two million at retail value.

	(£'000)	(£'000)
Sell at 33·3%		666·6
Buy at 20%		400·0
Gross Profit:		266·6
Less:		
Transport	17·5	
Insurance	2·5	
Walter (?)	10·0	
		30·0
Trading Profit:		236·6
Less: Spaghetti Jim		
(10%)		23·6
Net Profit:		213·0
MY SHARE:		106.5

106.5 – *say*, £100,000

Walter and Terry were in deep conversation. They talked like ventriloquists, not moving their lips. Then Terry turned to Ricky.

'We can't take in any sale goods after the 10th. That's a fortnight.'

'Has Ricky ever let you down?'

Walter looked up from his jottings.

'There's another problem.'

'Problems, problems. Don't you ever give up worryin', Walt? You're dead a long time, boy. The gear will be in on time . . .'

'The sealing wax.'

Simon's stomach turned to lead. He scratched out a nought on the final figure. Well, ten grand was something. Better than a kick in the orchestras, as Ricky would say.

But Ricky was tapping the side of his nose and smiling.

'You're dealin' with Ricky Stone, darlin'! Think I

haven't thought of that?' He leaned forward. 'Listen! Call it . . . "*Passion Black, Limited Edition*." They'll be collectors' items in no time.'

'Passion Black.' Walter rolled the phrase around his tongue.

'Limited Edition,' savoured Terry.

They exchanged an almost imperceptible nod.

'You're on,' said Walter wearily.

'When I get your proforma,' said Terry, 'I'll issue a purchase order. Should I send it to Panama?'

For a fifty percent surcharge, the printers had done a rush job, and at six o'clock Simon had picked up his new business card. It read:

Simon J. Brotherton
Chief Executive
TRANSCOSMOS TRADING LTD.,
Transcosmos House,
Poonah Mansions,
London SW15 7TL.

The new invoices contained a telex number – Eli and Abby's – and a note in minuscule print declaring that the company was a subsidiary of Transcosmos Trading Inc. (Panama).

Back home, Simon set up the typewriter he'd bought from an office equipment retailer that Steinman and Co. had liquidated (everyone else had got theirs at half price before the auction), and he spent three hours re-typing the multinational cosmetic firm's offer, marking up the prices as he went.

In the morning he showed it to Ricky.

'You can't send that!' cried Ricky. 'Not with that number!'

The invoice bore the number 0001.

Simon spent the morning re-typing the proforma on a sheet drawn from the bottom of the pad, number 0099.

The firm might not be going public any day, but at least it had transacted a deal or two before.

In the Merc that afternoon on the way to Eli and Abby's, Ricky said that Spaghetti Jim had called. Seventh Heaven Ltd were now demanding to see their customer's purchase order. This meant a document originating in Nigeria, naturally. Not New Bond Street.

'I told him it was a telephone order,' said Ricky. 'He said they needed something in writing. "Them blackies don't know how to write," I told him. "Anyway, it's all pigeon post out there." "Use a courier," says Jim, the stupid berk. "Or get your bloke to send a telex." When we arrive, Sime, get on the blower to Mel. His girl can send us the necessary.'

Hang on, warned Simon. A telex machine automatically identified the sender by his number and answerback. You could always tell where a telex had come from. Melvyn's call-sign was MELHAR G, and G was the suffix for Great Britain.

Besides, it really wasn't ethical.

That side of things was beginning to worry him. His father, a business tycoon yet also an active lay preacher, had instilled in him the belief that a thing was either cricket or it was not. Forging a telex was close to body-line bowling. Forging bills of lading, as they planned to do, was like the umpire cheating.

'Ethical?' Ricky choked. 'This is business, boy, not religion.'

'If everyone did the same . . .'

'Everyone don't! They're sheep. No imagination. The world's full of very unintelligent people, Sime. Else how would we earn a livin'?'

Maybe everyone else was playing football. Or something even dirtier, like ice-hockey.

'It's a jungle out there,' said Ricky. 'Dog eats dog.'

Simon tightened his solar plexus and clenched his jaw. He was growing up fast.

71

OK, he'd find a way to fiddle the telex.

He found one in his briefcase. It was one Eli and Abby had sent to Ricky to deal with. Ricky had thrown it in the bin. Westminster Promotions were being sued. A box of BAR-B-Q LITASTICKS had spontaneously caught fire and burned down a lean-to garden shed. The garden shed happened to lean onto a garage which housed a vintage Lagonda and a power boat, and the garage itself abutted a six-bedroom stockbroker-Tudor villa set in 5.3 acres of very flammable pine-trees . . .

But right now, it was the form, not the content, that counted.

On an old telex machine, if you pressed the key marked LOCAL, it worked like a normal off-line typewriter. Pressing HERE IS automatically typed out your own call-sign, in black. The other person's call-sign, however, which came up automatically when you actually sent anything, was printed in red.

In a flash, he had it.

You put the machine on LOCAL and type out your own call-sign. You made a carriage return. You took the ribbon out and turned it upside down. Then you typed out a likely-looking Nigerian call-sign. In red. Carriage return. You reversed the ribbon back again. Typed the text of the purchase order, in black. At the end, you called off in the same way you signed on.

A spurt of excitement shot through him. He looked across to Ricky and felt a wave of fellow feeling. They were of the same fraternity.

'Leave it to me,' he said confidently.

They met Alex, the shipping agent, in a pub on neutral ground at the Elephant and Castle. Alex spoke with the menacing twang of the Gorbals and he rarely smiled. His head, with its bulging eyes and almost colourless hair, was out of all proportion to his skinny body. He reminded Simon of spermatozoa.

Seventh Heaven Ltd would only release the parcel in

Rotterdam on presentation of bills of lading showing onward shipment to Benin, Nigeria. These were the documents a ship's master signed as a true and correct record of what he had taken on board. At least, they were meant to be. In this case, of course, they'd be moodies. No perfume was going on board any ship to Nigeria. The load was doing an about-turn and coming back to Harwich.

Alex could fix it, but it would cost. There was a scale of fees.

'Two thousand pounds,' suggested Simon as an opener.

Ricky chimed in with his usual quip.

'Two grand? I ain't feelin' too grand.'

Alex didn't smile.

'What's the value of the consignment?' he demanded dourly.

'A century, give or take.'

Alex wasn't to be fooled.

'You want me to insure it for a hundred grand? Suppose the ship sank.'

'Well, let's say . . . six hundred.'

'At one percent, that's six thousand.'

Ricky almost exploded. Simon clicked his tongue supportively.

'That's for the master,' continued Alex. 'And the same again for me. How's your arithmetic?'

'Twelve,' choked Ricky. 'Robbery on the high seas!'

'A right snip,' said Ricky in the Merc outside.

'Well within budget,' agreed Simon. 'But what if Seventh Heaven sue us?'

'Let 'em. They won't find nothin' in the company.'

'Or put an injunction on the goods?'

'Darlin', you worry too much. First they'll ever hear of it is day one of the sale. By day two, the shops will have sold out.' Ricky pulled suddenly into the kerb. ''Ere, fancy some jellied eels?'

At Tubby Isaacs' jellied eels stall in Whitechapel, Ricky initiated Simon into one of life's greatest pleasures.

You were given a small bowl with hunks of blue-white eel in a soft, salty jelly. You soused the whole in vinegar, then slurped the eel into your mouth using a wedge of bread, finally spitting out the spines onto the ground to be trodden with the rest into the soft tarmac. Most of Ricky's bones landed on his crocodile shoes.

Simon was getting a flavour for fraternity food when Tubby began telling how his wife cooked the stuff fresh every night, and this broadened into a minor David Attenborough lecture on the peculiar living and eating habits of the common sewer eel . . .

Still mildly nauseous, Simon arrived home to find the flat in total darkness. He flicked a switch. Nothing happened. The lights must be fused, he thought. Suddenly, from deep inside, he heard a rustling movement. Burglars! Industrial spies! He inched forward, pressing himself flat against the corridor wall. There was a heavy glass vase in the sitting room . . .

Torchlight flashed in his face. Martha let out an exasperated sigh.

'What are you doing, creeping up on me?'

'What are *you* doing with the lights out?'

'Saving the family bread.'

'Martha, we're not *that* hard up . . .'

'Really you are a dumbo at times. Come on, give me a hand.'

She led the way to the small cupboard where the electricity meter was kept. The meter cover was off, exposing an array of terminals. She consulted a diagram scribbled on the back of a CND leaflet.

'It should be *this* one,' she said and unscrewed the terminal.

At once the low whir of the meter stopped.

'Eureka!' she cried. 'No more electricity bills.'

She pulled the mains switch and the flat suddenly lit

up. Carefully she replaced the cover and fitted the thin wires back into the round lead seal that were to prove the meter had not been tampered with.

I'm an accessory, thought Simon. Aiding and abetting a felony.

But instead of bringing him out in a guilty cold sweat, the thought left him mildly elated. He'd joined the underground. He was playing *their* game by *their* rules.

Up with the revolution! Down with the London Electricity Board!

But what about the gas? That burned night and day, all year round, for fires, hot water and central heating. Women never saw the big picture. They couldn't take the broad-brush approach.

'One should do an ABC cost analysis,' he said.

'Is that business school gobbledegook, Simon,' she asked, 'or are you trying to say something?'

'I mean, tackle the really big expenses first. Electricity is a flea-bite compared with gas.'

She gave him a withering look down her long nose.

'Sometimes I think I've been living with a total stranger for the past year,' she sighed. 'Follow me.'

She led him to the kitchen and opened the cupboard where the gas meter was housed.

He drew in his breath sharply.

The grey metal box was turned around to face the wall.

'They read it every quarter,' she explained in the tone of a sergeant briefing a raw recruit. 'So, we run it normally for the first six weeks, then turn it round for the next six. That way, the gas flows in the opposite direction and turns the meter back.'

He gave her a look of pure admiration.

'Direct action, huh?'

'Exactly. Use your opponent's strength against him.'

Ah, thought Simon. The game's not cricket or hockey: it's judo.

Martha knelt over her books, wearing just an African kekoi. The flat had been subtropical for the past two days. Simon lounged lengthways on the sofa, calculating his profits under all possible contingencies.

The phone rang. Martha answered it.

'Check with Directory Enquiries,' she said irritably and hung up. 'That's the third wrong number today.'

'Who was it for?'

'Transcosmos something-or-other.'

Simon sat bolt upright.

'Who was calling?' he cried.

'No idea.' She looked up. 'Sorry. Next time I'll get their age and marital status, too.'

It must be Peabody's! Simon lunged for the phone. He dialled the company and was put through to Terry.

'You *do* keep a low profile,' said Terry drily. 'Wrong numbers all the time.'

'Ah, that's our new temp. Taking time to settle in.'

Martha glared at him. He looked away.

'Wrong address as well,' continued Terry. 'Our order came back marked Return to Sender. Temporary postman, too?'

'The holiday season,' gulped Simon. 'You know how it is.'

'Well, if you want the order, I suggest you come and collect it yourself. Don't send the temp, she might get lost.' He paused. 'You're not going to let us down, are you? We're committing a big slice of our budget to this. I turned down three other offers today . . .'

'Terry, just leave it to us.'

'It's a comfort to feel we're in such professional hands.'

As usual, Ricky spent Wednesday afternoon down at the club. He wanted to take his mind off the deal.

The club was a prefabricated annexe at the back of a betting shop just off Norwood High Street. Smoke thickened the air. In one corner, a group of men in shirt-bands and sleeked-back hair huddled around a television on which there was dog racing from White City. In the background, a speaker piped across a race-track commentary from Newmarket.

Ricky sat playing kaluki with three others. One had lost the fingers of one hand in a razor fight. Another had a prosthetic on his leg and, being thereby beyond reasonable suspicion, was regularly used as the bag-man after a bank or jeweller's had been hit. The third man, a better dresser and a better player than the other two, said he was in insurance but it seemed to be mostly night work. His name was Morris.

Ricky was finishing telling how Alfie Steinman had ripped him off.

Morris played a winning card and swept the pound coins off the table.

'The bigger they are, the harder they fall,' he pronounced. 'They all have their little foibles.'

'You don't know Alfie Steinman,' responded Ricky warmly.

'I do, as it happens. Rather well.'

'He done you up, too?'

'Let's just say we have an interest in common.'

'You owe him dough? Pay it over to me instead, Morrie. I'll cover you.'

'No, the interest is more . . . personal.'

'A bird,' guessed Ricky.

Morris looked up sharply. He made a small signal to the other two players and suggested they might have a race to back. When they'd left the table, he leaned forward towards Ricky.

'You never met my Lucy, did you? Lucy's what you might call a *protijay* of mine. Works up the West End. Very fancy clientele, Rick, I can tell you. Top people only. The cream de la cream . . .'

Two days later, on Friday 3rd June, Alex called Ricky.

The forty-foot container of *Passion* had been offloaded in Rotterdam. Bills of lading had been presented to

77

Seventh Heaven Ltd's shippers and the goods released into Transcosmos's ownership. The container was now on board a ship bound for Harwich. He estimated it would clear Customs over the weekend and be on its way to Peabody's central depot in Milton Keynes by mid-day on the Monday. That was a full working week before the deadline of the 10th.

Only an act of God could now stand between the two men and their money.

That afternoon, Simon went to the agents and paid £2,000 out of his redundancy money and got a further twenty-eight days' extension on the farmhouse completion. By then, the profit would be in. It would leave a surplus of £60-70,000. He'd spend half on refurbishing the place and live off the balance. That would give him time to build up a body of work for a one-man exhibition in Florence, possibly even in Rome.

On the tube home, Simon dreamed of all the receptions at which he'd be lionised and all the reviews in which he'd be acclaimed.

Simon Brotherton: A Prospective.

He could see it now.

Why a Prospective? Because Retrospectives are for painters whose best work is behind them. Simon Brotherton's greatest oeuvre lies ahead of him. This talented newcomer to the Italian art scene is offering us a chance to witness the process of an artist's development. 'Potential' is the keynote of this exhibition.

Innocent of the preconceptions of a formal art training, Simon Brotherton brings us a fresh and, dare one say, romantic vision of the countryside of his adopted Toscana . . .

He took out a pen and began writing his name in various styles on the back of his newspaper. He drew a large square around the one that pleased him best and started designing the poster.

The same afternoon, Ricky visited Sonia.

He picked her up from her shop and, because her two teenage sons were at home, he took her to a large hotel in Marble Arch where, for a score over the counter and a tenner under it, he hired a room for the afternoon.

The bedside radio played Clayderman, a bottle of Spumanti lay chilling in the ice bucket and there was only the tearful urchin above the bed to witness their act of unbridled lust or to blush at the obscenities that Ricky loved to hear her utter in her posh accent.

Afterwards, as she lay with her head on his chest, her thinning fair hair tangled and clinging to her damp forehead, he lit a cigarette and told her about the fortune that would shortly be his.

'Fifty grand,' he said. 'Our running-away money.'

He'd give the other fifty to Beryl, to see her all right.

'South of France, Ricky?' she cooed.

'San Tropay. We'll get a nice little pad on the sea-front.'

'Ooh, so you can see the yachts from the bed.'

'We'll live nice and quiet.'

She put on a little-girl voice.

'We'll get to know all the right people and there'll be lots of cocktail parties and people to dinner every night, and I'll open up a Pin Cushion . . .'

Ricky eased his body from under hers. He didn't go for all that cuddling number after a bunk-up. He held back a fart.

'Plenty of time for golf. No distractions.'

'Don't you go getting distracted by those topless girls, darling.'

'Jealous? I'll pull one and have her join us. We'll have a scene.'

'Oh, Ricky, you are awful!'

But Ricky was warming up. He rolled one of her large, brown nipples between his fingers until she squealed.

'They go in for all that *ménage à trois* stuff, them French birds.'

'Well, I don't,' said Sonia, pulling the covers up to her neck.

'A couple of drinks inside you, darlin' . . .'

'Stop it, Ricky.'

'And you'd be beggin' me to give the little bird a seein'-to.'

'You're crude!'

'You love it, don't you, doll?'

'There's a time and a place.' She drew away. 'I'm going to order some tea.'

He lit another cigarette and thought about Beryl. If he took Beryl instead, he'd have the full hundred grand to play with.

'Course,' he said, already preparing a line of retreat, 'fifty grand sounds a lot, but it don't buy you much these days.'

On the Saturday night, after the news came through that the container had arrived in Harwich, Ricky, Beryl, Simon and Martha went out to the Thirty-Three Club in Mayfair. A celebration was called for.

This was a haunt of boxing promoters, property racketeers and money launderers. Over discreetly lit tables and from deep velvet plush chairs, the talk was all in big figures. Ricky nodded greetings and exchanged the odd word. He was at home here.

The drinks arrived. He proposed a toast.

'To health and a long life.'

'To *Passion*,' said Simon.

'To true love,' said Beryl. 'Please God.'

'To the future,' said Martha.

They drank. Beryl tapped Martha on the arm.

'The future's been before,' she said. 'History repeats itself.'

Ricky corrected her.

'Every start is a new beginnin'. When one door shuts, another one closes.'

'I've seen it all before,' said Beryl wearily. 'Nothin' changes.'

'Nobody knows what tomorrow brings, Beryl.'

'Tomorrow is the first day of the rest of your life.'

'You can't teach an old dog new tricks.'

'Nah, but each day is a fresh start,' said Beryl.

'Fresh start? Nothin's new, Beryl. You don't need the brain of a Lord George to know that. History repeats itself.'

Simon exchanged a glance with Martha. She looked dizzy, like a tennis umpire after an especially long rally.

A waiter brought the menus. Ricky ordered a prawn cocktail and well-done steak, and the same for Beryl. She protested.

'Avocado vinaigrette and Dover sole,' she told the waiter.

'Fish gives you heartburn,' said Ricky.

'I don't need fish to give me heartburn,' she said. 'I get all I need from livin' with Ricky Stone.'

'No-one's forcin' you. Money buys freedom.'

Beryl turned to Simon.

'Freedom from the pain? All the money in the world can't buy that. Am I right, Sime?'

'Well . . .' began Simon.

'Money can buy anything,' interjected Ricky roughly. 'Ain't that so, Martha?'

'If you mean the tokens of exchange in a capitalist society,' replied Martha with a half wink at Simon.

'See?' said Ricky to Beryl.

'Can't buy you love,' said Beryl doggedly.

'Beryl, love is not a commodity.'

The *maître d'hotel* arrived and ushered them to their table. Liveried waiters hovered at every elbow. One carved from a beef trolley, another lit a copper pan of *crêpes suzette* in a whoosh of flame. The wine waiter, his silver tasting-cup around his neck like a bull at auction, asked if they wanted any advice.

'Two Niersteiners,' ordered Ricky. 'That do you, Martha?'

'Can money buy claret?' asked Martha.

'Sure, darlin'. Or do you want somethin' red?'

'The house claret will be fine,' she told the waiter,

then turned back to Ricky. 'So, what will you do with your new-found riches?'

'Pack in everythin' in this effin' country, excuse my French, and retire somewhere warm.'

'Pack in Lady Muck?' hissed Beryl. 'I've heard all that before. Talk about history repeatin' itself!'

'Beryl, can I please have a conversation with my friends here without you always puttin' in the nause?' He turned to Simon. 'What you two goin' to do? Get married and settle down?'

'Martha doesn't believe in marriage,' said Simon.

'Marriage is born out of fear,' said Martha. 'You're afraid of losing your partner, so you build this cage with big bars so they can't escape. Marriage is a prison.'

Simon knew this was directed at him. She refused to marry him. If he ever managed to demolish this argument, then she'd rely on the marriage-is-property-exchange angle, and in combating that the path was very narrow and very full of snakes.

'Yeah,' agreed Beryl. 'Prison, that's what it is.'

Ricky wasn't to be drawn on this, though he was especially well qualified on the subjects both of marriage and of passion.

'What about your dough?' he asked.

'With *his* new-found riches,' said Martha with a sly smile, 'Simon is becoming a landowner in Italy. He put some more down on the deposit today.'

Simon glared at her.

'You never know when they'll slap exchange controls back on,' he said to Ricky. 'One's hedging one's bets.'

'That is,' continued Martha with a touch of sarcasm, 'if he doesn't fall for another unbeatable roulette system.'

Ricky raised an eyebrow at Simon.

'Walk before you run, boy,' he said.

Beryl's mind was still on an earlier conversation.

'Don't listen to Ricky,' she said. 'All them dreams of retirin' to the South of France is fairy tales. Even if he makes enough, he won't keep it. He'll do the lot on horses. Or give it to that Alfie Steinman, like the last bit.'

Simon raised an eyebrow at Ricky.

'Walk before you run?'

Ricky smiled.

'*Touché*, kid.'

And slowly they raised their glasses and chinked them together in a salute. They were a team.

Just as Simon was drinking, he noticed a well-fed, well-dressed man getting up from a table in the far corner behind Ricky. A waiter held out a fur stole for his young companion. There was something familiar about the angle of this man's head and shoulders. As he turned and glanced around the room, he caught Simon's eye. He froze. Then he saw Ricky and blanched. With a brief word to the waiter, he hurried the girl to the door and out of the room.

'Speak of the devil,' breathed Simon. 'You'll never guess who I've just seen leaving. Our old friend Alfred Steinman!'

Ricky was on his feet in a flash, but Alfie Steinman had already disappeared.

8

Shortly after ten o'clock on the morning of Monday 6th June, Simon was getting out after an hour's soaking in the bath when Alex the Sperm called to say they'd hit a snag.

'Alcohol duty,' he said succinctly.

Simon wrapped the towel around his waist and laughed. It was to be the last time he'd laugh for many weeks.

'Wrong gear. Ours is perfume.'

'Perfume is alcohol. If you import alcohol, you pay duty.'

'Hold on! We're not importing anything. The stuff was made here.'

'How do Customs know that?'

'Well, it must say so on the packs.'

'It doesn't. It could be made in Bongobongoland for all they know. We don't have a Certificate of Origin.'

'Why not?'

'Your Nigerian customer didn't seem to need one.'

'I'll get one.'

'You'll tell Seventh Heaven you need a certificate to get the gear back in?'

Simon gulped. Something crazy was going on here.

'This is perfume, not booze! Do they think we're flogging it into pubs?'

'They're the Customs: they don't think. They go by the book. The book says, unless the alcohol is denatured, you pay duty.'

'Unless it's what?'

To prevent the Al Capones of this country from selling 100-proof spirit in the disguise of Chanel No. 5 and thereby doing the Revenue out of its lawful taxes, the basic ethyl alcohol was mixed with five percent of methanol. This made the perfume bitter and foul-tasting and unfit for human consumption by anyone but a meths drinker, who presumably couldn't afford it anyway. Denatured in this way, alcohol went free of duty.

'Seventh Heaven *must* have used the proper alcohol,' protested Simon.

'You and I know that,' said Alex. 'But *they* don't. As far as they are concerned, it could be triple-distilled arak from Timbuktu.'

'But it's only been out of the country a couple of days!'

'How do they know that?'

'Show them the bloody shipping documents.'

'Can you prove it's the same load? It could have been switched at Rotterdam. Irregularities do occur,' he added pointedly.

'Look, if it's not at Peabody's by Friday, we're fucked.'

There was a moment's pause at the other end.

'Then you'll have to pay the duty to get the goods released,' said Alex. 'Give them samples to test and when they clear them you'll get your money back.'

'What's the duty?'

'About a hundred grand, give or take.'

'Jesus Christ!'

Simon slumped into a chair. The receiver dropped from his grasp. He was having a stroke. Death would be sweet.

Ricky was exercising the Alsatian in Norwood Park. Simon stood behind a tree some distance away, steeling his nerve.

Ricky took a golf ball out of his pocket, teed up and drove it a hundred yards across the park. The dog circled frenziedly, then spotted the ball and bounded off after it. Ricky sauntered on until the Alsatian brought it back. Retrieving it from its jaws, he chose another target and began the game again. Today, he sported a jaunty suede jacket and new check golfing trousers. He didn't have a care in the world, and when he wasn't calling after the dog, he was whistling tunes from *Oklahoma*.

'Look who's here!' he exclaimed when Simon showed himself. 'Fancy a putt? No money on it, I promise.'

Simon shook his head.

'We've got problems,' he said dolefully.

Biting the bullet, he told him the news.

Ricky could never distinguish between the messenger and the message. Bad news was the bearer's fault. Especially here, since documentation was tacitly Simon's province. Ricky hated paperwork. Orders and invoices were just about OK. But tax forms, VAT returns, HP agreements, lease contracts, company accounts – none of these really existed for him. A problem of the present kind was literally outside his comprehension.

'You told them we was goin' to *drink* the crap?' he exploded. 'What are you, some kind of berk?'

Simon explained again, simplifying it further.

'They've got no right holdin' up other people's goods!' cried Ricky.

'That's the rules,' said Simon.

'Cobblers to your rules.'

'They're not *my* rules, Ricky. It's what the book says.'

'But Rotterdam's in the Common Market, ain't it?'

'Yes, but that's not the point . . .'

'If you can get the gear out, how come you can't get it in again?'

'Customs aren't to know it was the same gear.'

'Course it bloody is! Are they stupid or what?'

'They hold the cards, I'm afraid. They've got the stock and all the time in the world. We've only got till Friday.'

'The fuckin' pricks in this fuckin' country . . .'

Ricky ranted for five minutes. Then he dug the half-chewed golf-ball from the Alsatian's slobbery mouth, set it up on the tee and smote it with such force that it soared way over the roof of the tea pavilion, over the line of poplars by the road and disappeared into a far distant housing estate.

Ricky was around at Spaghetti Jim's house that evening. A new baby Volvo stood in the driveway alongside Jim's company Rover, and on the occasional table in the lounge lay a stack of brochures for Caribbean cruises. Jim had been spending his profits in advance.

He turned first red, then yellow, then green, like a traffic-light. His bald patch sweated. His hand trembled as he poured himself a third Scotch.

Distribution Department had gone into it carefully and provided all the documents required for Nigeria. What could he do?

'Earn your fuckin' dough,' growled Ricky.

Jim slipped a pill-box out of his pocket and took one. He thought again, and took another.

'I wish I'd never set eyes on you,' he moaned.

Tuesday came and went. Wednesday morning, Jim called Simon. He didn't dare call Ricky, for the news was bad.

No way could he get the certificates. Even mentioning it had raised suspicions and questions were being asked.

They'd have to find the money for the duty.

'It's got to be Billy,' pronounced Ricky, 'or we're snookered.'

Billy was short and tough. He wore his hair close-cropped and seldom blinked. Because his face never betrayed the slightest expression, it was smooth and unlined, giving him the look of an adolescent psychopath, rather than a mature one.

Billy had had a spell in the Foreign Legion – he'd done a runner after six months – and, later, a spell of detention at Her Majesty's pleasure. He owned a stable and half a dozen racehorses. He never boasted and never blabbed – except once, and then only for high literary motives, when Dick Francis came to ask him how he'd fixed a race. Careless of the risks, he let himself be seen at racecourses all over the country, betting in tens of thousands. William Hill's regularly accepted fifty grand on a single horse. The weight of his own money dramatically changed the odds, of course, and his constant problem was how to get large sums of money on without disclosing that the money was his. In this, Ricky regularly helped him, and half the faces playing kaluki at the club on any given afternoon were betting as proxies for Billy.

Billy lived high, higher even than the law. In many ways he was above the law. His immunity was aided by a certain Detective Superintendent in the Metropolitan Police. Unfortunately, the man had earned so well he was shortly retiring to his villa in Spain. But he was grooming a successor.

Billy lived in a Mexican-style villa behind a tall security fence in a wooded enclave near Esher. It was here that Ricky and Simon came to sue for help.

Billy was doing lengths in his covered pool, under the eye of Winston, his big black in-house bouncer, when they arrived. He got out and lay on a towelled bench while a blonde girl in nurse's uniform gave him an unconvincing massage.

Ricky introduced Simon. Billy repeated his name carefully; no doubt he'd have him checked out afterwards.

Simon described the problem. Billy listened without apparent interest. He asked no questions.

'A hundred G's,' said Ricky. 'That's what we've got to pull up.'

'It'll be out for two weeks,' said Simon. 'Maximum three.'

'We'll split the bunce down the middle. Even Stevens. You have half whack.'

'And security on the stock, too . . .'

Billy rolled over to let the masseuse work on his hairless, cherubic front. At last he spoke.

'Security? You're my security. Ain't that so, Winston?'

Winston grinned and strangled a wet towel.

Billy didn't have it in the house. In suitcases in lock-up garages, yes. In holdalls in left-luggage lockers and in bank accounts under any of twenty names, certainly. He needed time to put it all together. Moving around large sums of cash anonymously was an art in itself.

On Thursday morning, Ricky received a call from a phone box.

'Deliverin' the groceries at four o'clock,' said a voice and hung up.

At four, a black cab pulled up. The driver unloaded three large cartons of Jacob's cream crackers. Ricky signed for them and the man drove away.

A few minutes later, Simon called Alex and told him to lay on a truck first thing in the morning. The goods had to be in Milton Keynes by the close of business that day.

At five-thirty, Simon finished counting the first carton and started on the second. At six, Beryl brought him in another cup of tannin liqueur. At seven, he was into the third carton and already past the hundred thousand pounds mark. His fingers were sore and filthy.

Billy obviously hadn't counted the money. He'd have no idea how much was there. A devious thought flashed across Simon's mind, but he overrode it at once. He remembered the security. Every pound was a drop of blood.

Simon stayed over at Ricky's house and got up before dawn. By six he was in the Merc, heading for Harwich with the money in two suitcases in the boot.

Ricky stayed behind to liaise with Alex. Or so he said. In fact, Ricky had a deep-rooted dislike of Fridays. It wasn't to do with working on the Sabbath eve, for he was as lapsed in his faith as a Jew could be. No: Fridays were the start of the weekend, just as Mondays were the end of it. The working week was from Tuesday to Thursday, with Wednesday afternoons spent down at the club.

The sun rose ahead into a cloudless sky as Simon drove through the flat wastes of East Anglia. He tuned in to the news, but was too on edge to concentrate. He studiously ignored a pair of hitch-hiking nymphettes, and when he pulled in for petrol he didn't dare leave the car unguarded to take a leak.

Some time after ten, he reached the docks and parked the car.

He saw a sign, CUSTOMS, and joined a slow-moving queue. Eventually his turn came and he was asked to open his suitcases. He tried to explain, but at the sight of bundles of dirty banknotes, the supervisor was called, who in turn called the superintendent. It took Simon twenty minutes to convince them he wasn't a currency smuggler just come in from the Hook of Holland.

He was in the wrong building. Commercial Imports were across the way.

Shortly before eleven, Simon found a man who seemed to recall the consignment. With a sigh of relief, Simon opened the suitcases again.

The man tapped a notice on the wall.

'HM Customs and Excise,' it read, 'require payment by cleared cheque or banker's draft. Cash, coin and other specie is only acceptable to a maximum of £1,000.'

Simon broke into a sweat. He looked around him for a bank. Would they exchange the cash for a draft?

The man was rummaging through a box file marked 'Movements'. His face lengthened. He told Simon to wait. He was gone for several minutes. When he returned, he was shaking his head.

'The paperwork's gone up to London Head Office,' he said.

Simon pays in the cash at the Harwich branch of the Midland Bank. Two tellers take twenty-five minutes to count it.

Harwich branch phones Simon's own branch in East Putney. A code word is exchanged. East Putney branch phones back, repeating the code. Yes, they will issue a draft in favour of HM Customs and Excise for £105,320.67p.

Simon phones Ricky. Ricky is on the phone to a pal at the club, going through the *Sporting Life*. Eventually Simon gets through.

Ricky dresses. He jumps in Simon's car and goes to pick up the draft.

East Putney branch does not know Mr Richard Stone.

East Putney calls Harwich. They have a man causing a public disturbance in the bank, calling himself Mr Richard Stone. Would Mr Brotherton give a personal description? Simon says, 'Imagine Henry Cooper with a nicotine-stained mouthguard.' The description tallies. They accept Simon's instructions to release the draft to Mr Stone.

Simon's car is not automatic and Ricky drives all the way to Kings Beam House, EC3, the customs headquarters, in first gear. It stalls on Blackfriars Bridge. Ricky rides it onto the pavement on the starter motor, abandons it and catches a cab.

The paperwork hasn't arrived in London.

Ricky uses certain abusive language and the commissionnaire is called. He gives the commissionnaire a smack on the ear. The superintendent is called. Ricky shakes the superintendent vigorously by the lapels and his top dentures fall out. The deputy chief collector is called.

The deputy chief collector phones Harwich. Harwich says that their own copies of the paperwork have been sent down for microfilming. The DCC tells Ricky there is nothing he can do.

Ricky is then understood to make certain improper suggestions that might be construed by a suspicious mind as constituting an inducement. A verbal caution is issued and an assistant called into the room, who remains present for the rest of the meeting.

At twelve forty-five, the DCC goes to lunch.

At two-thirty, the DCC returns from lunch.

A search of the incoming mail room now reveals that the paperwork has arrived but has been mistakenly placed in the Southampton pile.

Ricky delivers a speech on bureaucratic inefficiency and the state of the country.

The DCC has had a good lunch and doesn't want more argument. He takes the draft and has the assistant show Ricky out. On the file he marks a large red cross. He calls Harwich and instructs the goods to be released.

At four-thirty, the superintendent at Harwich customs signs the release forms. The goods are free to be loaded and removed.

At five to five, Simon calls Peabody's. They have five minutes in which to cover a good hundred and fifty miles. He reckons they have missed the deadline.

Terry reckons so, too. Simon uses certain unprintable expletives and Terry suggests he speak to the warehouse manager himself.

Simon calls the warehouse manager. The manager consults his lads. For treble rates plus a pony in the hand, they'll stop behind and unload the vehicle.

The container is sealed. The driver climbs into his cab. He starts up and drives to the gate. He presents the release docket. The boom is raised and the way lies open. And at five-twenty-four the truck is heading west and into the declining sun.

Peabody's didn't get round to counting the stock until the Monday.

It was short. By £75,000-worth.

Ricky himself went up to Milton Keynes to check. He snooped around the back of the warehouse complex; he'd played that trick himself before. But no, there was no hidden gear. The count was accurate.

There'd be fuckin' murders with Seventh Heaven Ltd, he swore as he belted back down the M1. They hadn't got their money yet. He'd pay them short.

But he thought again. The goods were still on their way to Nigeria, weren't they? He couldn't scream yet. How could he know they were short? Once the sale was on, it would be Seventh Heaven doing the screaming and murdering.

He'd have to wipe his mouth and swallow.

It knocked seventy-five grand off the profit. Still, even allowing for Billy's half share, that left a nice piece to cut up when the customs money came back.

Section 5(b)(ii) of Notice 64, a pamphlet issued by the Customs and Excise entitled 'Spirits in Imported Goods: Remission of Excise Duty', reads:

'If the goods originate from the European Community . . . the ethanol they contain must be denatured with:

- 10 microgrammes of solid denatonium benzoate ('Bitrex') per cubic centimetre; or
- 120 microgrammes of solid quassin per cubic centimetre; or
- 4000 microgrammes of solid ducrose octa-acetate per cubic centimetre.'

If so, the goods qualify for relief.

If not, they don't.

Ninety percent of the Seventh Heaven parcel didn't.

The customs passed one tenth of the samples and paid back £10,000. They retained £95,000.

Spaghetti Jim stayed late night after night, rooting around in the Purchasing Department. He found that, in order to meet the product launch date, *Passion* had been made with a base imported from Houston. It had been denatured according to US regulations, but these were not the same as the UK regulations. How it had slipped through untested and untaxed was a mystery. But it had. Sod's Law had only now brought it to light.

'They let the crap in before!' expostulated Ricky, beside

himself with incomprehension. 'You can't hang a man twice for the same crime.'

'They can do anything,' said Simon morosely.

Ricky got on the blower to the Deputy Chief Collector. He was tied up in meetings. He called back half an hour later but the man was out of the office. Ricky suspected a vendetta.

As far as the government chemist in Stamford Street, SE1, was concerned, his labs had done the tests. He was snowed under by a backlog of work and he wasn't going to do them again. Simon insisted on appointing an independent chemical analyst. He found a firm in Slough, but when they contacted the government labs for samples, they were told they'd all been used up in the tests.

'Nip round the corner,' said Ricky to Simon, 'and *buy* some bleedin' samples.'

The shops were empty. All the product had been recalled.

Simon grovelled to Terry. Could he have the samples they'd left in his offices back? Half had been nicked. Simon hurried the rest to Slough for testing.

But that wasn't acceptable either. How were the customs to know that *this* 7ml. perfume was the same as *that* 7ml. perfume they'd drawn from the consignment at Harwich?

'Fuckin' stupid fuckin' petty fuckin' tyrants,' raged Ricky, 'they fuckin' get on my fuckin' wick!'

Throughout those bleak days, Ricky lived on tranquillisers. But they did little to calm him down.

Then, across the length and breadth of the country, Peabody's Grand Summer Sale started. Full-page ads appeared in the dailies, offering half-price *Passion*.

Simon left his phone off the hook. He took a sketch pad and spent the days in Putney Cemetery, drawing cypress trees. It was the closest he was ever going to get to the Tuscan landscape.

Ricky went down to Brighton for a couple of days alone. He was going to play some golf and just relax by himself.

A few days later, a small package dropped through

the letterbox in Millionaire's Row, Norwood. It was addressed to Mrs Stone. Beryl opened it. It was from the manager of the Metropole Hotel, Brighton, returning a garment that had been left behind. The garment enclosed was a lady's silk slip. It was not Beryl's.

That night she wound the slip into a rope and eased it gently under her sleeping husband's neck. Looping it into a noose, she knelt with her full weight on his chest and set to work to throttle the life out of her perfidious husband. She would have succeeded in doing so had he not remembered that she was extremely ticklish and managed to get his fingers to her armpits in time.

But Ricky survived it all.

He survived, too, the writs and injunctions from Seventh Heaven. He almost enjoyed the threatening letters and the abusive phonecalls.

'Sue me,' he'd say expansively. 'I ain't got an Abergavenny.'

There was nothing they could do about it. He knew it, and they knew it.

As the days ground by, even Ricky came to accept that they'd kissed their ninety-five grand goodbye. Simon revised his calculations downwards for the final time.

	(£'000)	(£'000)
Gross Profit		213·0
Less:		
Shortages	75·0	
Duty	95·0	
Extras	10·0	
		180·0
Net Profit:		33·0
Less:		
Billy (50%)	16·5	
Jim (10%)	3·3	
		19·8
Final Profit:		12·8

My share = £6,400

Six thousand six hundred.

Not enough to pay the balance on the farmhouse. Not enough to run away to the South of France. Not enough to do anything except keep on going. Still, better than a kick in the orchestras.

9

'Out of the fire, into the fryin' pan.'

Ricky pulled a roll of notes out of his back pocket and handed it to Beryl. He'd done a couple of grand at the club that afternoon. What was he left with? Four grand. Piss all. It would hardly buy a dirty weekend with Sonia, let alone a lifetime in the sun. Beryl could have it for housekeeping. And he was potless again.

Beryl put the roll, uncounted, in her housecoat pocket.

'Eat your lox,' she said, hovering beside his elbow.

'Beryl, will you stop? You know I can't think with my belly full.'

'I got to build your strength up,' she said. 'To get back.'

He finished his tea. At once she took the cup away to brew him another.

'I should never have got in with that young ponce,' he complained. 'He's a right unlucky face.'

'He's a nice lad. He's got an education.'

'If he's so fuckin' smart, how come we did our dough?'

'It's in the stars. It wasn't to be.'

'Remind me to consult you next time.'

'Yeah, that's me, Madame Beryl, Astrologer.' She peered at the dregs in his cup where a teabag had burst. 'I see an 'orrible old slag with bottle-blonde hair. Ugh! She's dyin' in a pool of blood. There's a great big knife stickin' out of her back. "Goodbye, Ricky," she says, all posh. "Excuse me while I peg out."'

Her cackle of laughter turned into a racking cough.

He switched on the television to *Grandstand* and turned the volume up high.

But he couldn't stop his mind going over and over the deal. Why had it gone wrong? Deals like that didn't grow on trees. They should have had a right coup off. Nothing had gone right since that little touch at the casino. Horses or dogs, he hadn't had a winner in weeks. Why?

Because he was in with that wet-eared ponce.

Luck rubbed off. Some people were lucky, other people were boks. Simon Brotherton was a bok.

And when had Ricky Stone ever needed a partner?

Simon watched the yeast frothing in the jug of warm water. To his side stood a bowl of stone-ground, whole-grain natural flour. Today he was making the bread. Today he was in the dog house.

Martha sat on a bar stool with her knees tucked under her chin, looking through the fringe cinemas in *Time Out* behind the curtain of her dark wavy hair. She was going to a movie on her own.

They'd had a row. He'd put the six grand towards the other six on the farmhouse and bought a further month's extension.

'Throwing good money after bad!' she'd cried in rage. 'Here I am, struggling to keep us alive on a pittance, risking the fuzz each time I do a phone box or get us a food parcel' – she had a friend who worked in the kitchens of the Hilton and filched food for a small consideration – 'and there you are, with your hands on *six thousand pounds*, and what do you do? You chuck the whole lot away on this dope-headed escapist dream. Didn't you think of keeping *anything* back? Not sixty pounds? Not even *six*?'

She'd had a point. You couldn't eat off dreams. But without dreams, what kind of a life was it?

Red spots had begun to show on her freckled cheeks. He knew the only thing to do then: take hold of her and give her a French kiss in the ear. Sexist and macho it might be, but it worked every time. This time was no exception, and within two minutes they'd been making passionate love right there on the kelim. His elbows and knees were still sore. Of course, going to a movie on her own was her way of regaining her dignity. Fair enough. He wasn't going to deny her that.

Martha was great. Individual. Interesting. Difficult. Life with her was always a challenge and there was never a dull moment. Theirs was the attraction of opposites. They'd be eighty years old and in their bath chairs and still be bickering and arguing. That was what a dynamic relationship was about. They'd never run out of things to say, they'd never run out of each other. Well, *he* wouldn't.

Why wouldn't she say Yes to him?

If he'd made that hundred grand, she'd be singing a different tune now. Martha was a woman. Every woman basically only wanted to get married, settle down and have children. They were wired up that way. They might throw up intellectual barrage balloons, but ultimately it came down to inescapable instinct. If only he could bide his time, the biological imperative would do the work for him.

Maybe she was right about his motives for wanting to marry. Yes, she brought the light into his life and he was afraid of the dark without her. Why couldn't he see things in her uncompromising, fearless way? He tried hard to be self-dependent, to be caring and yet not clinging, to look upon love as an exchange between two people who respected each other's freedom and not as one more mode of exploitation and ownership . . .

But if he thought it right the way through, he came back to his starting-point. It all boiled down to money. Money was the lubricant that would ease the transition. Money meant Tuscany. It meant sunshine and art, wine and talk, hot nights and long siestas. It meant capuccino for breakfast and fresh pasta for lunch, vermouth at sundown and a cornucopia of home-grown vegetables for supper. The place would plead his suit for him.

But would he ever get it? He had a month to raise the balance of twenty-eight grand or the owners could make him forfeit the twelve he'd paid so far.

God *damn* it, why hadn't the deal come off?

Ricky had set it up; the flop was all due to him.

Ricky was a child. He only saw what he wanted to see. Unwelcome facts hit a blind spot. He wouldn't listen to caution. When the problems did arise, he simply wished them away. And if they didn't go away, he blamed somebody else. Ricky Stone was never wrong. Ricky Stone would never admit a mistake. It was always somebody else's fault.

Frankly, he was one of the wide boys. He belonged among the spivs in the street markets. That was his element. International business transactions? Forget it. The man was simply too *unsophisticated*. Simon should have seen it before.

Well, he'd seen it now. He wasn't going to make the mistake again. He was a quick learner. He knew how the game worked. He'd pull up a deal of his own and see it through all by himself.

Simon Brotherton, Chairman, Chief Executive and Managing Director of Transcosmos Trading Ltd, didn't need any partners.

'Never known an August like it, Rick.'

'Business? Dead as a dodo, Ricky me old mate. You'd think they'd dropped the bomb out there. Even the ice cream boys are emigratin'.'

''Ere Rick, we heard you'd teamed up with Alfie Steinman's boy . . .'

'Bleedin' heatwave, but can I shift a pair of sunglasses? Got a big daffy stuck up my arse. You what, Rick? You'll take them? Sorry, pal, I'm puttin' them by for a rainy day, aren't I?'

'What's with this young geezer, Ricky? You fraternisin' with the enemy, or what? Don't tell me you're jobbin' out Steinman's!'

'Ask that pal of yours to sort me out some *Passion*, will yer?'

'Like I told yer, Rick, it's me accountant. Can't serve no dodgy customers. Now, that young kid, the one what took them firelighters . . . All right, Ricky, keep yer barnet on! I know it was *your* deal. I was only sayin' I'd be happy to serve *him* . . .'

It was the same old story. Nobody wanted to know Ricky Stone. Worse, all he ever heard was the name of that wet-eared ponce.

'Haven't seen Ricky around for a while,' said Martha casually. 'Dropped him, have you?'

Simon looked up from his business school address book. He was searching for likely alumni who could find him a parcel of stock. They'd all become bankers, accountants, stock-brokers, corporate treasurers. Not one of them was in a sales or marketing department. That summed up the malaise of British industry.

'No. Actually, I'm not sure he's quite my type.'

'Your class, you mean.'

'Martha, do you have to reduce everything to politics?'

'Just because he doesn't speak like you.'

'He doesn't have a trained mind. It makes communication difficult.'

'Oh, and you do, huh? Yours, Simon, is the product of a narrow, blinkered, middle-class system . . .'

'*He* wouldn't call it that. He thinks an education is the crown jewels. He'd give anything to be able to express himself better. Talk properly. Even spell.'

'My God, you are an arrogant snob!'

'He told me so himself.' Simon stared into the yeast. 'Poor Ricky. Such an unawakened consciousness.'

At the sarcasm Martha let out a low, silvery chuckle and sat forward in her chair. She always enjoyed a game of Simon-baiting.

'What you really mean,' she said, 'is that your dad's a Member of the Professional Classes and his dad's a retired bus inspector.'

'And a Member of the Proletariat? You ask Ricky if he's a prole! You'll get a knuckle sandwich.'

'But that's how *you* see him. I saw your face the other night when he ordered white wine with his steak.'

'He's perfectly entitled to his own tastes. I don't expect everyone to share mine.'

'And as for the way he holds his knife . . .'

'Martha, shut up! I'm very fond of Ricky. He's great to be with and I genuinely like his company. It's only that . . .'

'Only that you think you don't need him.'

As always, Martha expressed his thought for him. Often better, too.

'Well, yes. I don't.'

'I think you'll find you do, Simon.'

He jabbed a wooden spoon savagely into the yeast and prodded it till it slopped over the edge of the jug. He was damned if he was going to be playing *this* game in his bath chair at eighty.

'And it's Winsome Lad, Winsome Lad by a furlong! Then Sir Galahad in second place, ahead of Road Runner in third . . .'

Billy lowered his binoculars. His face gave nothing away. He moved off towards the exit of the Members' Enclosure.

His own horse, Hot Tip, hadn't been placed.

Ricky walked beside him, a full head taller. He began to hope the boys down the club had not managed to get all the money on. Forty grand was a right bundle to do on a single punt.

'She wasn't tryin',' said Ricky. 'You could see that a mile off.'

Billy said nothing.

'I'd have paid that jockey a grand to stay at home,' Ricky added.

Billy shrugged and put on a pair of mirrored sunglasses. Ricky shook his head. If it had been his money, he'd be throttling the bookies right now.

'I mean, that's a lot of dough!' he went on.

'I need a winner,' said Billy impassively.

'Don't we all, old son!'

'To stop questions.'

'Ah.'

Ricky understood. Billy lived high and didn't trouble to hide it. The question being asked was, where did he get the money from? 'From winnings,' was his regular answer. But *what* winnings? Billy had had a lousy season.

'That young lad you're in with,' he said as they approached the Rolls. 'Got a company, you said?'

'Yeah, but . . .'

'Get him to put me on the payroll.'

'Billy . . .'

'Tell him I want a salary. I'll give him one for one.'

Ricky's brain clicked like a fruit machine. A nice little proposition: readies in return for tax-deductible wages. Handy for Billy to receive an income he could declare and help explain how he afforded to live. Handy for the company, too, to turn its profits into walking-about money. In fact, handy for everybody.

'You mean, a nicker in the hand for a nicker on the book?'

Billy nodded, searching his pockets for the car keys.

'I want a card, a stamp, PAYE, the lot. It's got to look kosher.' He went through his pockets again. 'Lost the fuckin' keys.'

'Maybe you dropped them. We'll go back.'

'Leave it,' said Billy, turning away. 'We'll get a cab.'

A taxi from Newmarket to London made even Ricky think twice.

'It's worth a look.'

As Ricky turned to retrace his steps, his eye caught a glint from the boot of the Roller. It was the key, left in the lock.

'You could have got your spare wheel nicked,' he said.

'And the rest,' said Billy without concern.

Back in London, Billy drove Ricky to his house. As he drew up outside, he asked if he would look after something for him for a day or two. He went to the boot of the car and took out two large holdalls.

'Don't forget to talk to your pal,' he said as he drove off.

Indoors, Ricky unzipped one of the holdalls. It burst open, releasing wads of dirty, crumpled twenty-pound notes.

Over the brandy and cigars they got down to business.

Julian Wetherby had never been a close friend of Simon's. Their sole bond was a year spent at business school together. Wetherby was Financial Controller of Britain's largest junk food conglommerate. He had a company BMW 525i, two point four children, a Laura Ashley wife, a house by Richmond park and a cottage in Gloucestershire, an expense account which he signed himself and the absolute certainty of a comfortable job until retirement. There were times when Simon envied Wetherby.

'Job buying,' replied Simon when asked about his new career step.

'Jobbing? On the stock market?'

'No, no. It's clearance lines. Redundant stock. Liquidations. I buy from major companies and sell through the street markets.'

Wetherby ordered another brandy. His incredulity grew exaggerated. Simon read the signs; *he* was going to pick up the tab. Well, lunch had been his suggestion. And the Connaught his choice. He might be skint, but in business appearances counted for everything.

'What, you a barrow boy, Simon?'

'Julian, there's a network of wholesalers up and down the country who supply the street markets. Do you know, probably *one fifth* of all toiletries are sold through that outlet! Amazing, isn't it? And no-one's done any market research. I call that a major business opportunity.'

Then Simon came to the point. He wanted Wetherby to introduce him to the managers of all the main brands – Frisbees, Crispos, Wafathins, Crinklies, Robot Rolls, Jumbly-tums, Popsitops. Introduce him to the men who made the big product decisions.

But then Simon almost blew it.

'Course,' he added casually, 'you'll be covered.'

'We'll take out a Dun and Bradstreet report, naturally.'

'No, I mean *you*. Personally.'

'I'm the chief, old man. Got indians to take care of the details.'

How would Ricky put it?

'What I mean is, if I get a nice day's work out of it, I'll want to show my appreciation, won't I? Get my drift?'

Julian Wetherby finally got his drift. Shock drained the colour from his face. He swallowed back his brandy and looked at his watch.

'I shall have to be getting back. Group budget meeting at four. Good to see the old business school spirit alive and well.'

Moments later, Simon was standing on the pavement outside, waving Wetherby off in a chauffeur-driven XJ6 and wondering how he should have phrased it. Or was Julian Wetherby the one exception to the rule?

'You should have stuck with that Simon,' said Beryl. 'He had a head on his shoulders. Kept you out of mischief.'

'Leave off, doll,' said Ricky from behind the *Sporting Life*. 'Can't you see I'm studyin'?'

'With him around, I felt easy. I knew you weren't gettin' in no trouble.'

'Beryl . . .'

'Half your age and twice your brains.'

Ricky crumpled up the paper suddenly and violently.

'Beryl!' he roared. 'I get the fuckin' prick-ache hearin' that name! Once more and there'll be bloody murders.'

'Are you going to sulk *all* evening?' asked Martha.

Simon bit a nail crossly. Martha had the knack of defining his mood so as somehow to co-opt it for herself. He was sulking, yes, but it was *his* mood and *he* wanted to decide when to stop.

'Just business,' he said.

She reached for his hand in a gesture of sympathy.

'Tell me.'

He'd managed to get one introduction out of Julian Wetherby, and it should have been an ace: Chris Collinson, the group's Marketing Director. Simon had fixed a meeting. Chris had told him they already used a firm to handle their discontinued lines. Simon had hinted there'd be something in it for him. This time the inducement fell on fertile ground and Chris promised to sort him out something.

He'd phoned back that afternoon offering a contract to clear all the biscuits that got broken during manufacture.

'Who the hell wants *broken* biscuits!' groaned Simon.

'I don't know. Ask Ricky. It's up his street.'

'Leave Ricky out of this.'

'He's the expert. He's got all the contacts.'

'Martha, there's no such thing as an expert in this business. Anyway, I can make all the contacts myself.'

'You're being pig-headed. Ask his advice.'

'I don't need his advice!'

'You do, and you know it. Go on, call him. Now.'

'Martha! If you mention that man once again, I'll scream!'

The first race of the day was not yet under starter's orders and, apart from three old boys in the far corner preparing their afternoon's betting, the club was empty.

A pencil beam of sunlight angled in high through the tarry windows.

Morris took a manilla envelope out of his cashmere jacket and laid it on the table between them. He tapped it with a manicured fingernail.

'It's all in there,' he said. 'You might say we have our pal Alfie Steinman nicely tied up.'

Morris smiled at his little joke. His face was rounded and slightly squashed, as if he'd just come back from a robbery and hadn't taken off the fine-denier stocking.

Ricky reached to pick the envelope up but Morris kept it pinned down under his finger. He shook his head.

'Uh-uh,' he reproved.

'Come on, Morrie, give us a butchers.'

'Alfie's a good customer of my Lucy. A nice steady little earner.' He met Ricky's eye. 'A girl's got her future to think of, hasn't she?'

'You know me, Morris. I ain't tight. I like to see a person cop.'

'Know what I mean by discounted cash flow? No?' He leaned back, letting the envelope lie there like an undeclared poker card. 'Suppose he avails himself of our Lucy's services once a fortnight and pays her a two-er for the privilege. She loses Alfie and she loses five grand a year, right?'

'You're askin' *five grand*?'

'And she loses another five grand next year. And another the year after. Then there's inflation . . .'

'Hold on, Morrie. You don't grow young in *her* game. They have a limited workin' life. Like footballers.'

Morris shook his smooth head.

'Not my Lucy. She's got enough mileage in her to keep me into my old age, and her alone. I consulted her. She's prepared to forego Alfie's company for twenty grand.'

'Twenty grand! But Alfie only owes me twenty-five! You said five. I'll do you five.'

'Fifteen.'

'Seven and a monkey.'

107

'Twelve.'

'Nine.'

'Eleven.'

'Morrie, take my shirt. Let's have a deal. Ten.'

'Ten it is.'

They slapped palms. Ricky lunged for the envelope but Morris whipped it away and held it out of reach.

'Money up front, Rick. You weren't expecting credit?'

'Aw, come on, I'll pay you out of Alfie's dough.'

'And if he doesn't oblige?'

'Then your gear ain't worth a light anyway.' Ricky tried another angle. 'You don't expect me to buy it sight unseen?'

Morris relented.

'Just so you know what you're paying for,' he said.

He opened the envelope and took out a small sheaf of colour photographs. He handed Ricky the first.

Ricky drew in his breath.

'Take a look at that! The dirty dog!'

Morris handed him a second.

'Cor! 'Ere, Morrie, what's she puttin' in his mouth?'

At the third, Ricky drew back in revulsion.

'And he pays *money* for that? The filthy perverted bastard! What is he, a man or an animal?'

Morris collected back the photos.

'Ten grand and he's yours,' he said.

'I'd give ten grand not to see his evil mug again.'

The odds were fair. Lay ten to win twenty-five. But where could he get the ten from? He was *potless*.

Pictures of holdalls stuffed with banknotes kept floating through his mind. Couldn't Billy do him a favour this once?

Billy was lying on a sun-bed by the pool when Ricky arrived. He'd had a small win, the first for months, and he was in a cheerful mood.

'Ten?' he responded at once. 'Winston will give it you on your way out. You brought the cards?'

'You want kaluki *now*?'

'My employment cards, cock. From that young lad of yours.'

'He's fixing them right this very minute,' lied Ricky.

'T'riffic. That's life, eh? Doin' each other little favours.'

'Yeah, it's what friendship's all about, Billy.'

Billy called to a girl lying in a sun-chair. She wore a white nurse's pinafore and little else. He introduced her as Samantha. She seemed to think she'd met him before, but he'd never have forgotten that pair of bristols. She carried them ahead of her like an offensive weapon.

'Sammy, give Rick here one of your massage specials.'

Ricky swallowed hard.

The chest rode towards him. He was seeing Sonia later that afternoon. These days he had to go more sparingly on the old lead in the pencil.

'I'm feelin' great, honest, Billy.'

'Fuck off. You're uptight and tense. Go on, relax. She's the best in the business.'

Ricky gave an uneasy laugh.

'I'm knackered, Billy.'

'See what I mean, Sammy? He's tense. Take him away and give him the works. Don't no-one say Billy don't show his appreciation.'

'Pig feed,' said Melvyn, scratching the thicket on his chest with the edge of his Star of David pendant. 'That's yer best bet. Or Poland.'

Simon loosened his tie. He was over-dressed. In a cracked mirror behind Melvyn he caught sight of faces peeping around the door, staring at him. Did he have two heads and an elephant's trunk?

He adjusted his vowels downwards.

'Melvyn, the gear is past the post. It'll go flyin' out.'

He could see Melvyn was chewing his lip to hold back a smile.

'You're sellin' broken Frisbees and you ain't got no samples, no packing specs, no delivery dates, no nothin'?' said the wholesaler. 'You're in the wrong business, mate.'

Sonia was all tarted up for a fashion show at Barker's. She was worried he'd mess up her hairdo, so she lay on her back with her eyes shut. She reminded Ricky fleetingly of the plastic doll Angelina once threw into the fire when she was a child. Her slip was neatly folded on a chair beside the Harrods bag that had a change of shoes, and on the dressing table a line of lipsticks and creams lay ready to repair the damage.

Today, however, Ricky's mind wasn't on it nor his heart in it. Each attempt to scale her softened into nothing. He grew mildly anxious. This wasn't the man his pals used to call Rick the Prick. Course, Samantha had serviced him dry. But there was more to it than that. He'd got that wet-eared ponce on the brain. He'd have to fix a meet. He wasn't going to disappoint Billy in a hurry, not with ten grand of his money riding on it.

'Let's just cuddle,' murmured Sonia comfortingly. 'Don't worry. St Tropez will work wonders.'

Ricky didn't feel like a cuddle. He rolled off her and reached for his cigarettes.

'Don't hold your breath waitin'.'

She opened her eyes wide.

'What do you mean, Ricky?' she said in her little-girl voice.

'What do I mean? What does it sound like I mean?'

'Don't raise your voice, Ricky. There's no need for that.'

'I'm not raisin' my voice!' he shouted.

She laid a hand on his arm.

'Work problems?' she asked sympathetically.

'Nothing Rick can't handle.'

'You're so clever, darling.'

She lay back again. He stroked her breast and watched the nipple erect. God knew why, but he was fond of the old bat.

110

'Do you love me?' she asked in a murmur.

'Course I do.'

'Why?'

'What do you mean, why?' He wasn't in the mood for philosophy.

'You used to say you loved me for my class.'

'You misheard,' he said, then mimicked her long 'a'. 'Arse, I said. Not class.'

She giggled and curled up close to him.

'Just think,' she sighed. 'All that sun and sea. And the siestas.'

'Yeah, doll,' he replied more tenderly and stroked her hip. 'Pray God we live that long.'

He stubbed out his cigarette. The touch of her skin had begun to arouse him. He reached across her and turned the muzak down. She wasn't so bad. She might be forty-six and act like a dead body sometimes, but she could also be twenty-six and act like a right little raver. She'd do him well enough for his retirement. But he wouldn't hold his breath waiting.

Simon arrived at the Lamplighter Club punctually at six-thirty to find Alfie Steinman hadn't left his name at the reception. He waited half an hour at the desk, still puzzling out the reason for the invitation. His old boss must want him back in the firm. He had his response ready. Just conceivably he might be interested in being a consultant trouble-shooter. Provided it was part-time and he reported direct to the Board.

When Alfie eventually turned up, he was effusive in his apologies. Putting a friendly arm on Simon's shoulder, he swept him off to the bar. A topless waitress seated them in a discreet cubicle and another took their drinks order.

'How's Mary?' asked Alfie conversationally. 'And the acrylics?'

'Martha's fine, thanks. The painting's taking rather a back seat, though. One can't eat pictures.'

'Duchamp once did, I believe.'

The waitress brought two vast, frothing cocktails. As she put Simon's down, one breast dipped into the foam. Alfie took out a silk handkerchief and gallantly wiped it off for her. Simon tried not to look.

Then he dropped another hint.

'I've set up a company. Consultancy, trading, that kind of thing. I'm busy, but – what do they say? – if you want a job done, give it to a busy man.'

He laughed. Alfie didn't. Instead, he gave him one of his steady eyeballings.

'That man Stone you were with the other night,' he began. 'See much of him, do you?'

Had he been summoned to blab on Ricky?

'We've worked together, yes.'

'I'm sure I don't need to remind you that your service contract excludes you from dealings with the firm's clients for a period of two years . . .'

'Ricky's hardly a client!'

'But we might overlook that. I hope your work was financially rewarding?'

Ah! Simon spotted the trap. Alfie wanted him to say that Ricky had been earning money. Any money a bankrupt earned belonged to the creditors.

'Can't say it was, actually.'

'And Ricky?'

'Leaning on his friends. Calling in his debts.'

Even in the low blue lamplight, Simon could see Alfie visibly blanching.

'He wouldn't have to,' Simon continued, 'if he hadn't paid over that money. He believes you cheated him.'

Alfie choked on his drink.

'Money? What has that crooked two-faced villain been telling you?'

Alfie would know perfectly well the hundred grand Ricky gave him from his casino winnings had been meant to pay off the creditors in full, not just on account. Why was he pretending not to understand? Besides,

Ricky was not a crooked two-faced villain. He was his pal. And Steinman *had* ripped him off.

'He's no more a villain than half the Directors in the City!' said Simon, feeling the heat rising under his collar. 'There's one law for him, another for them, that's all.'

The flood gates were unlocked. The more he went on, the more he warmed to his theme. He detected trace elements of Martha in the polemic, but it came from the heart. Ricky was worth a dozen Steinmans, Fothergills and Trelawneys! No-one paid *him* a fat fee to sit on his backside in a Boardroom. He grafted, he ducked and dived, he earned his living. OK, so he'd slipped up once, but then what? Banks could go bust owing billions and the club had a whip-round to save them. But when Ricky Stone went skint owing a couple of hundred grand, they threw him in jail, took every penny and watched him bleed to death.

Alfie's face wore a tight, fixed smile.

'I was wrong about painting,' he said. 'You should be teaching politics at a poly. But I was right about one thing. Firing you.' He rose to his feet. 'You can tell your beloved friend Ricky I'll be ready for him.'

Beloved he was. Simon drove home with his heart full of love for him. He'd championed him, fought his cause, defended his honour. One day, when he'd made his money, he'd invite him to Italy and tell him about the day he saw off Alfie Steinman. And Ricky would make him repeat the story over and over again and they'd laugh about it together until the moon rose high in the clear Tuscan sky.

'That young lad of yours has been down my manor,' said Melvyn.

'What was he doin' there?' asked Ricky.

'Offerin' me some crappo, I dunno. Sent him away

113

with a right flea in his ear, didn't I? Can't be doin' with all that hoity-toity lark.'

'That's no way to treat a fellow human bein', Mel.'

'The boys thought he was Prince Charles,' said Melvyn with a cackle. He put on a posh accent. '"Sorry, not today, your Royal Highness."'

'I don't like to hear you speak like that, Mel.'

'Where's yer sense of humour, Rick? The lad's a toff.'

'He's my pal.'

'Looks a right Alphonse to me.'

'Now look, Mel. You lay off of him! He's a decent lad and I won't have no-one slaggin' him off . . .'

'Hang on to yer barnet! I was only sayin' . . .'

'Just bottle it, OK?'

Martha came into the small, windowless box room Simon had converted into an office. It had space only for a school desk, a fold-away chair and a filing cabinet. When it arrived, the telex machine would have to go in the bedroom.

'You've been on the phone for ages,' she said.

'Can't get through,' he replied. 'It's always engaged.'

'Who are you calling?'

'Oh, just a chap about something.'

Ricky slammed the receiver down. Beryl started, spilling his tea in the saucer.

'The effin' phones in this effin' country!' he raged. 'People waste *years* of their lives tryin' to get through! Phones should be free so everyone could have two lines.'

'You should go easy on yourself, pet,' said Beryl. 'At your age all that nervous tension can do you in. Don't I know!'

He dialled again and the line was still engaged. With a supreme effort he controlled himself. It was like bottling a volcano.

'Thank you, Beryl,' he said primly. 'Should I require any further advice, I shall send you a postcard.'

'Who was you callin' anyway?'

'Just business, Beryl.'

GIRL 1:	You seein' him tonight again, then?
GIRL 2:	Nah. Tonight's Greg, innit?
SIMON:	Hello? Hello?
GIRL 2:	Someone's listenin' in.
GIRL 1:	You've got a crossed line!
RICKY:	Ullo? What's this fuckin' carry-on, eh?
GIRL 2:	There's two of them!
GIRL 1:	He's using language!
GIRL 2:	Clear the line, whoever you are!
SIMON:	Hello? Are you 758 3565?
RICKY:	Who's that?
GIRL 2:	He's askin' who we are! None of your business! Go away!
RICKY:	Not you. *Him.*
SIMON:	Me?
GIRL 2:	You still there, Carol? Like I was sayin' about Greg . . .
GIRL 1:	'Goin' to the pictures, then?
GIRL 2:	It's his snooker night, innit?
RICKY:	Christ, how many people are there on this bleedin' line?
GIRL 2:	It's him again! He's still there!
SIMON:	Hey, Ricky! Is that you?
GIRL 1:	Both of them!
RICKY:	Sime! That you, Sime?
SIMON:	Yes, it's me. Simon.
RICKY:	You been on the trumpet all mornin'!
SIMON:	So have you.
GIRL 2:	Get off the line! I'm talking to my friend Carol.
RICKY:	Sime, hang up. I'll call you right back. (There's a click.) Carol?
GIRL 1:	You what?'
RICKY:	Sorry, darlin'. Just a bit of a mix-up.

GIRL 1:	That's all right. No harm done.
RICKY:	You sound a good sort, Carol. Blonde, are you?
GIRL 1:	How can you tell?
RICKY:	It's the voice, doll. Bet you got a nice figure, too.
GIRL 2:	Carol? Put the phone down! We got a dirty old man here.
GIRL 1:	OK. You put yours down and I'll call you back. (There's another click, then a pause.) You still there? What's your name?
RICKY:	Rick. Ricky. Mister Mystery. Whatever you like.
GIRL 1:	You married, Rick?
RICKY:	Course not! Can't you tell from my voice? Where you from, Carol?
GIRL 1:	Streatham. Work in Clapham here.
RICKY:	Round the corner! 'Ere, fancy a drink?
GIRL 1:	I don't know you.
RICKY:	You soon will. I'm Ricky Stone. Everyone knows me. What time you get off work?
GIRL 1:	Five-thirty.
RICKY:	Meet you outside the tube. I've got a blue Merc. Can't miss it.
GIRL 1:	Well, maybe.
RICKY:	Maybe's no good in this life, doll.
GIRL 1:	(pauses) OK then, Rick. Why not?
RICKY:	See you then. Bye, darlin'.

10

'Broken biscuits?' cried Ricky. 'I love it!'

Simon shrugged dolefully.

''Fraid so. That was all my man could offer.'

Ricky took his hand off the wheel and clapped him on the knee.

'We'll have a right touch here, boy!'

'But Melvyn said there was no market.'

'Melvyn's a fat prick who don't know nothin'. He said there was no market for them firelighters, remember? Listen, you ever seen a person eat a biscuit *whole*? Nah, they *break* it first! We're savin' them the trouble. Ought to charge a premium.'

Simon broke into a laugh.

'What's funny?' demanded Ricky. ''Ere, come on. Let's sort that Mel out. Rick'll show you.'

With a howl of tyres, he hurled the car into an about-turn and tore off towards the East End.

'Mel, I'm offerin' you *exclusive*. There won't be nobody else puntin' the gear south of Birmingham. You got the pitch to yourself.'

'Send me in a gross,' said Melvyn. 'Trial run.'

Ricky staggered back as if he'd been delivered a right-hander.

'Do me a favour! I'm talking *volume*! It's a container a week or nothin'. All the boys'll want a daffy at that price! It'll fly out like it's got wings. Believe me, Mel.' He turned to Simon. 'Can we serve him at them prices?'

Simon finished punching figures into his calculator. The margins were small, but the volume made up for that. He scratched his head.

'Depends on the cash flow position.'

'Yer what?' demanded Melvyn.

Ricky leaned forward.

'You heard what he said. Depends on the cash position. Terms, Mel, terms.'

'I pay thirty days,' said Melvyn.

'Sorry, darlin'. I love you, but I got to listen to my accountant here. Cash on the nail, Mel my boy.'

Cash on the nail, thought Ricky happily as he sped off towards his five-thirty rendezvous. He'd die a happy man after seeing the look on Melvyn's face. Got him by the cobblers, hadn't he? The prick deserved to get some of his own treatment.

He sat in the Merc with the air conditioning full on, watching the entrance of Clapham Common tube from behind a copy of the *Standard*. His eye picked out all the blonde ones: small, fat, tall, skinny, old, young, pimply, smart, petite, buxom, tarty and classy. Then one stepped out from the rest. She saw the blue Merc and started hesitantly forward.

She was a right livin' doll. If you'd made her yourself, you couldn't have made her more beautiful.

First thing Friday morning, a forty-foot flat loader rolled into Melvyn Harris' warehouse yard with two thousand ten-pound cartons of broken Frisbees. All through the day the street-traders poured in, and by dusk he was cleaned out. The following morning, in the street markets of Acton and Arsenal, of Uxbridge and Upminster, the boys began pitching their broken biscuits.

'All perfects, ladies. A few's a bit broke but you'd 'ardly notice. All right, darlin', I'm comin' to it. Am I

118

sayin' 50p a pound? Am I sayin' *40p*? No, just *35p a pound! A nicker for three!* Got yer purse ready, darlin'? OK, one at a time now!'

Ricky paid a visit to Berwick Market. He parked the Merc on the pavement and strolled through the teeming crowd. Second to watching the horse he'd backed sailing past the post, the greatest sight in the world was money being taken – tills opening and shutting and pockets and pouches swelling.

He bought a pound of the biscuits, gave a quid and left the change. As he sauntered back to the car, he reached inside the bag. The chocolate had melted in the heat and run into the marshmallow, the biggest bits were not much more than fragments and the whole lot was sticky and coated in a fine dust. He dropped the bag in a litter bin. It would do for the poor saps who only had a few coppers a week to live on. But not Ricky Stone. He was on the way back up.

'Your Martha,' said Ricky as they headed out towards Esher to deliver Billy his first salary cheque. 'She play, does she?'

'Play what?' asked Simon.

'*Play.* You know, fancy a little scene.' He looked across at Simon. 'Bit of a prude, is she, then?'

'Martha's strong-minded about that kind of thing.'

Ricky sucked his teeth.

'Don't let you have nothing on the side neither?'

'It's never actually come up.'

Ricky shook his head in awe.

'And you two have been goin' a year!'

'I don't really miss it.'

'You will when you see the bird I've got sorted out for you, boy! A real peach. Right up your alley. I told her all about you.' He reached into his inside pocket and took out a Polaroid. 'Cop a load of that!'

The girl wore a Father Christmas cloak, opened to reveal a red waspie, red stockings and red high-heel shoes. She was blonde and had a wide-eyed baby face and an egg-timer figure. In her hand she held a bottle of aftershave.

'Her name's Carol,' Ricky was saying. 'She does promotions. Pity. She was dyin' to meet you. I'll tell her you're takin' holy orders.'

'She looks more Billy's type.'

'Billy?' exploded Ricky. 'I wouldn't let my worst enemy's girl in a mile of him! Fuck 'em and chuck 'em, that's Billy. She's too good, this one. Real reem doll. Deserves a gentleman.'

Something in the girl's smile held Simon's attention. He flipped it over. On the back was a phone number, signed with an 'X'. He turned it back. Perhaps it wasn't only her smile.

'Steady on, you'll wear it out with starin'!' Ricky took the photo back and tossed it into the dashboard tray. 'Forget I mentioned it.'

'Well, no harm in meeting up for a drink sometime.'

'I wouldn't offend Martha for the world.'

'I wasn't thinking we'd invite Martha along, too.'

Ricky threw him a sideways smile.

'Glad to know you're flesh and blood, Sime.'

Simon laughed.

'Isn't she *your* sort, then?'

'Give us a break! Think I haven't enough headaches with women? She's only a kid, anyway. Same age as my Angelina. And she calls me Dad.'

The box room office – which Ricky referred to as the 'khazi' – became the epicentre of Transcosmos Trading's burgeoning business activities. However, only one person could sit down there at a time, and as Ricky twice broke the chair, Simon made sure he bagged it, leaving Ricky to stand half in the hallway. As a major investment, following a full financial appraisal, he bought a cordless telephone and now Ricky roamed all over the flat, shouting and swearing into it and stubbing his cigarettes out into coffee mugs and plant pots.

But Ricky was not happy.

He wanted to move to proper offices. They'd get a good-looker on the reception desk and kit out a show-room with all the samples, and in no time at all they'd have buyers coming in from all over the world. Already a workable game plan was emerging. Simon would open the doors into the big companies, they'd do their two-man act and nick a load of gear for nothing, then Ricky would get to work flogging it into the street markets. The key was to get in with the manufacturers. There were a dozen more where Chris came from – Chris the Crisp, as Martha had dubbed him – but they couldn't pull them in while they operated out of a khazi.

Martha was not happy either.

The raised voices and the stink of cigarettes drove her out of the flat. She spent the days in the reading room of the local library. When it closed, she returned to a litter of betting slips and scrap paper, to overflowing saucers and ashtrays and a sink clogged with tea bags. She'd clear up the worst, wipe down the loo where Ricky had misfired and burn joss sticks and open windows until some semblance of freshness returned to the place. She put up with this because Simon had an individual's right to elect his own lifestyle. In that she had an equal right, too, she wasn't going to put up with it much longer.

And nor was Simon happy.

The telex machine arrived and was sited in a corner of the bedroom. Perhaps it was because Ricky had told the world he'd done a big cosmetics deal in Lagos and somehow, in the re-telling, this got corrupted to Laos, but telexes suddenly started arriving from the Far East offering silks, spices, crackers, rice, soya beans, teak . . . A lively exchange began between Ricky and a mystery Bangkok agent. That would have merely entailed high telex bills had it not been for the difference in time zones. At the very moment Simon and Martha had reached their deepest sleep, there'd be a sudden whirr and a sharp ping and for fifteen minutes they'd be under heavy machine-gun fire, at the end of which a bell would ring, and continue ringing, until Simon crawled out of bed and signed off. He tried everything. He unplugged the machine, but Ricky found him out. He smothered it in pillows, but they merely blocked the paper and the type over-printed. He placed an order for an acoustic hood but there was a two months' delivery delay. Someone was going to end up in a pool of blood before two months were up.

In fact, no-one was happy.

But Simon persisted. Until they made money, they mustn't spend it. It was the price you paid for starting at the bottom.

It rapidly transpired that broken biscuits would *not* do for the poor saps with only a few coppers to live on. The younger housewives preferred junk food in glamorous packs to nourishing food in plain paper bags, and for the older housewives it brought back bad memories of post-war austerity.

Melvyn began backing containers.

Ricky was beside himself. What was wrong with the berk? Any dumb-wit could sell pound notes for 50p!

Simon unhappily re-drew his supply-demand graph to reflect the price inelasticity of the broken biscuit market.

A meeting with Chris the Crisp was urgently needed.

The three men met in Ricky's favourite nosh house, the Peking Duck at Richmond.

The Chinese staff there were all avid gamblers. Ricky had once given the manager a tip and the boys put their wages on it. There'd been some confusion between 'l's and 'r's and the horse they backed was not actually Ricky's choice, but it won by five lengths and ever since, although he never gave them a winner again, he received royal treatment and all but ate free.

Chris was a broad, jovial, bushy-browed bear. He'd

got the wind-surfing bug and drank only Perrier so as to cut a trimmer figure down at the club on Kingston reservoir, but he got quickly into the party spirit and soon was protesting with quasi-drunken incredulity at Ricky's tall stories of the great coups he'd pulled off in the past.

As etiquette demanded, the real business was left to the end.

'Forget them broken biscuits, Chris,' said Ricky. 'The market's dead. Sort us out some regular gear. Jumbly-tums in economy size. Or family-pack Wafathins. Special for the market boys.'

Chris shrugged. His hands were tied.

'My brand managers make those decisions,' he said.

'You're the boss or ain't you?'

Simon said, 'That's not quite how things work in big companies.'

Ricky glared at him.

'Listen, if he wants something done, he gives the order. Am I right, Chris?'

'I have some influence . . .'

'Terrific. You're cut in for your whack. Sime's got your piece of dough from the Frisbees. Right, Sime?'

Simon tapped the envelope in his inside pocket.

Chris was subtle. He smoothly changed the subject and it wasn't until the toffee apples were cleared away that he excused himself to go to the toilet.

'Go on, now!' whispered Ricky loudly to Simon.

Simon followed Chris to the gents. He had never passed a schmeer before.

This was the time he bungled the bung.

There he was, standing at one stall, working hard at relaxing. Chris stood on his right, long finished and playing for time. Simon reached into his inside pocket for the plump brown envelope. He was in the very act of handing it over when it caught the edge of the metal screen, slipped out of his grasp and fell to the bottom of the trough. At that moment, all the pipes flushed in unison. Under this small Niagara, the glue came instantly unstuck and the envelope burst open like a ripe seed-pod, sending a flotilla of banknotes sailing away on a frothy yellow tide of cigarette butts and coughings.

Chris was at the door in a flash.

'I'll say the prawn balls disagreed with you,' he offered generously.

'I'll be quick.'

'Quick? You'd bloody better not be!'

Ramming a chair against the door, Simon retrieved the soggy, reeking notes and dunked them in a wash-basin. Then, one by one, he held them under the hot air hand-dryer. Scottish fivers . . . Bank of Ireland tenners . . . Twenties, all torn and scribbled-on, one with a dubious watermark, another without a silver filament. All smelly, greasy, germ-infested . . . but *money*!

It took him twenty minutes to salvage the notes, but the envelope was beyond repair. What could he put them in instead? Then he had an inspiration. Slipping down to the kitchen, he stuffed the lot into a foil tray, fitted a card lid on top and put it in a small carrier bag.

Back at the table, he handed the carrier to Chris.

'Your take-away, sir.'

'What's that?' demanded Ricky. 'Sweet and sour?'

'Toffee apples,' said Chris. 'Peace offering for the old lady.'

'Next time, bring her with,' said Ricky and rubbed his hands. 'We'll soon be poppin' the champagne, please God.'

'Oh?' queried Simon.

'Chris is goin' to get us all the firm's redundant gear. Exclusive.'

Somehow in those twenty minutes, Chris's hand had come untied. Simon knew it was no miracle. Money spoke all languages.

Life was on the up and, as if to do its part, the sun outshone itself that Wednesday.

Telling Beryl he was going down to the club and telling

the club that if she called to tell her he'd just popped out for some cigs, Ricky jumped in the Merc and drove over to Roehampton High Street. He'd take Sonia out for a ride in the country. There was a little hotel down in Hampshire where he knew the boss . . .

He put his head round the door of the small shop.

'Knock knock, who's there?' he chimed.

'Ricky!' she squealed.

He turned the sign on the door around so it read CLOSED.

'C'mon, doll, we're goin' for a ride.'

She protested, but he grabbed her and gave her his Clark Gable kiss. She knocked over a seamstress's dummy, but by then he had his hand six inches up her skirt and she was melting.

She was a lady and liked it rough, but Ricky liked to take his time and do it in comfort. He was too old for quickies up against the wall or in the back of cars. As usual he had his way, and within a few minutes they were in the Merc, with the sun roof down, heading for the south-west.

They'd just joined the M3 and he was putting his foot down when she asked if there were any peppermints. 'Sure,' he said. 'In the dashboard tray.'

He was quickly to regret that.

He went on talking and didn't realise for a while that she'd grown silent. A sudden sob made him look across. Rivulets of mascara were trickling down her face. Her bottom lip was trembling. In her hand she held the Polaroid.

His brain revved wildly.

'That's Carol,' he said. 'My Angelina's best friend.'

'How *could* you?' she wailed.

'How could I what? She's in the promotions game. I was settin' her up with Eli and Abby . . .'

'*Fibber!*'

She hurled herself on him, nails clawing, teeth biting, fists pummelling. The car lurched across three lanes of motorway and onto the hard shoulder and back again, dodging between juggernauts and caravans and leaving a wake of screeching tyres and howling horns. Finally he silenced her with a belt across the face and, taking the next exit, headed back to London in silence.

Ricky arrived home at Millionaire's Row, Norwood, with a vast bunch of flowers. After his shower, he hung up the wet towel and put his dirty underpants in the linen basket. He watched *Match of the Day* with the volume down, ate a double helping of lox and discussed where the new freezer would go.

Beryl watched him from behind narrowed eyes. She stubbed out her cigarettes thoughtfully. She listened to the new note in his voice and heard a warning in it.

She was not to be fooled. She knew he hadn't been down the club that afternoon. She had her friends there, too.

He'd had a ruck with Lady Muck and now he was crawling back to her. Well, after all the grief and heartache he'd put her through, let him crawl.

Ricky had a photographic memory for football results. He'd lay wagers on a Saturday evening that he could recite the score of every match played that day. The skill often came in useful; at one time or another, he'd stung everyone he knew.

Simon, on the other hand, had a photographic memory for numbers. He could reel off the digits of his bank account, passport, driving licence, National Insurance and Premium Bonds, as well as the registration numbers of all his previous cars and the dates of past girlfriends' birthdays. This talent came in useful now. Sonia had torn up the Polaroid in her teeth and scattered little red fragments all down the M3. But Simon had remembered the phone number on the back.

Simon had ambitions for Carol.

Like any company in its growth phase, Transcosmos

Trading needed promotion. It needed sales aids, colour brochures, product leaflets. This was where Carol came in. He'd have Carol in her Father Christmas outfit, stuffing a stocking with SuperPacks of Wafathins. Carol in pigtails and pinny, tucking into a bag of Popsitops. Carol dressed in silver lamé with an antenna on her head, breaking the seal on a packet of Robot Rolls.

'If we capture just *two percent* of the market trade,' he told Ricky excitedly, 'within three years we could go on the USM!'

'We'll go skint in three weeks without another line,' Ricky replied.

The trouble with Ricky was that he could never see beyond the deal of the moment. Someone had to do the strategic thinking. Fortunately, Simon had the vision. He stayed up late all one night and drew up a corporate plan. Phase one was promotion.

He met Carol at a wine bar round the corner from his flat. One bottle became two and he invited her back for a bite. She'd had her tea at seven but she didn't mind watching him eat. Martha was out at her Aerobics and Consciousness class.

With his Marks and Spencer chicken Kiev he opened a third bottle. He was starting into his black cherry yoghurt and trying to keep track of whether it was Phil or Tim or Jeff who was the one she'd fancied in Benidorm when, with a little gurgle, she toppled off her chair and passed right out on the Afghan kelim.

He grabbed a pillow from the bedroom and put it under her head. He dampened a tea cloth and dabbed her forehead. Gradually she came round. He had to get her back home. He tried to lift her bodily to her feet but she was surprisingly heavy. Looping her arm around his neck and supporting her under the ledge of her breasts, he managed to ease her upright and, staggering up the stairs, crossed the yard to his car.

He drove to Streatham, delivered her into the safe-keeping of a flatmate and returned home.

By then Martha was back.

Martha had tidied away the chicken Kiev and the half-eaten yoghurt and the two wine glasses and the damp tea towel and the pillow on the floor. She was now in the bathroom with the door locked. She stayed there for almost an hour. When she came out, she went straight to bed without addressing Simon a single word.

He cleaned his teeth, gargled, squeezed a small spot, sluiced his armpits and put on the silk happy coat she'd bought him for his birthday. In the bedroom the light was off. Martha was asleep. At any rate, she didn't answer when he asked if she was awake. He got in beside her. She lay as stiff as a board. She wasn't breathing. He nudged her. She rolled over with a grunt and kept her back to him all night.

'I'm going to Terry and Tasha's for a bit,' said Martha the next morning as she poured the goat's milk over her muesli.

Terry and Tasha's meant he'd hit a boa constrictor and gone clean off the board. These were friends of hers who had a derelict farm in the Black Mountains and kept goats. They gave Martha sanctuary from Simon and other alienating elements of bourgeois capitalist society.

'For a bit?' he echoed.

'To sort things out.'

He put out a hand towards her but she moved out of reach.

'Martha, what's wrong?'

'If you can't see you must be blind.'

The old panic grabbed his guts. He pushed aside his toast, uneaten, and leaned forward.

'Look, I know things aren't easy, with the place turned into an office. It's awful for you, living like this, and it's all my fault, and I'm not expecting you to put up with it just because it's technically my flat, it isn't, it's yours as well, at least that's how I think of it, but one has got to put up with things when one's starting up, and I

128

know it's *my* business and not yours and you don't want anything to do with it, but it's not for ever, I promise you, and if it works we'll have plenty of money and, you'll see, money's not such a bad thing and you don't *have* to get it by exploiting other people . . .'

'Simon . . .'

'I know you think I've only left one rat race to join another, and it's money, money, money all the time, but we're buying our freedom, well, I know you think freedom's an inner thing, but I mean think of Tuscany and everything. Think how you'll have figs with your muesli, and peaches and grapes as well, and instead of going to that stuffy library you'll sit under an olive tree and read, and there's a mill pond to cool off in, and real people in the village to talk to . . .'

'Please stop, Simon.'

There were tears in her eyes.

'Well,' he said, scuffing the carpet with his toe, 'I just hoped you might see it that way a bit.'

She wiped her eyes and shook her head.

'Simon, you really don't understand, do you?'

'Understand *what*?'

'Exactly.'

She left, taking a large suitcase.

As the door shut, Simon felt a sudden, shameful wave of relief. He was liberated. If that was how she wanted to behave, then let her.

Besides, he had work to do. Work came before women. Love was *not* free. It was one of the luxuries of life, and everything in life cost. People spent far too much time obsessed with their relationships. In the old days, there simply wasn't time. Life was hard then and they had to get on with it. There were far fewer divorces and the mental hospitals were a whole lot emptier. But these days, everyone had too much time and too many expectations. No wonder one in three marriages broke up and people all over the place were living off tranquillisers and going to shrinks. Men and women should get together and agree a simple contract and stick to it. Think of all the time and energy and aggro that would save! It would run into billions of pounds a year.

He spent the morning making phone calls. At lunch he had a pint and a pie at the pub and then decided, as it was Friday and Ricky hadn't shown up, to take the afternoon off and paint.

Ricky's ten grand grew to fourteen at the casino, then dropped to five at Epsom racecourse. It rose to seven with a pools win but slumped back to four after a night at White City. A small cut-up from the first consignment of Popsitops just out of shelf-life raised the figure to eight but a peace offering to Sonia, bought from a furrier pal of his whose firm went belly-up regularly every summer, lowered it to six.

He called Morris.

.'Morrie, I'll give you six grand for half them pictures.'

'I've got my Lucy to think of,' protested Morris.

'Six now and six when Alfie coughs up.'

'Six and eight.'

'Right. See you down the club, you poxy bastard.'

Simon laid out his watercolours in a spectrum, the cool colours on the left and the warm ones on the right. Brown, being a mix of red and green, was hard to place, and he wasn't sure about Payne's Grey and Mars Violet either. Lamp Black stayed in the box; technically, it wasn't a colour at all.

Next the brushes, sable one side and squirrel the other. Then two jam jars of water, one for dirty, the other for clean. Finally, a sheet of Watman's hot-pressed paper, ready taped to a drawing board.

He looked about him.

From where he sat on the patch of threadbare grass at the front of the apartment block, he could see through a row of iron railings and across the street to a pair of yellow-grey brick houses, set back from the road by an unkempt garden in which a rusting Cortina stood washed up among a flotsam of beer cans. A baby was crying in a pram and the trees bore a dusty, late summer weariness.

He looked up. The sky was darkening. A light drop of rain hit him in the face, then another. He'd survive a shower. Turner used to stick it out in hail and blizzards.

He had an idea. Why not actually *paint the rain*! Or better still, let the rain itself spatter the paper! Let the image create itself!

The vermilion had dried hard, the cap on the cobalt was stuck fast and the gamboge had to be unpicked from the end. The rain was falling more heavily now. A drop fell just where he was painting a tree and granulated the pigment with ravishing beauty.

He worked fast, boldly. The results that grew before his eyes were breathtakingly thrilling. This was water-colour in its true sense!

Choosing the moment carefully, he got up. He took the board indoors and nursed it in front of the fire until the painting had dried. Then he took it over to the window.

He gulped.

It had gone dead, flat, like a pebble that glistened on the seashore but turned dull at home. It was a washout, in its true sense.

He put it in his portfolio. He'd save the paper for the other side. He was out of practice. You couldn't expect to pick up a brush after years of neglect and toss off a masterpiece. You needed time to get your eye and hand back in. There'd be plenty of that in Italy. And better light. And more interesting subjects. And no bloody rain.

Simon poured himself a large whisky and went through his address book. It was conveniently arranged with men listed on one side and girls on the other. He made very sure Martha never saw it.

131

Tom and Antonia were going to a film he'd already seen. Justin and Julia had left for the weekend. Chubby Chesterton was off to a fetish party and Randy Rochester was taking his American chairman to the Mirabelle. By the W's, Simon was almost prepared to call Julian Wetherby.

It was Friday night and the rest of the world was at play. Well, he'd stay in, dig a Marks and Spencer boeuf bourgignon out of the freezer and watch telly. Martha was lucky he hadn't gone through the right-hand column of names. There were plenty of girls who'd understand what it took to build up a business.

He turned on the television. If Martha had been there, it would have had to be Channel 4's documentary on Gujarati teaching in Bradford schools, but he could now watch *Starsky and Hutch* and not answer to anyone. He piled his dirty plates in the sink, intending to have them stacked to the ceiling by the time she came back. Then he changed his mind and washed them; he could look after himself perfectly well.

Terry and Tasha's farm didn't have a phone, so he couldn't call her. Besides, *she* was the one to call *him*. He put the answering machine on in case she did; it would do her good to think he was out. He needed an early night anyway.

Just as he was cleaning his teeth, the phone rang. He ran to the office and listened in. It was Chubby Chesterton, against a background of drunken giggling, saying there was all this kinky spare skirt and not enough blokes to go round. He'd hung up without giving the address before Simon had rinsed his mouth to speak.

Then the telex machine started up. This time it was Hong Kong with an offer of frozen Cantonese ducks, Grade A, weight 2-4lbs, fully eviscerated with neck and giblets in polybags . . .

He sat on the bed, wreathed in sudden loneliness. He missed Martha badly. She gave everything he did its meaning. Without her, life was like a television with the colour turned down.

In the morning he'd call Ricky and they'd start looking for a proper office. Right now, though, he'd write her a letter. A self-criticism, like the Chinese did.

He picked a pillow off the floor and propped himself up in bed with a note-pad. Gradually he became aware of a pungent smell of perfume. He sniffed around for a while until he realised it came from the pillow. And on the pillow, too, were several long, blonde hairs.

Martha's words came back to him.

'Simon, you really don't understand, do you?'

At last the penny dropped.

His telegram brought a belated phonecall. Martha wasn't impressed by his account of the incident with Carol.

'It's the truth,' he persisted. 'Do you think I'd have brought her home otherwise? One doesn't foul one's own doorstep.'

He gave a small laugh, but it didn't lighten the leaden atmosphere.

'I don't know what "one" does, Simon,' she replied coolly. 'I'm not sure any of this matters anyway.'

'Of course it matters! You've pissed off to that bloody farm because it matters! That's escapism. Not like you to run away from issues.'

'Is this what you wanted to tell me?'

'I just want to explain things.'

'Well, I accept your explanation, if that makes you feel better.'

'Martha, I need you.'

'You need me to absolve your conscience, that's all.'

'I *love* you.'

'You only love the bit of me you can't control.'

'I see, so I love you more than ever now because you're not here, where I want you, huh?'

'Very possibly.'

Simon snorted. Why did his arguments never leave a dent?

'I'm coming to get you,' he said defiantly.

'Don't be absurd. Go back to Carol and Ricky and your other friends. Do your deals and make your money . . .'

'You don't believe me, do you?'

'I've told you, Simon, I do. There's nothing more to be said.'

The pips went.

'I've got no more money anyway,' she said.

'Wait! Give me your number.'

'There isn't one on this phone.'

'Then reverse the charges!'

But the line had already gone dead.

'One for you, one for me.'

The Wafathins and the Jumbly-tums, the Crispos and the Popsitops were quite a different story. They flew out. This was date-expired stock, production over-runs, offer-flashed packs from discontinued promotions and large pack sizes made specially for the market trade. All of it was regular stock, most was fresh and none was broken.

And the money began to fly in. They awarded Billy a salary bonus to mop up some profits. Simon went to the bank to draw it out.

A pile of fresh tens and twenties now lay on the table in Ricky's front room. They were having a little cut-up.

'One for you, one for me.'

Ricky went on until the pile was divided in two. He put half his share in an empty tennis ball box and the rest in a roll in his back pocket.

He called to Beryl in the next room.

'Fetch us a cuppa, doll.'

'Get your own!' she snapped back. 'I'm busy.'

He pulled a face at Simon.

'Poxy women,' he muttered. 'Rucks with her in there, rucks with the other, I dunno.'

'Same here. Martha's in a huff.'

'Caught you with that bird Carol?'

'Sort of. And you?'

'Sonia only had to find that bleedin' photo, didn't she? There was murders! Then Beryl gets the hump.' He shook his head. 'What's it all about, eh, Sime? What are we here for?'

Simon put his share of the money in his briefcase.

'Search me,' he said.

'You should know. You went to school.'

'They teach you to ask questions, they don't give you the answers.'

'That's stupid! If I was there, I'd get hold of the professor and say, "If you're so bright, mate, then why was we put on this planet? Just to duck and dive and then one day drop dead?"'

'You wouldn't get much of an answer.'

'I mean, no-one consulted me. No-one asked if I wanted to come onto this earth.'

'You can always get off it.'

'God, religion, it's all cobblers. My Kev says it's pot for the people. All them wars and injustice, it's religion what makes people evil. If there is a God up there, why does he permit it?'

Simon shrugged. He was sitting this one out.

The puzzlement on Ricky's face deepened.

'And this marriage lark,' he went on. 'If God had meant a man and a woman to stop together for ever, he'd have made 'em of flesh and blood. It ain't fair, danglin' a carrot and sayin' you can't have it.'

'Don't listen to him, Sime!'

Beryl stood in the doorway. She was wearing her purple housecoat and carried a cigarette and ashtray.

'He can talk the hind leg off an Irishman,' she went on, 'and the pants off an 'ore. I should never have listened to him!'

'Beryl, could Simon and I please have an intelligent conversation without you openin' your North an' South . . .'

'I could have saved myself all the pain, Sime. Lived happy ever after, please God.'

Simon stood up and took a step towards the door. In

this household an arbitrator's life was short. He said the most anodyne thing he could think of.

'Well, no-one said life was going to be easy.'

'Easy?' cried Beryl. 'Livin' with Ricky Stone is psychological torture! 'Ere, Rick, where's the freezer money?'

'What freezer money?' said Ricky.

'See what I mean? Come on, Rick, hand it over.'

Reluctantly, Ricky reached into his back pocket and handed the roll of notes to her.

'God didn't make women,' he groaned. 'He made vampires.'

He pulled out his pockets to show they were quite empty. Then, with a wink to Simon, he casually picked up the tennis ball box and put it on a shelf with the other samples.

11

Particulars of offices to let began arriving in the post. Every day for a week, Ricky and Simon went viewing. Ricky was all for a former sanitary ware showroom in the West End. Simon wanted the two rooms above a shop in Battersea.

'With the kind of business we're goin' to do,' insisted Ricky, 'we need a decent gaff.'

'But not at fifteen pounds a square foot!' protested Simon.

'You got to lay out to earn.'

'Plus we're tied in for fifteen years with rent reviews every three.'

'You'll die worryin', Sime. We can piss off after one year. They can't stop us.'

'They're asking for personal guarantees.'

'So sign. What's the difference?'

No difference to Ricky. There was the rub. Ricky couldn't give a personal guarantee because he was a bankrupt. He couldn't be a director of the company either. If it traded insolvently, if bills went unpaid and agreements dishonoured, no-one would come knocking at *his* door. The firm could fold and he'd just walk away. Simon would carry the can alone.

'Suppose we don't do so well after all . . .'

'You're a right pessimistic bastard, Sime. If that's how you feel, we'll close down right here and now.'

'I was only planning for contingencies.'

'Yeah. Maybe they'll drop the bomb. Maybe little

137

green men will come down from outer space and do us all in.' He sucked his teeth. 'You should have stayed out there with them faceless gits doin' their nine-to-five.'

'It's easy for you to say that,' responded Simon hotly, 'but you're not the one signing the lease.'

Ricky leaned forward. His mouth had an ugly curl.

'And if I was, I'd tell the lot of 'em to sod off. They got no right to dictate! Let 'em come and get me! I ain't payin'!'

'They'd take your house . . .'

'The house is in Beryl's name.'

'Remember the trouble Mr Steinman caused you . . .'

'Alfie Steinman's a dirty, perverted bastard.'

'Yes, but look what he did to you.'

'He didn't do nothin'! I'm back, aren't I?'

'With undischarged debts.'

''Ere, wait a minute! The customs has got ninety-five grand of my money. I call that quits.'

'But it's Beecham's and Lever's you owe . . .'

'So? Let 'em collect from the customs. I'm all paid up.'

'Mr Steinman wouldn't see it that way.'

Ricky tapped his breast pocket.

'Alfie Steinman's soon goin' to be seein' things *my* way. I've got him by the cobblers.'

A smug grin spread across his face. He wasn't going to divulge his secret. But he would divulge a little paternal advice.

'So long as you've got your name, boy,' he said, 'you'll always climb back. Remember that.'

The next day, Ricky told Simon their prayers were answered. A right tasty gaff was coming up. In the West End, yes, but a *steal*. A pal of his in the furniture business had got tired of working and wanted to swap his warehouse in Marylebone for a villa in Majorca. The trouble was, he was up to his bushel in debt and his stock wasn't worth a light.

Ricky lowered his voice.

'Right, Sime, this is the S.P. You give my pal a couple of moody invoices for a hundred grand. Plus delivery notes, to show the gear went in. He'll do the necessary, right? And afterwards, we'll nick the lease for nothin'.'

'The necessary?'

'Use your crust, Sime. 'Course, there'll be some redecoratin' to do. Could be a spot of damage, see. The state this country's in, I'd lay ten to one the firemen will be out on strike.'

'The *firemen*? But that's . . . !'

'Right, son, right! It's *business*.'

It was no business Simon was getting involved in. He wasn't going to be tarred with Ricky's brush. Had Ricky still got his good name? Like hell he had! He'd climbed back on Simon's shoulders.

Simon also firmly refused that his own flat should serve as their office any longer. Until they found a gaff they could agree on, they'd use Ricky's house. That was the most cost effective solution.

The telex would take six weeks to transfer to Norwood. Meanwhile, he bought several eight-by-four sheets of soundproofing board and spent a morning battening them to the box room walls. He wheeled the telex in there on an extension lead.

Then he repainted the kitchen walls Spring Primrose yellow. He fitted a cat-flap in the back door. He regrouted the bathroom tiles, hung a Victorian pub mirror in the hallway and switched the sofa and hi-fi around in the living room. He bought two rubber plants and a weeping fig, put up more bookshelves and redeployed the kelims about the place. He changed the daily paper order from the *Mail* to the *Guardian* and sent off for a subscription to *New Society*.

Martha would find a new home when she came back.

Ricky began getting a curious itch. Something about the present business was leaving him frustrated.

Sure, it was easy enough. All he'd do was call up Marty

139

Silverman in Manchester or Ray Rogers in Birmingham, take their orders and phone them through to the company's distribution department. He didn't even need to send out samples since the lines were on every shelf in Tesco's and heavily plugged on television every night. The cases of samples Chris the Crisp had sent round stayed at home and became part of the general household supplies. Beryl was forever complaining at half-eaten packs of Popsitops in the loo and how she hurt her back bending down for bits of Crispos deep in the carpet pile. Even the Alsatian had a tooth for the Robot Rolls, which it would sniff out of the carton and chew in their wrappers.

The containers of Wafathins and Jumbly-tums went direct from factory to wholesaler. Ricky never saw a biscuit or a crisp he sold. The deals were all done on the phone and the stock only existed on paper. That was the source of his frustration.

Everyone else had their gear under their own eyes. Eli and Abby had a showroom like Aladdin's cave, and behind it a warehouse as big as an aircraft hangar with racks and shelves and fork-lift trucks and cartons that reached to the ceiling. Even Melvyn Harris could get out of his chair among the nose-pickings in his office cubby-hole and take twenty steps into his derelict Victorian spice factory and actually see and touch and count the stacked pallets.

Ricky wanted a parcel he could *get his hands on*. He'd sit on it and milk it out nice and slowly, in his own time.

The itch grew as his old contacts began phoning him with irresistible deals. Every line had its price. Buy better than that and you couldn't afford *not* to take a daffy.

Hello, Alfie, the note read. *Photigenic, aren't we? Time for a little chat about your career prospeckts. How about a pot of tea? Let's say the Hilton lobby, 6 p.m. Tuesday. Signed, your old pal R.*

Alfie Steinman felt a blade of sweat down his spine.

His lunch rose an inch. He looked closer. No mistaking Lucinda in the crotchless jodhpurs and the riding crop. And the figure on all fours, being ridden? Depended if you recognised the birthmark among the weals on the left bum cheek.

Just a single snap. But if there was one, there'd be others. Side shots, frontal shots, full-face shots.

The note had come in the general mail. His secretary had opened it. She'd said nothing, but merely slipped it in a folder among the letters to be signed. She'd have to go. She was no stranger to that birthmark.

For the tenth time he read the poorly typed note.

R?

Ronald? No, Ronald could spell. Roy was still inside, Randolph was exiled in a tax haven. Robbie was in a Moroccan hospital awaiting extradition.

Signed, your old pal R. That rang bells.

Ricky! Ricky Stone.

'Feel that gusset!' exclaimed Ricky, spreading a pair of blue jeans at the crotch. 'All machine hand-stitching. That's top quality gear there, boy.'

Simon frowned. The material was cardboard, a button was coming loose and the legs were flared in sixties style.

'I wouldn't wear them,' he said.

'You don't know from nothin', Sime! Wait till you hear what I paid.'

'You *paid* for them?'

'A nicker a lump! We'll go two quid – one-seventy-five for volume. There's a nice day's work in this. Could earn thirty grand if we do it right.'

Simon's throat went dry.

'How many did you . . . ?'

'Dunno. Forty thousand pieces, maybe more. All large sizes. That's why they're the price.'

'Where will we sell them? Outsize shops?'

'Give over! That's blackies' gear. We'll do a bit down

the Brixton market. Export, too. My pal Mo's got a big buyer in from Nigeria . . .'

'His customers had better be big, too.'

'Just leave it to Ricky, son.'

Morris was on the line. There was a sinister note in his voice.

'That you, Ricky?' he said. 'Hold on. I've got someone wants to speak to you.'

The girl that came on was sobbing hysterically.

'Bastards!' she shrieked.

Ricky held the phone away and looked into the ear-piece.

'Hello?' he said. 'Who's there?'

'They done me place over!' she wailed. 'Tore up me drapes, smashed me mirrors, chucked paint over me ridin' gear . . .'

Morris came back on.

'See what you done, Ricky? You've upset my little Lucy. She could have a nervous breakdown.'

The girl's voice howled in the background.

'An' they shat all over me zebra . . . !'

Ricky broke in.

'Hang on, Morrie! *I* ain't done any of this!'

'Just start savin', me old china, because this is goin' to cost you.'

The line went dead.

Ricky put the receiver down slowly. The bill was going up. Twenty-five grand for the initial bung. Another five, say, for interest. Fourteen for the snaps. Plus, what?, ten or fifteen for today's aggro at Lucinda's little sex parlour. Let the culprit pay for his damage.

Not much change out of sixty grand, Alfie.

Martha turned up one morning, out of the blue. She wore dungaree battle fatigues and had her hair tied back in a rubber band. Her freckly face glowed with vitality. She was with a bloke called Trev, a pushy dwarf who wore a Gentle Giant tee-shirt and a small black beret.

She'd come to get her things.

'You're . . . moving out?' said Simon, his throat lumping. 'Why? I mean, where?'

Zeal shone in her eyes.

'Hunter Street!' she said. 'The protest squat.'

Trev was rubbing his hands.

'Grass-roots action,' said Trev.

Simon cast about him helplessly. His eye flitted from the weeping fig to the rubber plants and to a pile of *Guardians* lying unread on the floor. The smell of fresh paint hung in the air.

He was incredulous.

'You're moving into a *squat*?'

'Simon, do you have any idea how many people are homeless in London?'

'But you aren't! You've got a home right here.'

Trev looked at Martha in amazement.

'He a scab, or what?'

Simon turned his back on the odious little man. No doubt he'd pay a penance later for his insensitivity, but this was a crisis. His perplexity was verging on panic. He blundered on, heedless of the pythons he was treading on.

'I don't see how leaving here's going to help! You'd only be taking a bed from someone who *is* homeless. You could be putting a whole family of Pakistanis on the streets.'

'Simon!'

'I mean why can't you just *visit* the place? Surely you don't have to live in to help.'

Martha gave him one of her fond, pitying, down-the-nose looks.

'There are thirty families in that block facing eviction, Simon. They have over fifty children between them, mostly under ten. The Council sent in the bailiffs today. We fought them off. They could come again any time, day or night. We've got to be ready. You can't change society by commuting.'

'That's not really why,' he said sulkily. 'It's this other business, isn't it . . .'

'Long forgotten.'

'Forgotten but not forgiven?'

'Simon, all that's quite unimportant.'

'Not to me.'

'And of course you're the only person in the world.'

She led Trev into the bedroom. Simon plunged his hands into his pockets and kicked at the pile of *Guardian*s. What was going on? Some great message was passing him by. He was missing the *point*. His whole life often seemed to be like that.

In three weeks she'd phoned just that once. She'd sent two postcards, one of a sunset behind Snowdon, the other of a Dada typewriter made from a lavatory seat. He'd searched vainly for the hidden meaning. The text had contained no clue to her mood or any reference to the issue between them. She'd opened just with 'Simon' and closed merely with her name and a single kiss followed by a full-stop, as though her name were Martha X. This was her usual form. He'd tried hard not to let himself read any special significance into it.

Trev came back in carrying a sleeping bag, pillow, kettle and several mugs.

'I'd watch that back window,' he said as he passed. 'You might come back one day and find a few of your Paki families in residence.'

Martha came through, her arms full of books. Was she expecting a siege?

'You've done wonders to the place,' she said generously.

'Martha, you will come back, won't you?'

'Especially the cat-flap.'

'Shall I come and see you?'

'Come and see me? If you want to. Go to Door G. It's the only one unbarricaded. Be careful, they're suspicious of strangers.'

144

'I'll wear my CND badge.'

She let out a silvery chortle and went to the door.

Suddenly he sprang into action. He ran into the kitchen and stuffed a carton with cans of fruit and soup and packets of rice and muesli. He put in two good bottles of wine, then swapped them for *ordinaire*. Why. waste decent stuff on squatters? Ashamed, he swapped them back again. But fine wine would make Martha look bourgeois, so he put back the plonk. Finally, he compromised with one of each. They'd probably be mixed anyway.

When she came back down he handed her the box.

'I do love you, Martha,' he mumbled, close to tears.

She gave him a soft kiss on the lips.

'Take care of yourself,' she said. 'And thanks for the food aid.'

'Shouldn't they be, er, lubricated?' asked Simon.

Ricky snatched back the shrink-wrap pack of condoms. He glared back, affronted.

'What you on about? Think a geezer's goin' to ask *that* when his dick is up and beggin'?'

'The girl might. You know, it's mainly the women who buy them. They have machines in ladies' loos.'

'And how would you know? Teach it in school, do they?'

'I was only saying the market may be more limited than . . .'

'You was complainin' again! You've always got to find a problem, Sime. You think crappo don't sell because you wouldn't buy it yourself. Anything sells at a price. I nicked them johnnies. Paid two-fifty a gross. They could be salt-and-vinegared and they'd still walk out. Everythin's relevant, Sime.'

That afternoon, a Friday, Ricky had a major ruck with Beryl. He drove to the club and called the Pin Cushion.

145

The girl left minding the shop told him that Sonia had gone away for a few days' rest. He knew where that meant he'd find her.

After the little misunderstanding over the photo, she'd sent his things round by cab – a couple of ties, a pair of golf shoes, a lightweight jacket and some shirts, but not the fur stole, the Capodimonte courting shepherdess, the onyx cigarette box that played the *Blue Danube* or any of his other gifts, some of love and some of guilt. He'd been out when the cab arrived. But Beryl had been in. From that moment on, domestic life had become a living hell. Beryl had the hump all day and the weepies all night. Any more and he'd bloody top himself. Or her.

He jumped in the Merc and headed for the health farm. Even if Sonia held out on him, he could use a weekend unwinding in the solarium.

As Ricky was driving to Hampshire, Simon was walking home from the wine bar at the end of the road, morose with drink and rejection.

He'd called up a fluffy little brunette who'd once been his secretary at Steinman's. She used to stay late and they'd have it off on the carpet behind the desk. After lunch that day he'd asked her back to the flat, more to hear her say Yes than to do anything about it, but she was seeing this fellow, an ex-black belt who got very jealous . . .

He'd just reached the entrance to the mansions when he saw a man in a car parked across the road, reading a newspaper. He'd noticed the very same man, *reading the very same newspaper*, two or three hours before when he'd left the building. Not even an illiterate could take that long over a tabloid.

He hurried down the stairs to his basement door. As he slipped the latch-key in, he noticed marks in the wood surrounding the lock. Someone had forced it.

146

He stepped tentatively inside and listened for sounds of movement. Emboldened by the wine, he snapped on the light.

'Anyone there?'

All was silent.

There were dusty footprints on the hall linoleum. He went into the living room.

Nothing was obviously out of place, yet things seemed to have been shifted slightly. The picture over the gas fire hung crooked, revealing a slip of white wall unmarked by the rising fumes. Books were not properly lined up against the front of the shelves. Martha wouldn't have done that. Had she sent Trev back?

He thought of the man in the car outside, and shivered. Carefully, without disturbing anything, he checked the rest of the flat.

He went into his box room office.

Most of the files were now at Ricky's house. But those that remained had been taken out of the cabinet and systematically rifled. The contents of the waste-paper basket lay on the table. Letters in the in-tray, telexes in the pending, brochures in the out-tray, all had been sorted through. But nothing seemed to have been taken.

This wasn't a visit from a felon or the VAT-man. It was the work of an industrial spy.

Ricky checked the treatments schedule and picked his moment. Sonia couldn't give him lip if she was having a mud facial.

He put his head round the salon door and drew his breath.

'This the Black and White Minstrel Show, or what?'

There were three of them in a row, three bodies swaddled from head to toe in white towels. Only their faces showed, thickly caked in black mud with just a thin white rim left around the eyes and mouth.

Six eyes opened simultaneously. Which were hers?

'Sonia?' he called tentatively.

Three pairs of white-rimmed lips remained firmly shut. Then one of the beauticians spoke.

'Gentlemen's hour is eleven in the morning, sir.'

'You'd need the whole of the Black Sea for me, darlin',' he said. 'Carry on. I'm just lookin' for a friend.' He saw a wisp of blonde hair peeping out from under the head towel of the nearest mummy and took a step forward. 'That's her! Sonia? Surprised to see me, doll?'

The lips parted and the head turned to the girl behind the chair.

'I think he wants the mental hospital down the road.'

It wasn't Sonia.

Sonia's voice came from the far chair.

'Ricky!' she hissed. 'What are you doing here?'

'Easy on,' he said. 'Cor, talk about black looks!'

'Go away!'

'But I only just got here! Booked myself in for a spot of relaxation, didn't I? What's the nosh like? Still carrot juice and rabbit feed?'

'You're causing a scene!'

'No I'm not. Am I, girls?'

'Go, or I will!'

She struggled to get up out of the reclining chair, shedding towels as she went. Her hair was straggly with mud and tears made two pathways down her cheeks, but she looked gorgeous, standing there in just a bathing-suit, shielding herself with her hands like a right fancy Venus.

'Don't worry, darlin',' he said soothingly. 'They can't see you blush.'

With a little squeal, she turned about and fled into the changing rooms.

When Ricky had had a massage and spruced up for dinner, he went to reception and ordered flowers to be sent up to Sonia's room. He'd give it ten or fifteen minutes then take up a bottle of Spumanti and tap on her door, pretending to be room service. He'd grab her, give her a bit of the rough, just how she liked it, he'd

148

find some Mantovani on the radio and before you could say Rudolf Valentino, she'd be begging him to have those big silk camiknickers off of her.

The man behind the reception desk shook his head.

Sonia had checked out an hour before.

'I thought the trend was towards LCDs,' said Simon.

'That's what I said,' responded Ricky. 'LEDs.'

'Liquid Crystal. It's not the same thing.'

'Sime, this here is a watch, right? It tells the time, right?'

'It doesn't, to me.'

'Well, *this* one don't because it needs a battery. Look, everyone's got to have a watch, right? Some people ain't got the dough for a Rolex Oyster,' he tapped his wrist, 'so they go for somethin' cheap. Right?'

'Yes, but . . .'

'Right or wrong?'

'I suppose there's a market at *some* price.'

'Right! I bought 'em at twenty percent of retail. Four quid a lump. Don't look like that, Sime. Twenty percent's a right steal on electrical.'

Simon took another out of its plastic box. The face was dark. A third blinked like a guttering candle.

'They're under guarantee?'

''Course they are.'

'We'd better send them back.'

'Can't do that.' Ricky grabbed the watch and cracked it hard on the table top. The flashing stopped and the watch went dead. 'See?' he said. 'Battery, like I said. One or two are bound to be duff.'

'One or two?'

'Sime, are you in this deal or aren't you? Say the word and I'll put Abby in it instead.'

'OK,' said Simon wearily. 'How many of these trendy little success stories do we own?'

'About five.'

'Five cartons? That can't come to too much.'

149

'Give over! Five *thousand*. You think I'd waste my time?'

Ricky dressed carefully. He put a handkerchief in his top pocket and rubbed the toes of his crocodile shoes on the back of his trouser legs. He dabbed Gold Spot on his tongue and braced his inside pocket with several tubes of cigars. He didn't smoke cigars, but you had to feel right to tap a man for sixty grand.

He drove slowly to the West End, letting cars pull out and pedestrians cross ahead of him, and he arrived in Park Lane at just a few minutes to six o'clock.

At five-fifteen, Alfie called down to his driver to bring the car round. He'd better leave right away, to allow for the rush-hour traffic across London.

He skimmed the confidential report once again.

They'd found the camera behind a two-way mirror in Lucinda's apartment and smashed it, but there'd been no photos or other compromising evidence. His enquiries into Transcosmos Trading and the watching brief on its Poonah Mansions office had drawn a total blank. The Brotherton boy seemed to live a predictably dreary life. A girlfriend who seemed to be moving out. The odd dolly bird in for a drink and out an hour later without a ruffled feather. A lot of early nights. And the office, some kind of converted broom cupboard, hadn't yielded any useful secrets. Certainly nothing to suggest that Ricky was making a great deal of money which he was withholding from the creditors. You could only meet blackmail with counter-blackmail, and Alfie was going to the meeting badly short of fire power. He'd have to bluff it out.

The car was waiting at the main door. He climbed in. 'The Hilton,' he said. 'Kensington.'

From six to six-fifteen, Ricky sat in the coffee-shop on the first floor, watching the girls and working out which were the out-calls.

From six-fifteen to six-twenty, he drank a second pot of tea.

At six-twenty-five, he ordered a large brandy.

At six-thirty, he slipped downstairs to the lobby to check.

By six-forty-five, he was about to explode. The bastard had asked for it! He'd had his chance. It would now go to the newspapers, his wife, his chairman, the stock exchange, the Bank of England and the board of every company in the City.

Alfred Steinman, That *Was* Your Life.

At six-ten, Alfie ordered a gin and tonic. He was told the bar wasn't yet open to non-residents. He swore, and asked for a Perrier instead. From where he sat in the coffee-shop, he could see all the comings and goings in the lobby.

Between six-ten and six-twenty, he watched the air crews checking in and amused himself taking his pick of the hostesses.

At six-twenty-five, he re-read the message.

A pot of tea . . . the Hilton lobby.

There were two London Hiltons. Only the Kensington one served tea in the lobby. In the Park Lane Hilton, the coffee-shop was on the first floor.

But did Ricky Stone know that?

By six-twenty-nine, the suspicion had become a certainty. He was in the wrong bloody place!

Alfie Steinman was known for his cool nerve. Stories abounded in the City of his icy control and unvacillating brinkmanship. He never panicked.

By six-thirty-one, he'd leaped from his seat, thrown a fiver onto the table, bolted down the hall, knocked over a flower arrangement, spun a porter dizzy in the revolving door and was yelling at his driver to do an

151

illegal U-turn in the thick of the Holland Park Avenue traffic.

By six-forty-seven Alfie was pounding up the stairs to the coffee-shop on the first floor of the West End Hilton.

But at six-forty-six, Ricky had slipped out of the back entrance and made his way purposefully towards the Merc.

12

'Mrs Stone?' asked the sleek gent on the doorstep.

'Could be,' answered Beryl cautiously. Then she saw the Rolls parked in the road. She must have won the bingo! 'That's me,' she said promptly.

'I'm Alfred Steinman. Is your husband in?'

Beryl let out a small cry. Her hand flew to protect her throat.

'Who is it?' bellowed Ricky from inside.

Signalling for the man to wait there, she hurried indoors. Ricky lay sprawled in a chair in front of the telly, eating from two packets of Popsitops at the same time.

'It's *him*!' she hissed. 'That man!'

'Beryl, am I supposed to be psychic?'

'Alfie Steinman!'

Ricky shot upright. He pointed towards the door.

'Tell him to eff off! I'm not havin' that filthy ponce in this house!'

'Evening, Ricky,' said Alfie affably from the doorway. He looked about him. 'Nice place you've got here. Tasteful, too.'

'You like my new curtains?' said Beryl.

Ricky jumped to his feet. He stepped forward, knotting his fists.

'Get out of my house!' he bawled.

Alfie stepped back into the corridor. He paused and his smooth brow momentarily puckered.

'You *did* send that note?'

'And where was you?'

'At the Hilton. Both Hiltons, in fact.'

'No you wasn't, you poxy bastard . . .'

Alfie was at the front door by now. He became conciliatory.

'Look, let's talk this thing over calmly.'

'Not in Beryl's house we don't!'

'My car's outside. Shall we?'

The Rolls purred slowly around the local streets. Heads turned to see who was in the fancy motor.

'Take a left,' Ricky ordered the driver. He didn't want to go past the club.

He turned back to Alfie and took out an envelope from his pocket.

'I'm askin' seventy-five Gs, Alfie,' he said. 'Five percent discount for prompt payment.'

Alfie smiled and shook his head. His jowels quivered over his stiff collar like fish's gills. He reached into his briefcase and took out a file marked, TRANSCOSMOS TRADING LTD/R. STONE.

'Sorry, Ricky,' he said. 'I've got you trumped.'

'Bullshit.'

'"Seventh Heaven Ltd cosmetics,"' he read. '"Various biscuit products. Jeans and watches in a Croydon warehouse. Lawsuit re firelighters pending. Profits undeclared. Association with Billy Tanner for the purpose of tax evasion . . ."'

'You can't prove nothin'!'

'With *your* form, Ricky?'

'Go on, try! I challenge you. You go to the law with that and I'll go to the papers with this.' He tapped the envelope.

Alfie's smile had faded. He swallowed drily and reached for a decanter in the drinks compartment.

'You know, I'm closing down companies every day. Somebody's got to clear the stock. It doesn't have to go to auction.'

'You propositionin' me?'

'I'm suggesting we work together, not against each other.'

'So you can pay me off?'

'I don't accept I owe you anything, Ricky. Let's just say I want to see you earn, right?'

Ricky thought. With the negatives, he could milk Alfie for a lifetime. But right now, there was Billy and Morris to take care of.

'I'd need a downpayment,' he said. 'Ten grand. To show bona fides.'

Alfie reached into his inside pocket and handed him an envelope. Ricky could feel at once it wasn't money.

'Open it,' said Alfie.

Inside were details of a large shoe wholesaler in Manchester who was going bust.

'Make me any reasonable offer,' he went on. 'And now, *your* bona fides. I'll have those photographs.'

Ricky faltered. The shoes looked a right tasty deal. Could be thirty or forty grand in it, if handled right. But could he trust Alfie to accept his offer? Better give him just one snap now. He could spin this out till he was down to the last.

'Don't let's be greedy,' he said, opening his own envelope. 'One at a time, eh?'

Returning from Manchester the following afternoon, Simon and Ricky got held up in a six-mile tailback on the M6. Eventually they came to the roadworks. Four men lounged on shovels, smoking. The heavy plant was idle.

'Three million on the dole!' fumed Ricky. 'They got no brains, this government, or what?'

Simon shrugged. He was dreaming of Italy. He'd paid another three thousand to hold the villa, leaving a balance of twenty-five. A few more weeks of Wafathins and Popsitops, plus a lucky touch on the shoes, and he'd be in the clear. He'd pack up the flat and close the company. He enjoyed imagining the scene when he went round to the squat and handed Martha her airline ticket to freedom.

'The country's too full of people with no brains,' Ricky was saying. 'If that's democracy, give me Russia. Mind you, I'm not against the blacks and the yellows, but they've got a different mentality. They shouldn't be allowed to vote, not without an intelligence test. Plus they breed like rabbits. You won't see a white face in a maternity ward. There should be a means test before anyone can have kids.'

Did that mean a bankrupt should forfeit his family? Simon refrained from asking. He looked out of the window at a housing estate crouching in the lee of a great slag heap.

'We should just consider ourselves lucky,' he said.

'You make your own luck, boy.'

Silence fell between them. Ricky sucked his teeth. He was wrestling with the eternal puzzle.

'If they're so bloody educated, why did they let all them foreigners in after the war? That's what I'd like to ask. If they wasn't here, you wouldn't have no unemployment.'

Simon thought of Martha and how patiently she would dismantle Ricky's thinking and reassemble it for him. He hadn't the energy.

'Without them, who would we sell our jeans to?' he asked with a shrug.

'We wouldn't have bought them in the first place. In Switzerland there ain't no nigs, and look how rich they are.' Ricky shook his head. 'It don't make sense.'

'Nothing makes sense if you really look into it.'

'Then what are we here for? If God's out for a lark, I'd like to be informed.'

'We're here to buy and sell shoes. Shoes and ships and sealing wax, cabbages and kings.'

Ricky looked more puzzled than ever. He opened his mouth but shut it again. And for the next few miles, as they crawled past the roadworks, he was silent.

'Ten percent across the board, Alfie, and ninety days' terms.'

There was an audible gulp at the other end of the line. Ricky held the car phone away from his ear and winked at Simon. Ten percent was daylight robbery.

'Make it fifteen?' pleaded Alfie.

'Go on like that and I'll make it five.'

'And no credit. You know the game, Ricky.'

'I thought this was *our* game, Alfie.'

When Alfie spoke, his tone was weary with defeat.

'When will you collect the goods?'

'You send 'em in to Croydon. The address is on your file.'

Ricky put the phone down in its cradle and clapped his knee. He began to whistle a Charles Aznavour tune. The motorway stretched clear ahead of them. He put his foot down. Suddenly his thoughts went to Sonia. Sonia and the South of France.

'Of course,' said Simon cautiously, 'we won't have trouble selling sandals at this time of year, will we? The summer season being over, I mean.'

Ricky stopped whistling. He looked across to Simon and scowled.

'Sime, you're a right miserable bastard! Always knockin' a deal. You think there ain't goin' to be another summer again? We can sit on the stock for ever. It's pound notes in the bank.'

'But I thought the idea was to do some quick deals and then quit.'

'Who was always sayin' we should re-invest the profit?'

'Up to a point, yes. But we don't want to get locked in, do we?'

'We're onto a run of luck and you're saying break it?' Ricky shook his head. 'I sometimes wonder about you, Sime.'

Ricky dropped Simon on the corner of his street and sped off. As Simon strolled towards the mansion block,

157

he saw a large truck unloading cartons onto the pavement. *Melvyn Harris (Wholesale) Ltd* was painted on the sides. He hurried forward and stopped one of the men.

The man pulled out a scrap of paper.

'This *is* the registered office of Transcosmos Tradin'?'

'Yes, but what's going on?'

'Search me. Ask the guv.'

'Hang on right there!'

Simon bolted downstairs into the flat. He grabbed the phone and called Melvyn.

'Them jeans,' cried the wholesaler. 'They fuckin' shrink!'

'All jeans shrink, Mel.'

'Nor four fuckin' sizes they don't!'

'Wait a minute . . .'

'I'm backin' the lot, get me? And you tell Rick he's sewn me up for the last time, right?'

The line went dead.

Simon raced upstairs. The truck was disappearing down the street. On the pavement were a dozen cartons, each the size of an armchair.

He went slowly back down. He phoned Beryl. Could Ricky call him the moment he got in?

'But I thought Ricky was with you, in Manchester,' she said. 'He said you was stayin' overnight.'

Simon swallowed.

'Ah, um, yes. I must be going loopy.'

But she was too sharp. She let fly for ten minutes before he was able to ring off.

He sat down and put his head in his hands. What the hell was he going to do with a couple of thousand pairs of un-pre-shrunk jeans causing an obstruction on the pavement?

Fifty quid's worth of flowers and Sonia had finally agreed to meet him. The time was seven p.m., the place the cocktail bar of Rafters Hotel, East Sheen. Ricky had booked a room. He checked in, showered, changed and was downstairs in the bar with a bottle of Spanish champagne cooling in a bucket when she arrived.

The moment he saw her he knew he was in with a chance. The evening was swollen and sultry and she wore a frilly cotton dress, laced half-open across the bodice, and a shawl over her bare arms. She was freshly bronzed and blonded, and her curves were all in the right places. Today she wasn't a day over thirty.

He got up as she approached.

'Talk about an oil paintin'!' he breathed.

'Hello, Ricky,' she said coolly and offered him her hand.

She sat down at arm's length across the table. Her manner told him he was going to have to fight for it. But that was how he liked it.

Simon hauled the last of the cartons into the corridor and collapsed in exhaustion. Already in his mind he was rewriting the balance sheet, marking down the jeans stock. What about the watches, the condoms, the shoes . . . ? He broke out in a sweat. Was all the profit from the Popsitops being dribbled away on bum deals? In future he'd vet every parcel *before* it was bought. Ricky was trigger-happy with money. He didn't seem to realise that half of it was Simon's.

So, it was down to him. Brotherton to the rescue again.

First, the jeans. Over a large whisky, an idea slowly evolved.

What had Martha said? Thirty families in that squat? Fifty children under ten? They must have a few washing machines among them. If they didn't, they really *were* skint and they needed the money all the more.

How long would it take thirty women to wash and press two thousand pairs of jeans?

'Dorchester Hotel?' enquired Beryl, looking down at the well-thumbed list of numbers. 'Reception, please. Have you got a booking for a Mr Stone?'

There was no booking for a Mr Stone.

'That the Hilton? Has a Mr Ricky Stone booked in, please?'

No Ricky Stone had booked in.

'Inn on the Park? I'm looking for a Mr Stone . . .'

Brown's, Blake's, the Elisabetta, the Penta, the Intercontinental, the Coburg and St Ermin's took care of central London. She moved south-west. Then she tried the Regency in Putney, the Rest House in Cheam, Rafters Hotel in East Sheen . . .

The guard on Door G was a barefooted imp who sat emptying collection tins. She sized Simon up and down and demanded to see inside the carton he was carrying. Satisfied, she called to a little boy to take over and with a nod of her head told Simon to follow her.

'You Martha's boyfriend?' she asked. 'The fuddy-duddy one?'

'I expect that's me. What's your name?'

'Natasha, and I'm eight.'

'That's a nice name.'

'No, it isn't. It's a stupid name. How old are you?'

'Guess.'

'Fifty-five.'

She led him up concrete steps, along corridors semi-tiled like public lavatories, past walls of violent graffiti and rooms of blaring music and screaming babies, until they came to a large, steam-filled kitchen. Fumes from the gas cooker mingled with the smell of simmering beans and baking banana cake. At a table a woman with close-cropped hair sat breast-feeding. Beside her, Trev was busy with a drill and flexible cable, winding back a speedometer.

Martha stood over by the sink, chopping onions.

'Martha,' said the girl, 'your fuddy-duddy friend's here.'

Martha looked up and rubbed her watering eyes on her sleeve.

'Hi, Simon,' she said.

'Hi, Martha.'

'Aren't you going to kiss?' said the little girl.

'Natasha, fetch me the garlic squeezer, please,' said Martha sweetly. She saw the carton. 'Ah, more provisions?'

'No, it's just an idea really. Make a bit of money for you all.'

Simon outlined his scheme. He'd deliver the jeans in the morning. They'd then shrink-wash them, re-press them and sew on new size labels, and in a week's time he'd come and collect them back. He'd provide all the necessary materials and pay them either piece-rate or by the hour.

'Make a bit of money for *you*, you mean,' said Trev sourly.

The close-cropped woman drew her infant off the teat.

'That's how the rich get richer,' she told it. 'Exploiting working people.'

'I said I'll *pay* you for it!' protested Simon. 'Whatever's fair.'

'Fair?' scoffed Trev. 'Try your Paki friends, mate.'

Martha put down her knife and wiped her hands.

'Simon, come with me. I want to say something to you.'

She led him down the corridor, past a boy dismantling a bicycle and a man sawing up a door, and into a small cell-like room. He recognised the kettle and rugs from home. She closed the door and turned to face him. Her eyes were gravely beautiful. He yearned to kiss her.

'Simon,' she began, 'if we're ever to see each other again, will you please try and do one thing? Try and imagine what it's like to be in other people's shoes. Can't you see how *patronising* that was?'

Whoops! An anaconda this time. Those were the ones

161

that lurked unseen in rivers and when an animal went to drink, seized it by the nose and dragged it in . . .

He shook his head.

'One just can't win,' he said in a small voice. 'I came here with the best intentions. OK, my motives were partly selfish, but I was thinking of you, too.'

Drawing him towards her, she pressed his head against her shoulder and stroked his hair.

'You might just have *thought* first. It's obvious everyone's very uptight here.'

'Why do you put up with it?' He burrowed further into her body and drank in its sweet smell. 'No, don't answer. I just wish you'd come home, that's all. Where you belong. It's lonely without you.'

'This squat can't last for ever,' she admitted.

He pulled away.

'Maybe we'll have the villa by then! Wouldn't you rather wake up to crickets and birds singing then bawling children and bailiffs?' He managed a smile. 'No, I suppose you wouldn't.'

She kissed him lightly.

'I know it's not easy for you to understand, Simon.'

'If only you'd . . .'

She put a finger on his lips.

'Don't say it.'

She reached for the door handle.

'Now, bring that box in here and stay for supper.'

Sonia nestled into the crook of Ricky's arm. Her breath was hot on his chest and she toyed irritatingly with the hairs on his stomach. He wanted to pull away, but thought better of it. He was dying for a cigarette, too, but he wasn't going to risk undoing what it had taken hours of patient work to rebuild.

'I'm sorry,' she said.

'That's all right, doll,' he replied. 'We ain't all perfect.'

'I'm sorry for *us*, I mean. We can't go on like this. It's not fair.'

Now he drew away.

'Not fair on who?' he demanded.

'Beryl, for one.'

'Sonia, I thought we'd agreed: no names in bed.'

She had begun to shake. She was sobbing.

'I don't know what I'm doing here. I promised I'd have nothing to do with you until you'd left her. But I can't resist. I'm too weak. You've got to help me.'

He spread a hand over her rump. It quivered with every sob. A weeping woman always aroused him. He rolled her gently onto her back and gave her a handkerchief for her eyes, which she seized with puppy-like gratitude. She sniffed, then tried out a small laugh.

'I must look as awful as with that mud-pack on,' she said.

'Darlin', you look a million dollars.'

She put on her little-girl voice.

'You do love me, don't you? Even though I'm silly and weak?'

He took a nipple and watched it swell in his fingertips.

'You want me to tell you or show you?'

'Tell me we'll be together in St Tropez and everything's going to be lovely.'

'We'll be together in San Tropay and everythin's goin' to be lovely.'

'Promise.'

'I promise.'

'When?'

'Come on, Sonia,' he began, then bit his tongue. 'Soon as I get clear, darlin'. I'll throw it all up and we'll take off.'

'I mustn't see you till then, Ricky.'

'Course you must. Stop rabbitin' on, doll, and make your lovely mouth useful.'

'I really mustn't . . .' she began in a mumble.

But by then there was no room for the words to come out.

They came down in the lift together in silence. She'd repeated her ultimatum: no more meeting up till he was free. She was only saying that, of course. Give her a week or so and she'd be begging for it. No woman who'd been given a right good seeing-to could say No to another.

He watched the floor numbers slowly descending. At the ground floor, the door opened. Suddenly he grabbed her by the sleeve and pulled her back inside. He hammered the buttons.

Beryl!

Beryl was standing in the centre of the lobby. She looked like she was plugged into the mains. Her coppery hair stuck out wildly and her pitch-black eyes darted here and there like lasers.

Too late. She had seen them.

'There she is!' she bawled. 'The filthy 'ore! Leave my husband alone, you dirty old slag!'

She charged forward. The lift doors wouldn't shut in time. Sonia screamed. Beryl came for her with her handbag. Ricky grabbed her and pushed her back. He pinned her down by the arms. Sonia slipped out of the lift and began running down the lobby. Beryl brought her knee up into his groin. He let out a howl and released his grip. She broke free and belted after Sonia. Sonia was hampered by high heeled shoes. Beryl kicked off her own shoes and closed the gap. She pounced like a lioness, dragging Sonia to the ground by her hair.

'Fuckin' 'ore!' she screamed, pummelling her face. 'I'll kill yer!'

Sonia struggled to save herself. A hair-piece came away in Beryl's hands. She shrieked.

They fought like cats. The reception manager hovered helplessly by, dodging from foot to foot like a referee. People in the lobby melted away and took refuge behind armchairs and grandfather clocks.

Ricky sauntered over. He watched them for a moment. His money was on Beryl. He'd have liked to see it go to the finish.

'Stop them!' cried the manager.

'Time, ladies,' called Ricky, intervening at last.

He grabbed Beryl from behind and lifted her bodily away, still kicking and clawing. Sonia slithered aside, got to her feet and fled without handbag or shoes down the corridor.

Beryl watched her go. Jabbing her elbow in Ricky's ribs, she freed herself and brought her hand up in a sweeping, stinging slap full across his face. He reeled back.

'You touch her again, Rick,' she hissed, 'and I'll kill yer both!'

Then with great dignity she picked up her bag, collected her shoes and walked calmly down the lobby and out of the front door to a waiting taxi.

Ricky knocked on the boiler room door. He could hear the whimpering inside.

'Open up, doll.'

'She's there, I know she is!' howled Sonia. 'Don't let her near me!'

'It's only me. She's gone. It's all OK. C'mon, open the door.'

But she wouldn't. Ricky had to get the manager to unlock it with a pass key. Sonia shrank back against the boiler as he entered. Her white dress was torn and her hair all tangled and askew. She sucked her knuckles like a terrified child and made high-pitched squealing noises. She looked demented. Christ, had she gone off her rocker?

A fine drizzle had set in and the night bore the hint of autumn when Ricky finally arrived in Norwood. He'd taken Sonia home, put her to bed with hot milk and a valium – luckily, her teenage sons were both out – and beaten a smart retreat.

As he drove home, he considered the angle to take

with Beryl. The only policy was to keep absolutely *schtumm*.

He pulled into the carport and got out. He walked up the front path and almost tripped. There, on the doorstep lay a large pile of shirts, golf-clubs, suits, jackets, shoes, underpants, shaving gear, all growing sodden in the rain.

There wasn't a light on in the house. The front door was on the chain. He rang the bell, to signal he'd at least tried to come back, then drove away, leaving the things where they were.

He'd tackle Beryl in the morning. Right now he was dog tired. Where could he go? Not back to the hotel. No, he'd knock up young Sime and nick a bed off him for the night. Martha was off somewhere, so he'd be spared flapjacks for breakfast.

He stopped at a call-box on the way. The answering machine was on. Likely as dammit, the wet-eared ponce was in bed, getting his leg over. Ricky had had enough to do with sex for one night. He'd slip over to the club and get a bed off Bert.

As he headed back to Norwood, the thought uppermost in his mind was *dough*. Only a nice piece of money would get him out of the shit. And this time, no messing about. He'd pull out all the stops.

13

The club's guest suite was a one-bed cell with a chipped basin in the corner, in which Ricky took a jimmy during the night. The room lay over a fish and chip shop and stank of stale frying. The stair carpet was spongy with fat and grease, and coming downstairs in the morning, Ricky followed the imprint of the shop manager's shoes before him.

He found Bert in a back room of the club. Bert offered him breakfast: two cold saveloys from next door and a tin mug of tea with the milk curdling. Ricky had no appetite. It was like being back in the nick when he should be out celebrating his freedom.

He'd hole up at the club for a few days until things had blown over. Beryl would soon realise she couldn't do without him. She'd have him back, even if he had to sit it out until they cut her gas and electric off.

He slipped round the corner to Joe the barber's for a shave. Next he studied the *Sporting Life* over a salt-beef sandwich at Solly's caff. Then he went back to the club. He'd call Sime and get him busy on the trumpet, punting the shoes.

Ricky Stone was back in business.

As he opened the door, he came face to face with Morris. Morris wore a smile like a false moustache. Ricky swallowed. He was going to have to front this one out. He pulled out his paper.

'Ullo, Morrie,' he said cheerily. 'Want a hot one for the 2.15?'

Beryl woke to hear the dust cart grinding in the street outside. She pulled back the net curtain. Ricky's things still lay in a pile outside the front door, now completely sodden.

Tying a scarf over her curlers and slipping on her purple housecoat, she hurried downstairs to the kitchen. She had money squirrelled away all over the house. She pulled out a cookbook and shook it upside down. Fivers fell out like confetti.

She went to the front door and called to a dustman.

'Oi!'

She waved a note at him. He came over.

'Take this garbage, too,' she said. 'And here's for your trouble.'

At three in the morning, a domestic row in the next room woke Simon. At five, it was a chorus of howling babies. At six, a ghetto-blaster. Martha slept like a child through it all. She didn't even stir when he drew his dead arm from under her head and eased himself out of bed. He dressed quickly, then stood for a moment looking at her. Poor love, she was so tired. Too tired even to make love. There was a soft, vulnerable expression on her sweetly sleeping face. This was the real Martha.

Picking up the carton of jeans, he slipped out of the room and down the corridor. He went past little Natasha, who was playing with the dismantled bicycle and gave him a long and knowing look, past the kitchen where nappies were now steaming on the stove, past Trev going through his night's haul of car radios, past windows curtained with torn sheets, past a bed-sweaty group queuing up outside the latrines and finally out through the barricades of jagged timber and broken glass and into the daylight and air.

How could he let Martha live among such ugliness? These might be her principles but they weren't her people. She deserved beauty, calm, grace. She deserved Italy.

As he joined the early morning city traffic, he realised what had to be done. He'd nip down to Croydon and do a stock-take, revise the balance sheet and then go and see Billy. He'd sell out his share in the company.

'It's *circumstantial*, Morrie,' protested Ricky. 'You got no *proof* it was Alfie's boys duffin' up her place. One of her other customers might have got the needle.'

'Monday you put the lean on Alfie, and Tuesday my Lucy gets a visit from the heavy mob. You call that coincidence? In twenty years in the business I've had no trouble like this.'

'Times are changin', Morrie. You get a different class of punter these days.'

'Ricky,' warned Morris wearily.

'Anyway, if it *was* Alfie, it's down to him to pay the dammex.'

'My deal is with you, Rick.' He looked at his manicured fingertips and shook his head sentimentally. 'Cut me to the heart, it did, seeing my Lucy so upset. You could say I get over-protective. I've done things I'd rather not remember for her.'

Nor would Ricky. Rumour linked Morris's name with a pair of brothers from Bermondsey who were found floating to the surface in the foundations of a high-rise block not a million miles from where they sat.

'Course,' agreed Ricky piously, 'you've got to look after your girl. I'd be happy to make a small donation. Say, a monkey?'

'Add a nought and you're half way there.'

'Morrie, I ain't in the charity business!'

'Plus loss of earnings during the repairs.'

'Don't the poor kid ever get a holiday?'

'*And* a holiday. She's having a Caribbean cruise to get over it.'

'That's ain't no holiday! She works them cruises!'

'I'm looking at fifteen grand, Rick.'

'You're lookin' at a man who ain't got fifteen grand, Morrie.'

'He's about to become a very unhappy man, then.'

'Two grand, Morrie.'

'Two grand will do for starters.'

'Next week.'

'Today.'

'Tomorrow.'

'Tomorrow noon.'

'We had to shift your gear into the hangar,' said the foreman.

He led the way across the cracked concrete taxiway to a vast, crumbling building with metal doors that both of them could barely slide open. He switched the lights on. Pallets of cartons rose to the roof, one stacked upon another so they obscured the lighting.

Simon took out a pad and a calculator.

'Which is our lot?' he asked.

'It's all your lot, mate.'

Simon gulped.

'*All* of it?'

'Here's the delivery dockets.'

Simon thanked the man as civilly as he could and strolled slowly around the warehouse. The stock there could have supplied a beleaguered city for a month.

Forty thousand pairs of jeans. Every one a shrinker. Stood them in a pound a lump. Worth 50p.

Five thousand LED watches. Majority requiring new batteries. Cost four quid each. Worth two?

Condoms, unlubricated. Enough said.

A hundred thousand pairs of shoes. All summer styles. Pound notes in the bank – next summer.

And then the stock he had never even seen.

Five pallets of ladies' toiletry bags, marked Faulty.

Fly sprays, a thousand gross of them, in Hindi and Arabic cans. Just in time for the winter season in Southall.

Golf practice kits, the ones he'd read about in the papers that flew apart, already killing one and maiming two others.

Barbie dolls, in squashed acetate presentation boxes. Children's pop-up books, water-damaged so that the glue had come unstuck. Plastic garden furniture, deleted records, rusting exercise weights, ladies' cotton blouses from Turkey, men's viscose suits from Poland, Loo-Blue lavatory freshener, bucket-and-spade sets, barbecue tongs, cake trays, vegetable slicers, baby rattles, car deodorants, Naked Venus can openers, kids' cricket bats, Miss Muffet make-up sets, novelty farting cushions, ping-pong balls, safety matches, kites . . .

'Hello, Beryl,' said Simon down the line. 'Is Ricky about?'

'Who?' she demanded. 'Ricky Stone don't live here no more!'

'Oh, er, um . . .'

Then Hurricane Beryl struck. He put the phone down on the blotter and for five minutes re-worked his balance sheet calculations. Finally the line went quiet and he picked up the receiver again.

'Sime?' she was calling. 'You still there? 'Ere, I was chuckin' out Mr Unmentionable's things when I found these letters for you.'

'Letters?'

'Well, bills. A whole load of 'em. You comin' by?'

'I'll send a bike around straight away.'

'Listen, Sime, don't have nothin' more to do with that man! He's *evil*. I should know. But I'm free of him now, please God. I'm a new person. It's like takin' off a pair of shoes that give you 'orrible achin' corns. The relief!'

And then came the fateful call from Chris the Crisp. He was being posted to the States to run a group of new acquisitions. His successor had his own pet firm who handled clearances. Transcosmos would lose their contract and there was absolutely nothing Chris could do.

The goose that laid the golden egg was dead.

Ricky breezed into the flat, sporting a floral tie and matching handkerchief. He took one look at Simon and clicked his tongue.

'You been on the nest all night, boy,' he said. 'Shows in your boat. Knocks you bandy, that lark. You want to pace yourself or you'll peg out.' He rubbed his hands. 'Right, what's in the kitty? I need a couple of grand. Urgent.'

Simon pushed the balance sheet across the table. Ricky studied it without making anything of it.

'The kitty's empty,' said Simon quietly.

Ricky turned on him angrily.

'What you talkin' about?'

'The firm's skint.'

'Fuck off, Sime. How can we be skint? I need some dough.'

'In fact, we're insolvent. The definition of insolvent is you can't pay your debts when they fall due . . .'

'Don't give me definitions!'

Simon went through the pile of invoices that had arrived by bike.

'Loo-Blue lavatory freshener, £8,458. Bucket-and-spade sets, £12,400. Ladies' cotton blouses, £15,750, invoiced as kids' clothes and no VAT. Garden furniture, £12,375. Barbecue tongs, £5,450 . . .'

'It's all past-the-post gear, Sime.'

'Naked Venus can openers, £7,650. Fly spray, £14,400 . . .'

'I've got a buyer for them!'

'Total, £115,745.50p.'

'We'll double it.'

'We can't pay for it. There is precisely £3,100 in the bank.'

'T'riffic! So write out my cheque for two grand.'

'That's preferring a creditor. It's a criminal offence.'

172

'Sime, you talk like one of them boks from the Inland Revenue! It's our fuckin' dough! We'll get by. I'll squeeze a bit more gear out of Chris . . .'

'You can't. He's being transferred. That's all drying up.'

Ricky's face grew brutish, his neck veins thickened and froth appeared at the corners of his mouth.

'What you been doin', you dumb prick?'

Simon stood up.

'What have *you* been doing, buying all that crap? That's why we're skint! Buying goods you know you can't pay for is *fraud*. Didn't your six-month sabbatical teach you anything? Or were you too busy sewing mail bags and studying form?'

Ricky balled his fist and took a step forward.

'You're askin' for a poke, boy.'

'That's it, lash out when you're losing the argument! Typical! Just like a stupid animal. No wonder your Kev left home . . .'

Wham! The blow caught him on the side of the face and sent him staggering backwards. He wiped a hand over his mouth and stared at the smear of blood with disbelief.

'Fuck off, clever dick!' shouted Ricky. 'You're a right unlucky face! Nothin' but problems and criticism. I don't need it. I don't need *you*. Keep your soddin' little firm and all your lovely paperwork and that fancy legal crap. You'll never make it, boy. You got no imagination. You're a *nonentity*!'

With that, Ricky turned on his heel and stormed out.

I shouldn't have hit him, thought Ricky as he drove angrily away. But he'd asked for it, the stuck-up prick. Who was he to judge, anyway? Who pulled up the deals? Who bought the gear, who found the customers? Who ducked and dived to earn a few quid and then shared it with the ungrateful berk?

Cobblers to him!

Ricky didn't need him. He didn't need anyone. He had his pension, didn't he? Alfie Steinman was going to keep him looked after into his old age. Alfie would provide the apartment in St Tropez and a nice piece of money to enjoy it with.

He patted his inside pocket.

He frowned.

He patted it again. It felt empty. He reached inside. It *was* empty. Of course! The snaps were in his blue blazer.

And all his jackets were lying in a mouldering pile on the front steps of the house that he used to call his home in Millionaire's Row, Norwood.

I should have hit him back, thought Simon as he slammed the front door angrily. That was the only language *he* understood. The man was as thick as two short planks. Who had to sort out the mess? Who had to deal with impatient creditors? Who was going to carry the can now? Ricky had bought stock in the company's name that it couldn't pay for and he'd swanned off, leaving Simon to face the music. The penalties for trading insolvently were severe: a hefty fine if you were lucky, a prison sentence as well if you weren't. With his background, Simon could hardly plead ignorance of that area of company law. And if he let the company simply fold, he could well be had up for fraud.

Bugger the man!

First thing, he'd write him a formal letter forbidding him to act in any way as agent for Transcosmos Trading Ltd or involve the company in any further liabilities.

He'd send back as much of the stock as he could and then set about settling the creditors one by one as he cleared the rest. Liquidating the firm could take a year and was bound to show a loss. *His* loss.

It meant goodbye to Italy, goodbye to a life of freedom and art, goodbye to all that destiny promised Martha and him. A weak man might have thought of ending it all. That day, Simon came close to his weakest hour. Only rage at finding Ricky had broken a tooth drove him to carry on.

174

'Beryl? 'Ullo, doll . . .'

The line went dead.

Ricky called again.

'Beryl, wait a minute! Listen to me . . .'

'Listen to more lies? Listen to Ricky Stone, Holy Friar? If you have anythin' to say, say it to my solicitors. Goodbye.'

Again the line went dead.

He dialled a third time. It was engaged and stayed engaged. She'd taken the phone off the hook.

'Sonia, darlin' . . . ?'

The line went dead.

Ricky called again.

'Sonia! Hold on, doll! Listen to me . . .'

'I have nothing to say to you, Ricky. Please go away.'

'I've got to speak to you . . .'

'I'm hanging up.'

She hung up.

He called again.

'Clear the line, please,' she said, 'or I'll have the calls intercepted.'

She then left her phone off the hook.

Ricky spent another night at the club. Billy sent the lame bag-man around with a reminder about his ten grand. Morris called to confirm their meeting at midday. The world was closing in.

A cockroach dropping from the ceiling woke him early. He leapt out of bed. He'd never spend another night in that poxy khazi. He'd go home. He'd smash the door down if need be. You couldn't arrest a man for breaking into his own house. Beryl would have to take out an injunction to stop him.

He arrived just as the milkman was delivering. The man had his book out, ready to collect the week's money. Putting his finger to his lips and giving him a broad, conspiratorial wink, Ricky hid behind the porch as he rang the bell.

Chains and bolts rattled as Beryl unlocked Fort Knox.

'Three pound seventy, missus,' said the man.

'Hang on while I print some money,' she replied and went back in.

Ricky slipped quickly in through the open door and slid unseen into the front room. Through the crack in the door he watched her come back down the hall and pay the bill.

'Just one pint a day from now on, please,' she said.

Then she re-bolted and chained the door and carried the milk into the kitchen.

But he was inside.

Two for me, two for Her Ladyship and two for the pot.

Ricky let the tea brew. He searched in the cupboards for the remnants of the bone china set he'd got off a dealer in Whitechapel as a trade sample and given her for their silver wedding. He accidentally knocked over a teapot. A roll of notes fell out. He quickly unpeeled a couple of twenties and put the rest back. They couldn't have you up for thieving your own money.

He poured the tea, then hesitated. Did she take sugar?

He carried the tray into the living room. Beryl sat on the sofa with her back to him, reading the *TV Times*. She pulled on a cigarette with that sucking noise she knew he couldn't bear.

'Tea's up,' he said cheerfully.

There was no reply.

'Beryl, I've made you a nice drop of tea.'

Wrapping her housecoat tightly around her, she got up. He had to move aside or she'd have walked into him. She looked right through him. He was invisible.

Two minutes later she came back in, a mug of coffee in her hand.

He went upstairs, past the bathroom door with its stabs and gashes and into the bedroom. He'd been wearing the double-breasted blazer. He opened the cupboard.

176

It was cleaned out. Not a tie, not a shirt, not a pair of shoes.

She must have brought his things indoors and dumped them in the garage.

Except for cases of samples and returns, the garage was empty.

He prowled into the living room. Beryl was now onto the *Reader's Digest*, tracing the words with her finger.

He winched his lips into a civil smile.

'What you done with my gear, doll?'

She turned a page noisily.

'I asked you a question, Beryl.'

She brushed a fleck of dust off her sleeve and went on reading.

He snatched the magazine and flung it across the room.

'Leave alone!' she screeched.

'My clothes, Beryl? Where are they? Where's my blazer?'

She glared back at him, her eyes afire.

'Ricky Stone don't live here no more. I threw his things out.'

'Threw 'em out?'

'Gave 'em to the garbage men, didn't I?'

He grabbed her shoulder.

'You know what you've done? Chucked away those photos! I had Alfie by the short and curlies, and now look what! You've fuckin' snookered me!'

She reared back defiantly.

'You brought it on yourself! It's His punishment!'

It wasn't under G for Garbage or R for Refuse. Directory Enquiries directed him to Norwood District Council who routed him to the Cleansing Department. He finally reached the supervisor and told him the cleaning lady had mistakenly thrown out some vitally important pictures.

'Works of art?' queried the man.

'You might say so,' said Ricky. 'It must have been yesterday mornin'.'

The man rustled some papers.

'Well, they won't have been incinerated yet.'

'T'riffic! I'll shoot right over.'

'Let me see. The barge should be passing the Isle of Dogs about now. You'll find them somewhere in among the rest of the three thousand tons on it.'

Ricky was beat. He picked up the phone, then put it down again. He didn't have a friend in the world.

Mavis, the cleaning woman, had left the hoover on just outside his door. She'd be in the kitchen with Beryl, tearing him to pieces over coffee and cake. Over the din, he heard Beryl's voice rising to a crescendo. He was trapped behind enemy lines.

His thoughts turned to Sonia, to other times in other hotels and to their dreams of a life of sunshine and relaxation together. Would she still have him if he left Beryl once and for all, for richer or poorer?

He called Florrie's Flower Shoppe and sent her the biggest bunch of roses two twenty-pound notes could buy.

Carefully he composed a note to go with it.

To the only woman in the world, it ran. *I can't live without your loving touch. Forgive a repentant heart. I swear to be true forever. Remember all those times we had together? Dreaming of St Tropez, with all my love, Rick.*

Simon picked up the phone, then put it down again. He didn't have a friend in the world.

Only Martha.

A forty-minute drive took him across London to the squat. Natasha was once again on sentry duty.

'Shouldn't you be at school?' he asked.

'The teachers are on strike,' replied the fair-haired imp. 'Martha's out with Roger, picketing.'

'Roger?'

'He's a social worker. He's writing a book on us. He's

178

nice. Not fuddy-duddy.' She looked up archly through her fringe. '*They* kiss.'

'I'm sure you'd know if they did.'

He gave her a 50p piece. She kept her hand out until he'd made it two pounds. Then he retreated to the pub on the corner and sat nursing a pint of lager.

He mustn't start imagining things. Little girls couldn't tell between one kind of kissing and another. Roger was probably one of those avant-garde types who'd been on a package holiday to France and come back kissing instead of shaking hands. Anyway, Martha was entitled to do what she pleased. *He* wasn't her keeper. And if things had gone further than just a greetings kiss, she would have good reason for it. Who knew, maybe this Roger only had a few weeks to live? Maybe he'd had a bad socio-political experience and needed his consciousness nursing? Or maybe it simply didn't *mean* anything to her, just as that hit-and-run job in Glasgow of his hadn't meant a thing to him. She'd formally forgiven him for that, though he'd never actually felt exonerated.

He shouldn't have come to see her anyway, not in his present state. Women shunned failure. They were venal, seduced by success, turned on by power. Martha was no different from the rest of them. He had to recoup his aces and win her back from a position of strength.

Sweeping up the debris of Transcosmos Trading Ltd wasn't going to help. He needed real success. He needed the Big One.

The doorbell rang. Ricky inched the ruched net curtain aside. In the street stood a van marked *Florrie's Flower Shoppe*.

He was at the front door in a flash.

A boy handed over a vast bouquet of red roses.

'The lady says to send them back,' he said in a loud voice.

Ricky could hear Beryl's cough advancing down the hallway. He pressed a quid into the boy's hand and slammed the door shut. Quickly he ripped off the label addressed to Mrs Sonia Pringle, The Pin Cushion, Roehampton High Street, and crumpled it up into his pocket. Inside the cellophane, way out of reach, he could see a small white envelope sticking out among the blooms.

Beryl snatched the bouquet from him.

'Don't think you can make up so easy! I've had it all before. Flowers, sob stories, the lot. It's too late.'

'Then give 'em back.'

He tried to take them, but she clung on tight.

'I'll keep 'em for your grave. Ricky Stone, RIP.'

'Let me put 'em in a vase for you.'

But she wouldn't hand them over. He tailed her into the kitchen. She cut the ribbon. She undid the wrapping. She leant forward and breathed in their scent. And then she reached for the white envelope. She tore it open.

For a moment, she was silent. He shut his eyes. It was like waiting for a doodlebug to land.

Then she let out a soft little *aaah*.

'"To the only woman in the world,"' she read. '"I can't live without your lovin' touch . . . I swear to be true forever . . . Dreamin' of San Tropay . . ."'

Her eyes had gone misty.

'You do have a way with words, Rick, you cunnin' bastard.'

He scuffed the table-leg with his toe.

'Comes from the heart,' he said.

'All them lovely silver beaches. And the night life.'

'Yeah, Beryl.'

Her tone crispened sharply. She rummaged in a tin for a thumb-tack and pinned the note in the centre of the trellis of plastic vines and fruit that separated the kitchen from the dining area.

She stood back and pointed her finger at it.

'I'm keepin' you to this, Rick. Every word of it. I'll be watchin' you. It's your twelve commandments.'

Ricky Stone was a fighter. He might be on Death Row but he'd find a way to escape. And if they did come with the black hood, they'd need a regiment to hold him down.

Beryl, Sonia, Morris, Billy, Simon, Alfie . . . there was only one way out of the spider's web. He'd said it before and he'd say it again.

Dough.

But not just a tickle here and there from Crispos and condoms. He needed *bundles* of it. One really tasty deal, and he'd be shot of the lot of 'em for good. Just one. The Big One.

14

'Cash with order, Ricky my son.'

'Gear, Rick? Got no gear, old mate. Business dead as a dodo. You'd think it was the kipper season.'

It was nowhere near the kipper season: it was September, with summer gliding into autumn. In Millionaire's Row, Norwood, the cherry trees were struggling into fruit, and in the park yellow blotches already foxed the maple trees and mist filmed the grass when Ricky walked the dog in the early morning.

Business was booming, and Ricky could see it. Melvyn had bought himself a second Roller and Eli and Abby were building a five thousand square foot extension to their gaff. Across the country, warehouses were emptying as fast as the wholesalers could fill them, and in the street markets cash pouches overflowed and tills rang red-hot.

But that wasn't the story Ricky heard.

In Shoreditch, business was slow. In Houndsditch, it was sticky. It was flat in Whitechapel and slack in the Angel. No-one had seen a September like it.

Ricky wasn't dumb; he got the message. Word was out that he had a warehouse full of goods bought on credit. He was still an undischarged bankrupt. Was he lining up another long-firm fraud?

What they all meant was, they had no business for Ricky Stone.

'Melvyn? Hello, Melvyn. Simon Brotherton here. Brotherton. Simon. You remember, Ricky Stone's partner. Sorry? No, don't worry, it's not jeans this time, ha ha. What? Yes, I'm sorry about that, too. Slight oversight. These things happen. A dropped thread in life's rich tapestry, eh? Compensation? No, that's not why I rang. Actually, I've got this other parcel. Just up your street, Melvyn. It's really great. Hello? Are you there? OK, it's stuff called Loo Blue. A sort of toilet deodorant. Colours the water blue at the same time. Quite clever, really. You what? You *sold* it to us? Ah. Oh. Well, would you like to buy it *back*? At a price, of course. You wouldn't. I see. What? The jeans? Yes, it's regrettable but what can one do? The man's *suing* you? Look, there's no *medical* evidence . . . Well, tell him to wear boxer shorts and he'll get it back in no time. He shouldn't have been jumping around the fountains in Trafalgar Square in the first place. They cut them off? All right, I'll pay for a new pair. They *what did you say*? Oh my God. Well, it's not your fault . . . No, it's not *my* fault either . . . I wasn't holding the scissors . . .'

'Leave it out, Eli. Don't give me that fanny about them firelighters. Affects my game.' Ricky jabbed his cue at the ball. It zig-zagged across the baize, missing every pocket. 'See?'

Eli sprawled his slabby chest over the table and took practice dabs along the cue-rest.

'Settle out of court, mate,' he wheezed.

'I ain't settlin' with no-one. Who is this geezer anyway?'

'The insurance company. The feller claims against them, they claim against us and we're claimin' against you.' Eli smacked the ball into a pocket. 'You should claim against the Polish manufacturers.'

'Fuck off, Eli. I didn't come here to discuss problems. I want to do business.'

Eli smacked another ball home. He chalked the tip of his cue and took aim again.

'Business is lousy.'

'Just give me the good news.'

Eli sent the last ball neatly away and stood up.

'I just won. That's the good news. So you owe me a tenner, Rick. You're slippin', son.'

Poxy bloody country, cursed Ricky and quickened his step across the park as the first light drops of rain fell. He didn't even enjoy these early morning walks with the Alsatian any more. What was the fun, without a club to swing at a ball?

Turning the corner into his street he saw the dust-cart doing its round. What kind of poxy country was it where they collected the garbage one day and dumped it on a barge the next? They should give people time to rectify mistakes.

As he drew alongside, he stopped dead in his tracks.

One of the men was wearing his blue double-breasted blazer!

He stepped forward, then faltered. How was he going to put it?

''Ere, Jim,' he called in a bluff tone. 'Looks like my jacket you're wearin'.'

The man emptied a bin into the cart before turning round.

'I don't know nothin' about no jacket,' he said in a surly tone.

'Steady, Jim. I ain't the law. You got it down the road, right?'

'The old girl at number 30 chucked it out,' he replied and went to get another bin. 'And my name ain't Jim.'

'No offence, John.' Ricky followed him to the house and back to the dust-cart. 'Find anything in the pocket, did you?'

'Such as?'

'Oh, anything. An envelope? A brown envelope? Belongs to a pal of mine, see.'

The man paused for a moment and gave Ricky a long, level stare.

'No, mate.'

'In the *inside* pocket? 'Ere, take a butchers now.'

Ricky unpeeled a pound note from a roll and held it out. The man stepped forward but didn't take the money.

'I wouldn't touch no dough from a dirty pervert!' he hissed in Ricky's face. 'Them photos is where *you* ought to be, mate. In the fuckin' trash.'

A girl in a silk sari led Simon into the penthouse office where Joe Patel sat in a white linen suit, chewing betel nuts. Brothers and cousins, dressed deferentially in shirtsleeves, jabbered on white telephones or sorted through the samples and brochures piled on white-framed glass tables. Beyond the window spread a breath-taking panorama of Hyde Park.

Joe waved Simon to a white-upholstered armchair. Simon handed over his card.

'Good of you to see me,' he began. 'Now, I believe you deal in . . .'

'Everything and anything, sir.'

Simon opened his suitcase and took out a small packet.

'Fancy a spot of Loo Blue? Your price to clear: £1.44 a dozen.'

'How much do you have?'

'Five thousand dozen.'

'One pound, I will take them all.'

'But they *cost* me one twenty-five!'

'I would be happy if you paid nothing at all, sir.'

'I might come down to one fifteen.'

'One pound, Mr Brotherton.'

'One *ten*?'

'Sir, please do not offend me.'

'All right, a quid. Done.' Simon gulped. He delved

185

deeper into the suitcase. 'Can I interest you in Barbie dolls? Or these handsome barbecue tongs? Naked Venus can openers, very handy around the house? Kids' cricket bats, ideal Christmas line? Garden furniture, an absolute flyer? Children's pop-up books? Men's suits? Ladies' blouses . . . ?'

Ricky sat uncomfortably in a low leather camel chair. The floors and walls of Mo's office were thickly covered in exotic Persian rugs. At the far end, beneath a portrait of the Shah, lay roll upon roll of priceless carpet. Through the modular steel window frame Ricky could see the dismal rooftops of Ealing.

A girl brought in a brass pot with a long curved spout. Her eyes flashed behind her yashmak and she moved like a belly dancer.

'Talk about Turkish Delight,' he breathed.

Mo smiled and adjusted the cuffs of his immaculate suit.

'She's from Iran, actually. You take Arabic coffee?'

Ricky looked up at the girl.

'Could you do me a nice little pot of tea, darlin'?'

Mo translated, and with a slight bow she left.

He then turned to the third man in the room and exchanged some words in Arabic.

The man was slight and wiry. He wore a white djellaba with a jacket, shoes and socks from an Oxfam shop. He sat across the low fretwork table, fiddling with worry beads and clearing his throat and swallowing. He'd hardly spoken a word since Ricky arrived, but merely sat watching him with hawk-like eyes. His name was Ahmed. Ricky had taken him for a refugee until Mo said he was a very important man in Libya – number two in Colonel Gadaffi's central buying office.

'Ahmed asks if you are Jewish,' said Mo.

'Tell him, business is business. Money speaks all religions.'

Mo jabbered away, then turned back to Ricky.

186

'He says, what is your position on the Palestinian cause?'

Ricky did a double-take. Mo had called him over urgently. Had he dropped everything and rushed over, only to be asked his views on world politics?

'Everybody's entitled to a place to live in. He's Libyan, right? Then he's entitled to live in Libanon.'

More yattering. This went on for five minutes. Ricky glanced at his watch. What the eff was going on? He had deals to do, dough to make. He had to graft, not sit on his fanny on a camel chair with his golf-swing muscles seizing up. They must get terrible arthritis, them nomads.

Finally Mo turned back. Ahmed was grinning a gold-toothed grin.

'Ahmed wants you to handle it personally,' said Mo.

'Sure. Handle what?'

'Let me explain. Libya wishes to send aid to the Palestinians. Not money, but goods. Things to eat, things to wear. Tools, cosmetics, hardware – items like that.'

This was music to Ricky's ears.

'I can get it all! Top quality gear. Cheap, too. How much does he want to spend? Ten grand? Twenty?'

'Five million.'

Ricky gulped.

'Five million?'

'It's too much for you?'

'Too much? You've got to be jokin'! That's peanuts! I've handled far bigger deals.'

Mo held up a warning finger.

'But time is of the absolute essence.'

'I'm lightnin' when I get goin', son. What are we talkin' about? A couple of months?'

'The letter of credit expires in fifteen days.'

Ricky nearly toppled out of the camel chair.

'Fifteen days?'

'Not possible?'

'Course it's possible! You're talkin' to Ricky Stone!'

187

'I should warn you,' said Mo as he followed Ricky to the Merc, 'the reward is great but so is the risk.'

'Nah! There ain't no risk, buyin' in them volumes.'

Mo drew him close by the elbow and spoke in his ear.

'You forget who these people are! Terrorists. Assassins. Killers. If you succeed, you may become a People's Hero.'

'Bollocks to that.'

'If you *fail* . . .' Mo drew his finger across his throat and made a garrotting sound. 'Easy as killing a fly, my friend.'

Fail? Ricky Stone wasn't going to fail, not over a five million nicker deal! It was the chance of fifty lifetimes.

This was it. The Big One.

Within minutes he had it all worked out.

Five million was the invoice price, but he'd buy well below that. He'd go to all the big companies and offer 25 percent of retail for any stock whatever, current or dead, delivered Portsmouth. He'd invoice it out to Ahmed at 50 percent of retail, across the board. Who, from Palestine to Peckham Rye, wouldn't be happy to pay half price?

Ahmed was taking £1,000,000 off the top. That left a gross £1,500,000. Alex, the shipping agent, would need his usual fee to arrange documentation, and there'd be bank interest on a bridging loan if cash had to be paid up front, but these expenses were a fleabite. Mo was on 33 percent of the net profit, but that still left going on for £1,000,000 for Ricky.

One million pounds!

ONE MILLION POUNDS!

That would take care of Beryl, Kev and Angelina for the rest of their natural. He'd see young Sime got his whack, too, to put him in the clear. The truth was, he felt really bad about the kid. Several times he'd picked up the phone, but he'd always hung up. He wasn't good at saying sorry; he really didn't know the words to use. Still, he'd make it up this way. He'd see the boy all right. And then, after everyone was looked after, there'd be a tasty bit left to buy himself and Sonia (or possibly not Sonia) a nice little pad overlooking the harbour in St Tropez.

'Anythin' you got, Chris. Anythin' at all! I'm payin' twenty-five percent.'

But it was Chris's last day in his present job. He wasn't going to commit his successor to any deals.

'Eli? I'm goin' to make your life! I got this big punter. Gadaffi's number two. Yeah, the boss of Libya. He's lookin' for gear, real big volume . . . You what? Fuck the firelighters! Ain't you listenin'?'

Eli wouldn't discuss new business before the old was cleared up.

'Ski suits, Phil? Sure, I'll take ski suits. We'll label 'em up as sleeping bags. Them nights in the desert get mighty nippy, mate. What d'you mean, you can't do twenty-five of retail? Give me a moody invoice showin' a higher retail price, you berk. You think they're goin' to ring up and check in the middle of the fuckin' desert?'

But Phil was a conscientious objector when it came to fiddles.

'Mel? How much do you want for your whole gaff? No, I am *not* pissed. And don't talk to me about them effin' jeans. What? You fall for a line like *that*? The geezer's probably a woofter anyway, and good riddance. Are you goin' to listen or are you not?'

No, Melvyn was not.

Ricky was growing alarmed. He stared at the phone. It was jinxed. Here was the deal of a lifetime, and he was still getting blanks. Of course, there was the gear he'd left with young Sime, but that wouldn't exactly knock a hole in a five-million-pound deal. If only he hadn't lost his hold over Alfie. Alfie would have been the answer.

His nerves were coming on and he took one of his pills, swallowing it in cold, scummy tea. Beryl was sitting in the next room, reading *True Romance* with the radio and the telly on both at once. Since he'd come back home, she'd treated him like a lodger. She would throw some food at him at six-thirty, but for the rest of the day he had to get his own. Couldn't she at least make him a cup of tea while he was grafting to get them all out of trouble?

He tore open one of the last remaining packets of Popsitops and waited until the pills took effect. Growing calmer, he picked up the phone again and looked at the next name on the list.

Chapati Joe.

Ricky got through and described the deal.

'You want Loo Blue?' said Joe.

'Loo Blue? How can they have toilets out there? They're starvin'! You should know that, bein' of the tribe.'

'I come from a high caste family in Bombay, sir, and my father . . .'

'OK, send it in. My people will take anything. How much?'

'One fifty.'

'Cobblers! I paid one twenty the other day. Or has there been a sudden run on the commodity?'

There was a brief pause at the other end.

'Did you say they will take *anything*?'

'Yeah. What else you got?'

'Oh, sir, I have a whole *warehouse* of wonderful items . . .'

'Is that Mr Simon Brotherton? Joe Patel here. And good afternoon to you too, sir. I have a big, big buyer. A close personal friend of Mr Gadaffi. Yes, sir, the Libyan leader, but do not mention that I told you. This man has need of *everything*. Excuse me? Perhaps they teach cricket in schools in Libya, I cannot say. I am telling you, though, he will buy everything you have. I will bring him to your warehouse tomorrow morning personally. For me, sir, it is pleasure enough to be of service. For my brothers, it is twenty percent.'

'You're askin' me twenty percent?' cried Ricky. 'You're jokin'!'

Chapati Joe pulled his white XJ6 into the side of the road.

'You wish me to turn back?'

'Come on then, you poxy wog, let's have a look at the gear.'

They headed south, following the signs for Croydon. Ricky fell silent. Joe had said there could be a couple of hundred grand's worth of gear in the warehouse. Bump up the invoice value to two-fifty and give them some moody retail prices, and he could have done ten percent of the load by the end of the morning.

They skirted Croydon and took the road for Gatwick. After a few miles Joe made a sharp right turn for the old airport.

'I know this place, as it happens,' mused Ricky.

Joe crossed a pitted old runway and swung left through some iron gates. Above, garlanded in coils of razor wire, was a name board.

Ricky now sat up.

'I've got gear in this gaff myself! There, in *that* one.'

He pointed to a small corrugated iron building. Joe, following a set of instructions, drove past it. Finally he drew up outside an old hangar. The massive sliding door was ajar. He led the way inside.

'This is the gentleman who owns the stock,' he announced.

A figure came forward out of the gloom. Ricky's eyes took a moment to adapt.

Christ Almighty, it was the wet-eared ponce himself!

'Sime!' he cried.

'Ricky!' cried Simon.

For a split second they stood frozen to the spot. Then

letting out a guffaw, Ricky stepped forwards and drew the boy into his arms.

When Chapati Joe found he was selling a company its own gear and, worse, it emerged that he was taking commission from both sides, he beat a tactical retreat.

Simon shut the warehouse up and drove Ricky home. It wasn't until they were approaching Norwood that he came out with it. It had been lying heavily on his heart.

'Listen,' he said, 'I'm sorry. I shouldn't have said those things.'

'That's OK,' responded Ricky. 'We all make mistakes.'

Simon bit his tongue. For a moment they were as far apart as ever.

Ricky broke the silence.

'Course, it takes two to have a ruck. Wrong ain't always on one side.' He struggled to say it. 'Sorry for what I did, like. Hope I didn't hurt you, Sime.'

'Hurt me? Never!'

'Liar! I could see your boat.'

'Well, maybe a bit,' Simon admitted, feeling his tooth. 'And you?'

Ricky chuckled.

'Thought I'd broke my knuckles.'

Back in Ricky's front room, Simon spread the stock list on the glass table between them.

'Fly spray in Arabic cans? The very thing!'

'We'll go double-bubble on that line,' said Ricky, rubbing his hands.

Simon looked for the next item.

'Golf practice kits?'

'Yeah, well . . .'

'Double-bubble there, too. Think of all the time they must have in those camps to improve their swing!'

'T'riffic, Sime. Next?'

'Naked Venus can openers.'

'We might have to leave them out, Sime. They don't go too strong on nudity out there.'

'No way! They're *educational*. We'll band them with those Discover Your Own Body children's pop-up books. The kids can have a Coke while they're discovering their bodies. A dual purpose line.'

'I like it, Sime.'

'Car deodorants?' Simon frowned. He reached into his suitcase and examined a sample. 'It doesn't actually *say* "car" on the label.' He amended the word on the stock-sheet. '*Tent* deodorants.'

'What's next?'

'Novelty farting cushions.'

'You got me beat there, son.'

'Just think of all that hummous they eat . . .'

Ricky stood back. A look close to wonder smoothed his craggy, lived-in face.

'What's happened to you, Sime? You used to give me a pain in the head with all them "ifs" and "buts". You said this gear was crappo.'

'It's crappo to *us*. But not if you're stuck in a crummy camp or wandering around the desert on a camel. Think what a fancy aluminium cake tray must mean to a no-mad! Or a set of plastic garden furniture!'

'Or a deleted record!'

'Or exercise weights!'

'Or a bucket-and-spade set!'

'Or ping-pong bats . . . !'

'Watches with no batteries!'

'Condoms!'

And the two men cracked up and laughed until the tears flowed.

193

15

The man who mass-murdered money was right off form.

Ricky had never had any problem spending dough before. Now, like the man with the million-pound note, he simply couldn't get rid of it. The days began to tick by. He flew around all his old contacts. He raced up to Manchester and buzzed from one wholesaler to another like a bee on heat. Even his Transcosmos Trading business card didn't help. He was still Ricky Stone who couldn't get tick.

Simon, in the meantime, was working his way through his business school address book. He packed his diary with appointments. Breakfast at the Ritz was the first meeting of the day, a nightcap at Tramp's the last. He covered the ground exhaustively – corporate treasurers, company secretaries, bankers, fund managers. Those that were neither cautious nor suspicious mostly mistook his meaning and thought he was after stocks of the kind traded on the Exchange. A lot of memos were written, calls made, introductions effected and internal studies set up, but no deals closed.

By the end of the first week, all they had in their shopping basket was thirty thousand metres of fire-scorched velveteen that Angelina had procured, a load of Muppet toys impounded following a copyright action and a container-load of cling peaches mistakenly canned in brine.

And all they'd spent was £150,000.

By careful fudging, Simon re-costed the stock in

Croydon at £250,000, to be invoiced out at £500,000. This textbook example of Added Value at least completed ten percent of the parcel.

The score at day seven stood at four hundred grand down and two point one million to go. And only eight days left.

It simply wasn't good enough.

Desperate measures were called for. Ricky phoned everyone he'd ever known or met.

Even Sonia.

Maybe she could lay her hands on a parcel of clothing through her suppliers and earn herself a bit of commission on the way. Anyway, it was a good excuse to call her. He had to get the softening up campaign into top gear right away. He could cop the dough and be a free man within the fortnight. Lovely month to be in the South of France, September.

'Pin Cushion, can I help you?' chimed a girl's voice he hadn't heard before.

'Is Sonia there, please?'

'You Mr Charles? She left a message if you rang. She says it's OK for tonight, the boys are away.'

Ricky's hand tightened around the receiver.

'This is Mr Ricky,' he said coldly. 'Mr Ricky Stone. As in stone dumb.'

Day nine, towards the middle of the morning, Martha called by Poonah Mansions.

She announced herself from a phone box around the corner, in case it was inconvenient. Simon replied he was alone.

The flat was piled with telexes and scrap-pads, days-old coffee mugs and ashtrays not emptied since Ricky was last there. He hurried round clearing away what he could and was in the middle of cleaning his teeth for her when the doorbell rang.

Her dark hair was fuller and somehow less severe, and her face was lightly made up. She wore a bedouin shawl over a long jacket and tight turquoise trousers that ended above the ankles. The effect was devastating.

'You look great, Martha,' he said.

'You look terrible,' she responded. 'Aren't you sleeping?'

'Working. It's shit or bust time.' He looked at her with admiration. 'Life in that squat can't be too bad. Or is it Roger?'

'Or is what Roger?'

He laughed to conceal the rising love panic.

'That bourgeois reactionary outfit, I mean. Clean hair, make-up . . .'

'Simon, that sounds like one of your devious compliments.'

'It sounds sexist, you mean.'

'Feminist doesn't mean not feminine.'

'That's news.'

She laid a hand on his arm and drew him down onto the sofa.

'You see why we can never be right together, Simon.'

'I *don't*! We're great together! Or, we *were*, until you upped and went.' He looked down at the floor and shook his head. 'I've tried to understand. I've wrestled this way and that. I was just getting back on the rails and now you come by and I start wobbling all over the place again.'

'I'll go if you like.'

'No! Stay. I'm sorry.'

'I was worried. I may not be living with you but I do care about you. I had a feeling something was wrong.'

'Well, things haven't been terrific.'

'Tell me.'

He told her about the bust-up with Ricky and the struggle to get clear of the millstone of debts, and now the sudden change of fortune, the chance of a reprieve and the promise of the dream coming true.

As he described the project, he grew less melancholy, almost enthusiastic. He might, he just might, become a very rich man.

'And it's all ideologically sound,' he added with a half smile.

She matched his ironic tone.

'Absolutely,' she agreed. 'It's aid.'

'No-one's getting ripped off.'

'You're not exploiting the proletariat, Simon.'

'It's for a good cause.'

'Those poor deprived Palestinians.'

'And if I happen to make a profit . . .'

'Profit? What's that?'

'Correction: wages. If I end up with a fat wage packet, no-one can knock that. A labourer is worthy of his hire.' He was laughing now. He squeezed her hand. 'Christ, Martha, it's good to see you.'

'You too, Simon.' She stood up. 'Hey, how about some coffee? Did you fix the expresso machine yet?'

He followed her to the kitchen.

'No point. We'll be having the real thing in a week or two. Well, *I* will. And if you won't share it with me, more fool you.'

She took him by both hands and looked him seriously in the eyes.

'Simon, can I say something? I know this deal is really important to you. I was thinking about what happened at the casino. This time, don't take a chance. Don't back red *or* black. Somehow find a way of backing both.'

He nodded.

'I know. This is my only shot. It's got to be fail-safe.'

She kissed him on the cheek.

'Come on, you make the coffee while I wash up, huh?'

Alfie hurried down the deep-carpeted stairs, past the travel agents and the employment bureau, along the narrow corridor that led to the back of the Italian restaurant and out through the side door into the street. He glanced up and down to make sure he wasn't spotted and slipped around the corner to where the driver was waiting with the Rolls.

197

He could only walk in very short steps. Sadie was no bloody good. Either she tickled or she hurt. Still, at least she didn't have any mirrors in her chamber. Nothing had been the same since Lucinda. Lucinda had had a knack. A lot of verbal in with the violence. Would she visit him on a call-out?

He eased himself gently into the Rolls, grateful for the soft leather upholstery, and took a bible-thick catalogue out of his briefcase. He wasn't looking forward to the meeting he was about to chair with the creditors of Bigwood's, the mail order giant that had recently gone bust. His firm were going to have to earn their fees on this one. Most of the stock was lightweight summer clothing, dead as doornails in September. Worse, it was going to be hell sitting down all afternoon.

Day ten, Ricky made a minor breakthrough. A pal of his had done a barter deal with Hungary and taken a parcel of luncheon meat in exchange for tractor parts. Ricky bought the parcel for £300,000. The retail price was anybody's guess.

He'd agreed with Mo that he'd check each item with him before having it sent into Portsmouth. So far everything, from Loo Blue to kids' cricket bats, had gone through smoothly.

Ricky sat in his front room and called up the Iranian carpet dealer. Opposite sat Simon, chewing his fingernails. On the glass-top table stood several cans of the product.

'Right, Mo,' began Ricky. 'Got your next line. Luncheon meat from Hungaria. Top quality, my boy.'

'What has it got in it?' asked Mo at once.

Ricky put on his glasses and held the can at a distance to read the label.

'Dunno. It's in Hungarian.'

'We must know.'

'Hang on, I'll open one.'

He picked up a can and unwound the top with a key.

Half way round, the key snapped. He prodded a biro into the slit and dug out a sliver. He tasted it.

'Kind of like Spam. You know, pork pie fillin'.'

'*Pork?*'

Out of the corner of his eye he saw Simon gesticulating frantically.

'Hang on, Mo, while I consult my Hungarian expert.' He put his hand over the mouthpiece.

'Say it's *beef*!' hissed Simon. 'Halal killed.'

Ricky uncovered the phone.

'My pal here is readin' the label. It's beef. Allah killed.'

That was fine.

It was fine as far as it went. It knocked off another three hundred clams, but still left one-point-eight million. And now only five days to go.

Ricky chain-smoked and swallowed mouthfuls of pills. Simon declared a state of emergency. It was beginning to look hopeless.

Day eleven, and gloom descended over the front room office. The morning went by without the phone ringing once. They'd come to the end of their contacts. Ricky paced up and down, irritably swiping things with a kid's cricket bat. Simon sat going through the figures once again as if by some alchemy of statistics he could turn a flea-bite into a fortune.

Finally he gave up and went into the kitchen for a coffee.

Beryl stood behind the bar, making sandwiches. He almost didn't recognise her. Her coppery hair was permed and the roots re-tinted, and in place of her usual purple housecoat and slippers she wore a figure-hugging red woollen dress with a black patent-leather belt and high-heeled shoes.

'You look terrific,' he said.

She screwed up her eyes to avoid the smoke from the cigarette burning low in her lips.

'Nah, but I can't bear to see him down, Sime. I'm too

soft-hearted. He's a right monster, but you can't go round like a zombie, all down in the mouth, when your man's graftin'.'

Simon spooned coffee into a mug.

'Yes, it's not going too well, I'm afraid.'

'He ain't eatin' properly. I've had to hide them Popsi-tops. Junk food, yuk! These sandwiches have got lovely jelly from the chicken. You've got to keep your strength up in this life, Sime, don't I know it!'

'We need just one lucky break.'

'He should have hung on to that Alfie. It's his own fault I chucked them photos out. He knows it, and don't let him tell you otherwise.'

'Oh? What photos?'

She turned in surprise. An inch of ash fell onto the sandwiches.

'Them indecent ones he was milkin' Alfie with.'

Simon listened with his mouth agape to the story that followed: Lucinda, Morris, Alfie's little kink, blackmail, how Lucinda's salon had been done over, how the shoe deal had come about and how the photos were thrown out with Ricky's belongings and had ended up in smoke.

He shook his head.

'That's really too bad.'

Beryl sighed.

'It's in the stars, Sime. God was lettin' Alfie off. Or puttin' Ricky on the rack.' She handed him the plate of sandwiches. 'Take these in with you. There's enough for both. 'Ere, say you made 'em yourself. He thinks I've got the hump, and I have! He can't expect no favours. But I've got to see he's fed, haven't I, Sime?'

'T'riffic grub,' said Ricky with his mouth full. 'We may soon be openin' a sandwich bar. What a game that is! All lovely cash. You put the coppers through the till and the pound notes in your pocket and nobody can touch you.'

Simon stood staring out of the window, deep in thought.

'Ain't you hungry, Sime?' asked Ricky.

Simon turned round slowly.

'Beryl just told me about Alfie and those photographs,' he began.

'What poxy luck *that* was!'

'Wait. Alfie doesn't *know* you don't still have them, right? As far as he's concerned, you do. We know he takes it seriously – witness the shoes. I think there may be a chance to bluff him.'

'He ain't so dumb. He'll want to see them.'

'But say you've lodged them at your bank in a sealed envelope. Better still, actually lodge something and get a receipt. Wave that in front of his nose. I know Alfie, he'll go for that. Then offer him a once-for-all deal: a really big parcel in return for the whole lot. He's bound to come up with something. Of course, you'll hand over the snaps only when the goods are in Portsmouth. By then it'll be too late for him to renege.' He paused. 'It'll only work once. But then, it only *needs* to work once.'

Ricky slowly put down the sandwich he was eating. His eyes widened and a grin spread over his craggy face.

'Sime, boy, I think you've aced it!'

Like any gambler, Ricky was attuned to the ebb and flow of his luck and he quickly sensed the tide was now turning in his favour. A host of small things confirmed it. Beryl discovered an old ticket from the cleaners, as a result of which he had a suit to wear to meet Alfie that evening. He'd put twenty quid to win on a horse in the 4.15 at Sandown Park and it had come in at eight to one. The Merc, which had been playing up, started on the button, and every single traffic light from Norwood to Mayfair was green.

There was only one Thirty-Three Club, and this time there was no mistake. Alfie was already at the bar when Ricky arrived.

Alfie extended his hand with something close to warmth. The scent on Ricky's after he withdrew it was not entirely unpleasant.

Alfie insisted the drinks were on him.

Alfie was the one who cut the social preamble and brought the conversation around to business.

He seemed not to need the encouragement when Ricky showed the bank receipt Simon had procured earlier that afternoon, and when Ricky suggested a sudden-death deal, he simply asked what kind of gear he was looking for.

He sat stroking his ivory jowls and nodding as Ricky described the Libyan aid deal.

'Any gear for a hot country,' concluded Ricky. 'All clean, no seconds or dammex. I'll pay twenty-five percent of retail across the board. That's fixed and no argy-bargy. You'll have your dough – and the other – when it's checked into the shipper's gaff in Portsmouth.'

'Go on.'

'I want exactly a million eight hundred grand's worth of gear and it's got to be in by Friday.'

'Not tomorrow?' asked Alfie with mild sarcasm.

'Tomorrow would do nicely. OK, Alf, what have you got?'

Alfie sized Ricky up and down, then caught the waiter's eye and ordered more drinks. He looked around the plush velvet room.

'Trouble with this place,' he said idly, 'is there's no girls.'

'Alfie, I'm here to talk business.'

'Relax. I've got it all sorted out for you.' He sipped his drink appreciatively. 'How's Bertha?'

'Beryl's fine. Look . . .'

'Still in with young Brotherton, are you? Bright lad. Not quite greedy enough, I used to think. Maybe the cold outside world has changed that. Has it?'

'Yes, Sime's in the deal. No, he don't know nothin' about our little transaction. Yes, he's a bright lad and a sight tougher than you reckon. OK? Right, you were sayin' . . .'

Alfie made a gesture of surrender, then suddenly his

manner grew serious. He leaned forwards and spoke in a low, confidential tone.

'You know the mail-order firm, Bigwood's . . . ?'

'Sime?' shouted Ricky into the call box phone. 'We're on!'

Simon let out a whoop at the other end.

'You've *done* it?'

'Course I have! What do you think I am?'

'A bloody genius. What's the firm?'

'Bigwood's!'

'What, the huge mail-order group?'

'He's liquidatin' the whole outfit! I got him to call the geezer in charge up there. We'll shoot up tomorrow mornin', you and me. There's bombs of gear! Clothin', footwear, beddin', the lot! We can have anythin' we want, at a quarter of retail.'

'But it's mail-order, not retail.'

'I know that, Sime, you berk. That's the whole point! There *ain't* no retail prices. We can pay what we want. How would quarter of catalogue sound?'

'Music to my ears, Ricky.'

The warehouse resembled an abandoned space city. The firm had died of hyper-technology. Robotic fork-lifts that once would have raced noiselessly down the avenues between the stacks, shooting up twenty feet to pincer out a single ladies' slip and darting back to earth for a gabardine coat, now stood idle and absurd. The computerised control room, installed at a cost of four million pounds, was dark, and the electronic packing line was shrouded in dust sheets.

Tony, the distribution director, showed them round. Back in his office, he gave them catalogues and a stack of printout. Simon took out his calculator, Ricky a couple of packs of cigarettes. They were going to be there a good while.

There were shirts, pinafores, sweaters, blouses, trousers, cardigans, shawls, tights, evening dresses, V-necked jumpers, disappearing pleat skirts, blouson dresses, herringbone coats, mink-look jackets, three-quarter coats, leather flattie shoes, ankle boots, fleecy housecoats, cotton briefs, lace-trimmed brief and sus-pender belt sets, pantie corselettes, seamfree crossover bras . . .

And that was only for the ladies of the camps.

'Why is Alfie being so co-operative?' asked Simon as they drove back from Manchester late that night. 'It's as if *we*'re doing *him* a favour.'

'If you'd seen them pictures, boy, you'd know why,' replied Ricky. 'Enough to put a man away for life.'

'Even so.'

'What matter? We got the gear, Mo is over the moon, Tone up there is gettin' it all packed and ready. We should worry!'

'Still . . .'

'Tony? Alfred Steinman here. Hope I didn't wake you. Just a thought. Remember our little chat the other day? Well, I've been thinking. This rush job for the Pales-tinians. The stock is going straight to the docks and onto the ship, right? Not much time for an accurate count. That occurred to you, too? Precisely. What if the parcel's *short*? Who's going to come back at the other end? If anyone did, well, the computer's been on the blink a lot recently, hasn't it? Exactly. It's a matter of packing. You know, just the top half of every carton. The rest can be old catalogues, anything. Sorry? Of course you'll have to match the weight and volume. I wasn't thinking you'd pack breeze blocks . . . though, on the other hand, building materials out there . . .'

Day thirteen. Simon spent the morning with Alex in his office in Holborn.

The bung had already been agreed over a beer at the pub in Elephant and Castle. Twenty grand, flat. For that, Alex would see that the warehouse boys at Portsmouth worked night and day to check the stock in and the manager signed the sheets without too close a scrutiny. If they had to count every pair of jeans and every Miss Muppet make-up set, they'd be at it for a month.

Once the stock sheets were signed and sealed, Simon would take them to Ahmed's bank in Cheapside. This would trigger payment of the letter of credit and the various parties would get paid.

Simon made a list of who was due for what:

	£'000	£'000
Total L/C value:		5,000
Ahmed's commission:	1,000	
Bigwood's:	1,800	
Peaches, Muppets, luncheon meat, material, etc:	450	
Transcosmos Trading:	500	
		3,750
Gross Profit:		1,250
Less: 33% for Mo:		416
Net Profit:		834

In addition, there was the hidden profit in their own stock from Croydon, costing something over £100,000 and invoiced at £500,000, making a nice little turn of about £400,000. Subtracting Alex's fees and incidentals, this gave an overall profit of very nearly £1.2 million.

£600,000 for Ricky.

£600,000 for Simon.

Twenty-five grand outstanding on the farmhouse in Tuscany suddenly looked insignificant. Rebuilding from scratch, adding a solarium patio and a heated swimming pool, re-stocking the terraces and laying down hogsheads of wine and olive oil couldn't take it much over a hundred grand.

He was looking at his dream come true, plus half a million in the pocket.

'There'll be tax to pay, of course,' said Simon over crispy pork at the Peking Duck that night. 'Sixty percent, top rate.'

'I'll be a tax exile,' said Ricky. 'In a tax heaven.'

'Then count St Tropez out.'

'Bollocks to that! Let 'em come and get me. They couldn't get Ronnie Biggs.'

'He was in Brazil. Extradition laws and all that.'

Ricky wiped his mouth with the back of his hand. Grains of rice lodged among the hairs. He gave Simon a despairing look.

'Know somethin', Sime? You ain't changed.'

'Tell me,' Simon persisted, 'how much would you pay to be sure they'd never come looking for you? Ten percent? Twenty?'

'Guaranteed no aggro? I might give ten.'

'I have a pal who's a trustee for a Dutch Antilles company. He'll invoice our own company for the amount of the profit as a management charge. Three percent to him, three percent tax there, total six. Guaranteed you can play golf in the South of France till the cows come home and no-one can touch you.'

Ricky broke into a grin.

'And don't you change either, Sime.'

Day fourteen was spent in Ricky's front room, manning the phones. All the stock from Bigwood's had now arrived at the dockside warehouse and was being checked in. Every half hour they called for a progress report. Everything was running smoothly.

That night Simon took the Merc and drove down to Portsmouth. He'd stay overnight, collect the signed stock sheets in the morning, drive back to London and present them personally to the Jamahiriya Bank in Cheapside.

Day fifteen. The big day.

Simon leaves the hotel at seven. At seven-thirty he is at the gates of the shipper's warehouse.

Bernie, the warehouse manager, has been working overnight with his boys. They're tired, and a fork-lift accidentally knocks over a stack of cartons. Watches spill everywhere. They appear to be broken: the lads can't get them to work. Simon persuades Bernie there's no reference on the invoice to the goods being in working order. Problem resolved. Counting and stacking recommences.

Eight o'clock, Simon calls Ricky. Ricky has been up half the night with Mo. Mo is ecstatic. So is Ahmed, who is now back in Libya. All is in order.

Nine-thirty, the warehouse dockets are being typed out. More coffee arrives. Simon tells Bernie about the farmhouse in Tuscany. Bernie tells Simon about his caravan in Wales.

Nine-fifty, Simon scribbles a postcard to Martha. They only had ones of Portsmouth Promenade in the hotel. Doesn't have quite the same signification as a Dada loo seat but the message is a paeon of triumph. He has *done it*!

At ten, however, Simon is growing anxious. London is three hours' drive away, and the documents must be presented at the bank by two-thirty.

But there's no hitch. The papers are ready on time. Bernie signs the sheets, in triplicate. Affixes the company seal. Puts them in an envelope. Hands it to Simon, keeping a hold of his end. 'Where's *my* envelope?' he asks. There's a slight altercation. Simon refers him to Alex in London. Alex is not at his desk. Simon leaves his watch as some kind of pledge.

It is ten-thirty-five. Simon is in good time for his two-thirty deadline. He calls Ricky again. He has the documents and he is on his way.

The countryside rolls away into the distance on either side of the motorway. Clouds roam across the blue sky, raking shadows along the fields of ripe corn. In Italy there'll be villages on the hill-tops and spiky cypresses along the roads and already the fields will be burned in black stripes. He'll have a Merc in Italy, too.

At eleven-forty by the dashboard clock, he pulls in to a service station to refuel. He keeps the buff envelope in his hands even while filling the car and paying for the petrol. He returns to the car, gets back in and puts on his seat belt.

It won't start.

The starting motor turns but the engine won't fire. Maybe it's flooded. He waits a minute. He tries again. Not a spark.

He breaks into a sweat. He turns the key in short bursts, long bursts, his foot on the accelerator and off it. Before long, the battery begins to flag.

He puts up the bonnet. A truck driver in overalls stops. He fiddles and pokes around.

'It's yer coil, mate,' he says.

Crisps, cassettes, chewing-gum, yes, and even car deodorant, but can you ever buy a coil for a Mercedes stretch-saloon with velour interior, air-conditioning, headlamp washers and driver's seat warmer in the kiosk of a service station on a motorway a million miles from anywhere?

Eleven fifty-nine, Simon is standing on the slip road with his thumb out. His toes hurt where he kicked the car and his shirt is drenched with sweat, but he has the envelope in his hand and he's damn well going to make it.

Twelve-ten, a white-haired parson stops in a F-registration Morris Minor. Simon has to think fast.

He opts for the known devil.

The parson chats pleasantly. He looks across at Simon rather than at the road. Cars swerve around him. They stop hooting when they see his dog collar. He says he's going flat out but the Morris seems to have a governor on the engine. It won't do more than fifty-five. Simon keeps reading the parson's watch. Twelve-thirty and it's still over twenty miles to the outskirts of London. Couldn't this man of God try a miracle?

Twelve-fifty-eight, the parson drops him at a bus-stop in Richmond. It's too far out to find a black cab passing. A bus arrives. He gets on. The conductor asks his destination. Anywhere central, he replies.

He spots a minicab on a rank and jumps out. As he reaches the car, it pulls away.

Half a mile away, he is told, there's an Underground station. He tucks the envelope under his arm and sets off at a run.

The station is at the end of a line and the train sits just whirring its generator. It's sixteen minutes before the doors close. He asks the woman next to him for the time. One thirty-one.

He counts nineteen stops to the City. On the basis of the first few, he calculates an average of three minutes between stops. That would get him to Mansion House at two twenty-eight. Could he run to Cheapside in two minutes?

As the train nears the centre of town, the stops get closer together and the average time-lapse shortens to two minutes forty seconds. At Westminster, he begins to think he might just make it. But outside Embankment, the train stops in a tunnel. He eyes the emergency cord. Minutes tick by. For the tenth time he asks the woman next to him the time. She glares at him and changes carriages at the next stop.

Temple at two nineteen.

Blackfriars at two twenty-two.

And finally Mansion House at two twenty-five.

Simon knows the City. He is up the escalator and across Queen Victoria Street in under two minutes. Bucklersbury into Poultry, Poultry into Cheapside. And a two hundred yard sprint down Cheapside to the Jamahiriya Bank.

He slumps over the Securities desk as the first clocks strike the half hour.

He's made it!

The clerk frowned.

After re-examining the documents once again, he took them away to the assistant manager. Through the glass wall partitioning of the office, Simon could see, though not hear, a dispute taking place. There was a lot of Arabic gesticulating and shaking of heads. The assistant manager kept comparing the papers with another set on his desk. At one point the clerk pointed to Simon and Simon unslouched and gave a smile. Finally, the assistant manager put the papers all together and left his office. He crossed the banking hall to a mahogany door marked 'Manager'. The clerk followed him inside.

Five minutes later, the assistant manager came out and went over to Simon.

'You have not supplied us with details of the lifting,' he said.

'You mean, the shipping? It's all there. The vessel is leaving for Tripoli by way of Genoa . . .'

'No, sir, the lifting of the oil.'

Simon afforded himself an indulgent smile. They'd got their paperwork mixed up. The Libyans buying oil? That would be the day!

'We're supplying clothing,' he explained patiently. 'Shoes, hardware, that kind of thing. For the Palestinian aid programme.'

'I am referring to your form of payment, sir.'

An icy hand was creeping up the base of Simon's spine.

'Payment has been agreed. Five million pounds sterling.'

'Five million pounds sterling in value, yes,' agreed the man. 'But paid in our fine Libyan crude oil.'

16

'Five million nicker of cookin' oil?' raged Ricky. 'What am I goin' to do with that? Serve all the fish and chip shops in the whole world? Offer Alfie Crisp'n'Dry in lieu? What do you mean, it's *crude*? I'm goin' to get crude with that Mo! Wait till I get my Germans on him. I'll make fuckin' kebabs of him.'

Simon knew it was unwise to interrupt Ricky in full spate. It was bad enough having been the carrier of the bad news. A paperwork foul-up was always implicitly his fault. Ricky hadn't said that yet, but there was an ominous 'I' and 'me' in his talk.

Through the door, Simon could see Beryl standing in the hallway, as white as a ghost, fingering her necklace like a rosary. She melted away when he caught her eye.

The house was like Hitler's bunker in the last hours. Ricky stormed around, blaming everyone for the catastrophe.

But maybe it was not so catastrophic. Their payment was a contract to lift five million pounds' worth of oil from Tripoli offshore terminal. The contract price was $29 a barrel, and with the pound at $1.75, that gave a total volume of around 300,000 barrels – a workable amount to offer on the Rotterdam spot market. Someone would buy it off them, even if it meant dropping a few cents.

In fact, it might be no catastrophe at all. But, Ricky couldn't see it yet.

Nor could Alfie.

When a memo arrived on his desk with the news that the payment to Bigwood's had not gone through, he cancelled all calls and paced up and down his office. His swelter increased as he saw the maze had no exit.

The goods belonged to Bigwood's until they'd been paid for. His duty now was to slap on an injunction to prevent them being loaded.

But then what?

He examined the terms of the letter of credit that had come with the memo. The oil contract was not transferable. Ricky and Simon couldn't sell the contract on until they'd actually lifted the oil. And they couldn't do that until the goods were on board ship at Portsmouth – and that meant paid for.

It was a very vicious circle.

The longer all that gear hung around, the more likely someone would dig a hand deeper into a carton and find something he shouldn't. And if the deal collapsed, Ricky would still be skint and lean on him harder than ever.

No, the goods *had* to be paid for. Through a bridging loan, by selling the oil forward . . . anything. But pretty damn quick.

Simon also quickly made the same unpleasant discovery that he did not have title to the oil until the stock at Portsmouth had been paid for. And he couldn't pay for that until he'd sold the oil. It was Catch 22.

It meant finding £1.8 million to finance one against the other.

He went back to his address book and did the rounds of the bankers.

Not one of them would touch a back-to-back deal.

'Bankers?' he stormed. 'Wankers!'

He reported back to Ricky. The unthinkable was staring them in the face. All that lovely dough and not a penny within reach.

'There's only one man for it,' said Ricky finally. 'And he'll want his whack.'

Simon guessed at his meaning.

'Billy?'

Ricky called round at Simon's late that night. He'd been to see Billy. Billy's latest trawler had just come in. He was flush.

'Nine hundred grand, that's all he can do straight away,' said Ricky. 'Alfie will have to swallow. We'll have it ready the day after tomorrow. Bring a couple of big suitcases.'

Alfie did swallow.

Tony had drawn up two sets of invoices. Nine hundred grand would just about cover the goods that had actually been despatched from Bigwood's. In a crisis, he'd switch invoices and pass the actuals through the books. But if all went as it should, there was another nine hundred grand's worth lying in the warehouse, and only Alfie and Tony knew about it.

Simon took charge of the arrangements for lifting the oil.

Alex took him to meet a Greek ship-owner called Costas Stefanidis, a pirate with protruding eyes, a bulging belly and a mask-like face that flashed from comic to tragic every few seconds.

'Tanker beessness very bad,' he sibilated, his face going tragic. 'Too many sheepss.'

He had a small tanker, the *Aphrodite*, rusting at anchor off Sicily. She could be made ready and reach Tripoli within six days. That was ideal.

There was some haggling over prices but eventually Alex approved the charges and they shook hands on the deal. As soon as the master of the *Aphrodite* cabled to confirm lifting had taken place, Simon would have title to the cargo. He could sell it there and then.

As he was seeing them out, Costas drew Simon aside.

'Take my advice,' he said. 'Don't sell at once. Sheep it to South Africa. You arrive, you unload, you get cash. They pay extra four or five dollarss. And no questionss.'

'Thanks,' replied Simon, 'but I'd rather not take the risk.'

Costas gave a knowing smile.

'Think about it. You know where to find me.'

It was a fatal mistake to tell Ricky.

'Four or five dollars a barrel?' he cried. 'What's that come to in English, Sime?'

'About seven hundred grand in total. But don't forget the extra shipping and insurance costs . . .'

'Listen, we've got to give a third whack away to Billy, right? This way, we'll keep our six hundred grand and he won't cost us nothin'.'

'But he'll want his money back right away.'

'Cobblers! How long to South Africa? A couple of weeks? Billy can hang on. Let him earn his dough! Just don't mention nothin' when we see him, OK?'

They met Billy at a run-down car repair garage under the railway arches in Lambeth. He led them across an oil-steeped mud floor, past wrecks with engines suspended on chains, through an office with grimy pin-up calendars and out to a small shed at the back.

Winston undid the padlock and switched on a light. He drew back a tarpaulin. Under it stood five or six heavy-duty crates, each the size of a tea-chest. In the light of a naked bulb Simon read the markings: *Ford Auto Parts*, *Handle With Care*, *This Side Up*.

At a sign from Billy, Winston dragged one out. On top lay a layer of cogs and ball-races in thick brown oil-paper. He tossed them aside.

Simon gasped involuntarily.

Underneath lay a jumble of banknotes, all crumpled and packed tight like waste paper.

How much was there in each crate? Three hundred grand? Four? They didn't look as if they'd even been counted.

'Hope you brought your sandwiches,' said Billy without expression.

Now this was a job Simon insisted on doing himself.

A new secretary, leggier than any before, showed him into the Partners' Room at Steinman, Fothergill, Trelawney and Co. While he waited for Alfie, he tried to puzzle out why the place *felt* different. The same sepia photographs, scrolls and charters still hung on the walls and the same mahogany table with its hallowed auctioneer's gavel still stood in the centre. Yet it all seemed smaller, meaner. The air of tradition and integrity went no deeper than the walnut veneer of the panelling. No, he realised, the place hadn't changed. He had.

Alfie came in and shook his hand warmly.

'Like old times, eh?' he beamed.

'Not quite like the last time we were in this room.'

'Ah, yes.' Alfie swallowed. 'Well, on to business. You've got a cheque for me, I believe.'

Simon hauled two vast suitcases onto the mahogany table, snapped open the locks and threw back the lids.

'It's all there. Nine hundred thousand pounds. And you've got a receipt for me, I believe?'

Alfie listened for footsteps. No-one was around. The suitcases lay open on the table. He moved carefully forward, almost on tiptoes, as if approaching a young and as yet unbroken girl.

He stroked his fingertips over the notes on top. He riffled his thumb along the edges of a bundle of tenners. He plucked the rubber band holding a sheaf of twenties. Gradually he worked his fingers in among the tight-packed bundles and felt the warm flesh of money. A kind of pain swelled in his abdomen.

The other nine hundred grand would feel like this. Only better, for after giving Tony a few quid, it would all be his.

By six o'clock that evening, the container ship *Galaxy* was fully loaded, and shortly after midnight, under a full moon and on a high tide, she let out three blasts of her horn, weighed anchor and slowly steamed out of Portsmouth harbour.

Her destination was Tripoli in the Socialist People's Libyan Arab Jamahiriya. She would stop once *en route*, at Genoa, Italy, where she'd pick up some other cargo.

At five the following morning, local time, as the sun rose over a mirror-flat sea and before the first *muezzin* in the towns and villages had begun calling the faithful to prayer, the tanker *Aphrodite*, one of the fleet of Stefanidis' ships, drew alongside a large buoy moored half a mile off the Libyan coast, some distance to the west of Tripoli.

The *Aphrodite* was old and her steering poor, and it took longer than usual to get her into position before the heavy-gauge hoses could be connected up. But by the time the sun was at its highest, the master had signed for receipt of three hundred thousand barrels of Libyan crude of the correct API and sulphur content, had drawn up all his anchors and given the engine room the order, Slow Ahead.

Mid-afternoon, Costas Stefanidis called Simon. The cargo, he confirmed, had been lifted. The *Aphrodite* was on her way to Durban, South Africa, a journey of eighteen days.

Costas did not ring off at once. A hesitant edge entered his voice.

'Simon,' he began. 'My sheep, she is old. If she were a horsse, I put her to grass. But then she is worth nothing. Simon . . . I have been thinking.'

'I've been thinking, too, Costa.'

'So, perhapss we can meet?'

'I think we should. As soon as possible.'

'I know a quiet little place . . .'

'Sonia? 'Ullo, darlin'. How you been?'

'Hang on. I'll take it upstairs.'

Ricky lit another cigarette off the butt he was smoking.

He knew what the hang-on-I'll-take-it-upstairs routine meant.

'Sonia, I gotta see you.'

'It's not easy right now.'

Ricky put on a posh voice.

'Mister Charles is it, tonight?'

'How did you . . . ? Well, yes. He's a good friend. I mean, he was. Of Horace's, my late husband.'

'Don't give me all that fanny! Anyway, it don't matter. I've only to come round and knock his block off, haven't I? OK, OK, take it easy! I was only jokin'. It don't matter, doll, because I've *bleedin' well done it*! Hit the jackpot! Say goodbye to your troubles, darlin'. We're in the bees!'

'Sorry?'

'The bees and honey. The money. The dough, the lolly, the jam.'

'I'm very happy for you, Ricky.'

'So am I. Right, when are we meetin' up? We've got to celebrate.'

'I'm not sure that's a good idea.'

'San Tropay not a good idea? All that lovely sun and siestas?'

'I've got to go now, Ricky.'

'Hang on! What about our deal . . . ?'

'I'll call you.'

'Sonia? 'Ullo? You still there?'

But all he heard was the dialling tone.

'Beryl?'

'Don't shout at me. I ain't your skivvy.'

'Beryl. I was about to say somethin' nice as it happens.'

'You want a loan. The answer's No.'

'I don't need no loans no more. Not from you, not from Billy, not from no-one.'

'Then I'll have that forty quid back you nicked out of the teapot.'

'You want forty? What would you say if I did you forty grand? Or *four hundred* grand?'

'I'd say, let me see it with my own minces first.'

'Beryl, you give me prick-ache. I just pulled off the biggest deal you'll ever see in your lifetime and all you can do is slag me off! I'm askin' you nicely to do yourself up and come out. We're goin' on the town.'

'When, I'd like to know.'

'When? Soon as you've tarted up, doll. We'll slip up to the Meribel . . .'

'When's the money comin' in?'

'Beryl, we don't need four hundred grand to have a meal out!'

'I ain't celebratin' till the money's in the hod. It's bad luck.'

'We'll have it in a fortnight . . .'

'Book a table for then. You hungry? I've got some nice chicken and barley soup . . .'

Somewhere towards nightfall on the tenth day, the *Galaxy* berthed at Genoa. The crew were given shore leave and told to return to the ship by seven the following morning, when there was cargo to be loaded.

What the crew were not told then, not that it would have concerned any of them but the master and the number two in Colonel Gadaffi's Central Buying Office, was that there was cargo to be *un*loaded, too.

A container or two wasn't going to be missed. The Palestinians should be grateful to get anything at all. Besides, a certain shrinkage was all part of the international aid game.

What was not part of the game, however, as the number two saw it, was to be clipped himself.

As the *Galaxy* was leaving port and cutting an azure furrow away into the Ligurian Sea, the shipping agent at Genoa docks made a routine check of the cargo he was holding. A clerk brought certain discrepancies to his attention. On the manifest there was no mention of lightweight building blocks and mail-order catalogues, and the clothing and footwear appeared to show considerable shortages . . .

A call was put through to Monaco, to a company owned by a man not entirely without a blood connection to the number two in the Libyan Central Buying Office, and some minutes later the phone was ringing on that very man's desk, beneath the smiling photograph of Colonel Muammar al-Gadaffi.

Ahmed did not echo his leader and guide's smile. He put the phone down with a scowl and fingered the ceremonial dagger he kept in his belt. After a moment, he picked the phone up again and dialled London.

Surely Martha would have received his postcard by now. Why hadn't she written back, or called?

Simon took the Underground to the nearest station to Hunter Street. It was going to be bus and tube until he heard from the Union Bank of Switzerland in Geneva that the funds were safely in his account. There were another eight days to go. The suspense was crucifying. He stayed in most of the time, with only the cats for company, living in constant terror of the phone. Every time it rang, he imagined some disaster he hadn't foreseen. Even if you really did play both red and black, that was only a ninety-seven percent certainty – there was always the three percent that went to the house.

As he approached the squat, he noticed rows of police buses parked in the nearby streets. Outside broadcast vans surrounded the pub on the corner. A crowd had gathered. A voice barked over a loudhailer and was answered by distant shouts.

He hurried closer. The street was littered with broken glass and smashed cars. Police, lined two deep, cordoned it off at either end.

Simon asked one if he could go inside to visit a friend.

'No-one's going in,' replied the policeman curtly. 'Them that's in are coming *out*.'

Simon waited an hour, two hours. Nothing seemed

to be happening. Bailiffs in bowler hats hung about in a corner. Police dogs yelped on their leashes. On the rooftops opposite, two men in army uniform with radios and binoculars took out their sandwiches. The police turned their backs on the street and chatted to the crowd.

Simon grew worried for Martha. He tried to persuade a television reporter to lend him his union card, but not even journalists were being allowed in. All the entrances would be either barricaded from the inside or guarded from the outside. He could do nothing.

'Watch it on the box tonight,' suggested the reporter.

And so began the Seige of Hunter Street.

'Yes?'

Beryl kept the door on the chain and drew her house-coat tight. She'd never seen this man before. Nor would want to again, either. He had the oily pocked skin of an Arab and the dark glasses and bulging shoulders of a villain.

'Mister Stone is in?'

'Who are you?'

'I ask, Mister Stone is in?'

Ricky was out in the back garden, swiping off daisy heads with a new golf club. The Merc stood very obviously in the car-port.

'No, he ain't.'

A boot stopped her shutting the door. With a sudden, swift movement the man produced a pair of wire cutters and neatly snipped the chain. He pushed the door open.

Beryl saw red.

She took the cigarette out of her mouth and rammed it in his face. Then, with a piercing screech, she flew at him. She clawed and bit, she spat and punched. She kneed him in the groin and as he bent over she gave him a shove that sent him tumbling back through the doorway. He tripped and began edging away. She followed after him like a tornado. Flailing her fists and screaming abuse, she chased him down the path, through the gate and along the street until he turned his back and fled in a lumbering run.

She brushed her hands and stomped back home. No-one was going to come barging in her home like that.

Deep in the darkest hour of the night, far out at sea in the uncharted region where the Gulf of Aden merges into the Indian Ocean, with no land in sight and no other vessels in the vicinity, the master of the *Aphrodite* gave the order, Slow Astern, to bring his ship to a standstill.

He pored over the radar screen. The blip was approaching on the port side. Turning to the prearranged frequency, he called for identification.

'*Poseidon*, calling *Poseidon*. This is *Aphrodite*. Do you read me?'

The confirmation came crackling over the radio. The *Poseidon* was closing on the rendezvous. She had been making good progress, for her tanks were empty and she rode high in the water.

'*Endaxi*,' responded the master, satisfied.

Inside the hour, the other tanker would be lying alongside her. The *Aphrodite* would pass a line across and winch over eight wide-bore hoses. And, with her pumps at full power, she'd have transferred ninety percent of her three hundred thousand barrels of Libyan crude to her sister ship before the first grey hints of dawn rose in the east.

The ten percent left was going to make a fine oil slick when she was scuttled.

Alfred Steinman was dictating to his secretary, standing behind her but slightly to the side so as to get a view through the parting of her blouse, when Ricky's call came through.

'Alfie?' shouted Ricky. 'That Tony at Bigwood's has conned us! I've just had a visit from the heavy mob. My pal Mo is jumpin' up and down, screamin' his head off.'

'What are you telling me?' snapped Alfie.

'They unloaded some gear at Genoa . . .'

'What for?'

'Maybe there's a load of them rag-heads livin' there. Or Ahmed was chisellin' out his whack. How do I know? They opened some cases. What did they find? Only fuckin' breeze blocks! I demand compensation!'

'You signed for the goods.'

'Don't fanny me, Alf. If I don't get paid up, they'll hear the bang on the fuckin' moon. Got me?'

At that, Ricky hung up.

Alfie dismissed the girl at once. He had to be alone to confront the truly disastrous implications.

Kissing goodbye to nine hundred grand was bad enough. But there'd be hints of complicity with a firm he was liquidating. Questions asked at the next creditors' meeting. Tony fired, and squealing. The Fraud Squad called in. And, if that didn't spell certain ruin, there was Ricky storming around like a mad bull and still in possession of the photos.

He looked at his wife and two children smiling trustingly at him from his desktop. They'd ask Stephanie to identify the man in the photos as her husband. At school, Jill and little Amos would hear that their father had been arrested on a fraud charge.

What in Christ's name could he do?

First, cover his traces. Get Tony to pass the fall-back invoice through the books. And destroy all copies of the invoice given to the Brotherton boy.

He unlocked a drawer in his desk and took out the file marked *Transcosmos Trading Ltd / R. Stone*. He reached for the phone. The man should have no trouble getting into the young lad's flat again.

From the shadows, the broad-shouldered Arab in the dark glasses watched the short, fat man cross the court-yard, cast a furtive glance behind him and disappear

222

into the basement of No. 5 Poonah Mansions. He cracked his knuckles and slowly lumbered forward.

From the top of the flight of stairs he saw the man bending over the lock. He seemed to be having some difficulty with his key. The Arab hung back. Let him get inside first. The kind of little chat he wanted didn't need witnesses and took place better in a flat with plenty of soft furnishings to muffle the noises.

He gave it a moment, then followed. The door was on the latch. He stepped inside.

A dark corridor stretched ahead into a dimly lit room where the man was bending over a stack of papers.

The Arab stumbled into a carton. The man whipped round like a startled rabbit. He looked desperately for a weapon. He made a grab for a heavy glass vase.

But the Arab was on him. He cuffed the vase out of his hand and lifted him up bodily by the shirt-front. The man lashed out at his face and managed to wriggle free. He darted across the room and hurled a table lamp. It crashed into the television, shattering the tube. A chair followed, then a plaster bust of Beethoven. The Arab cracked his knuckles louder. He was going to enjoy getting Mr Brotherton to sign.

Simon spent the afternoon with Costas Stefanidis. He arrived home at around six o'clock.

As he approached the entrance, he noticed to his horror a trail of blood leading down the steps into his flat. The door was ajar and smeared with bloody hand-prints.

He kicked it open and listened.

There was no sound.

He snapped on the light. A scene of devastation met him.

The blood led down the hall to the sitting room. Chairs lay smashed, tables overturned, mirrors and pictures shattered, the sofa was blood-marked and the phone ripped out. In the bedroom the wall hangings were down and the bedding was rumpled and stained with blood. He went into the bathroom. Gore spattered and blotched the white tiles surrounding the bath and basin.

Then, behind him, he heard a footstep.

He spun round.

In the doorway, his shoulders filling the frame, stood an olive-skinned man in dark glasses.

'Mr Brotherton,' he said. 'At last.'

At seven-thirty, Ricky received a call from Mo.

'I have to inform you,' said Mo, 'that Ahmed has taken steps to reclaim the cargo of oil. Mr Brotherton's signature to the transfer of title has just been obtained.'

Before Ricky could ask more, Mo had rung off.

Apoplectic with fury, he rang Simon's number. It was engaged. He rang incessantly but couldn't get through.

There would be murders, *real* murders. First he'd do Simon, the cowardly little prick. Then Alfie, the swindling bastard. Then Mo, the two-faced Judas. Then Ahmed, then Gadaffi, then the whole rest of the bleedin' world.

He'd lost the oil. He'd been done out of a fortune.

Billy lay on a towelling bench beside the pool while a buxom girl manicured his nails. Beside him stood a television on a trolley. A Princess Di look-alike was announcing the news: the teachers' strike, another victim of the masked rapist, the continuing siege of Hunter Street. Billy was more interested in contemplating the girl's cleavage. He was just wondering how far she'd really go when his attention was caught by an item in the bulletin.

'Fears that the Gulf War is spreading,' said the announcer, 'were fuelled last night by an incident in the north Indian Ocean. An oil tanker, the Aphrodite, was sunk after an explosion ripped a hole in her side. First reports suggest an attack by Iraqi jets equipped with Exocet missiles . . .'

Billy sat up, howling as the cuticle knife jabbed him. He turned to his burly black bodyguard.

'You hear that, Winston? That's our ship! I lent nine hundred fuckin' grand on that oil! 'Ere, give me the phone.'

He dialled first Ricky, then Simon. Both were engaged. He hurled the set on the floor.

'Get the motors out!' he yelled. 'I'll take care of Rick. You get over to Putney and sort out that young ponce.'

Martha took an hour and a half crossing London. The journey from Islington to East Putney involved three changes of tube and a bus at the end. It was too bad if the wine got warm.

The evening was mild and she was in no hurry. She wasn't even sure if Simon was in. She'd called repeatedly, then rung the operator and been told the line was out of order.

She reached Poonah Mansions at half past eight. It was quite likely he was out to supper, or had someone round. If so, she'd just leave the bottle with a note. His postcard of Portsmouth Promenade had been forwarded from the squat and arrived only that morning. Of course he didn't know her new address. It sounded as if he'd pulled off his big deal at last. She hoped his triumph would make it easier for him to bear the news she had to break.

As she turned the corner into the courtyard, she was aware of a beefy, coloured man just behind her. He followed her down the steps to the basement.

As she reached for the bell, a black hand closed over her mouth.

Rape! she thought at once.

She reacted violently, instinctively. She sank her teeth into the hand and twisted free.

'Simon!' she screamed.

The man let out a grunt of pain and grabbed her shoulder. Her jacket ripped. Something from her

Aerobics and Consciousness class came back to her now. She caught hold of his lapel in her left hand and, using his own weight, spun him towards her. As he toppled forward, she gripped the bottle in her right hand and brought it crashing down on the back of his head. The bottle shattered and the man sank to the ground with a guttural cry.

The door flew open and Simon stood there, aghast.

'Who is it?' called Beryl through the door.

'Billy.'

'Oh, Billy. Come in.'

She opened up.

'Rick at home?'

'Everyone's wantin' Ricky all of a sudden! Popular ain't in it!'

'I said, is Rick at home?'

'No, pet. He's gone up to see young Sime. He was in a right foul mood, too. The effin' and blindin'! I'd keep clear, if I was you.'

But Billy was already hurrying down the path to his car

Right, said Ricky to himself as he drew up outside Poonah Mansions. I won't lose my bottle, I won't break his face, I won't shove his teeth in, I won't stuff his Hampton up his Khyber. I'll be nice and cool and collected and just ask him, why? *Why did you sign our oil away, you fuckin' berk?*

Before he got out of the car, he took another four pills. A ton wouldn't do any good in his state.

As he went down the stairs he saw a trail of blood. Suddenly he realised: that Arab villain had done the poor kid over! He'd beaten him into signing! He hurried down. The door was covered in bloody hand-marks. On the floor lay a broken bottle and other signs of a struggle.

He rang the bell and hammered on the door.

Simon threw it open.

He was unharmed. Not a scratch nor a bruise.

'What the fuck is goin' on?' demanded Ricky.

'Come in,' said Simon. 'Join the party.'

'Don't give me Join the party, just give me an effin' reason! What you done, givin' our oil away . . . ?'

Fuming, he followed Simon into the flat. His eyes widened in disbelief. Someone had been having a right set-to there. The place had been done over good and proper. Blood and broken furniture everywhere. But there was not a hair out of place on Simon.

On the sofa sat Martha, white-faced, nursing a mug of tea.

'Whisky?' offered Simon. 'You missed the wine. It was a knock-out.'

The young girl was *smiling*!

Ricky shook his head in total bewilderment.

'Am I off my loaf? What's goin' on? This a wake, or what?'

Simon looked at his watch.

'Hang on three minutes,' he said, 'and you'll see.'

The pips heralded the nine o'clock news. Simon turned up the volume on the small transistor radio.

The teachers had issued an ultimatum. A nurse had been assaulted by the masked rapist of Ripon. In London, the siege of Hunter Street continued. Overseas, in the Indian Ocean, a tanker had been attacked and sunk.

'. . . no official confirmation from Baghdad . . . the tanker sank without loss of life . . . a ship in the area took off the crew . . .'

Simon turned off the radio.

'*That* ship was another of Costas' tankers, the *Poseidon*. And the crew wasn't all she took off.' He handed Ricky a document. 'Here's a copy of her bills of lading. You'll see she is carrying a cargo of oil. About two hundred and seventy thousand barrels. Look at the bottom and you'll see who it belongs to.'

Ricky stared.

'Transcosmos Tradin'!' he exclaimed. 'Sime, will you please . . .'

'Listen. I made a deal with Costas. The *Aphrodite* was on her last sea-legs. He could have sold her, but there's over-capacity in the market and she'd have fetched bugger all. So, he thought, why not arrange a small accident and claim the insurance on the hull?'

'Disgraceful,' muttered Martha.

'But what a waste of the oil! Why not offload most of it first and claim on the insurance for that as well? OK, so what happens? The *Aphrodite* meets up with another tanker, the *Poseidon*, and transfers the bulk of her cargo. They fix explosives below the water-line and down she goes, leaving a bloody great slick to prove the oil goes with her. The *Poseidon* does her mercy bit rescuing the crew and then sails on her merry way down to South Africa with our lovely oil on board. So you see, when that thug came round, I wasn't too upset about signing. Poor Ahmed. He believes his oil is lying at the bottom of the sea. He may try and claim on the insurance, of course, but I'm afraid if it's shown to be an act of war . . .'

'Amazin'!' breathed Ricky.

'Amazingly crooked,' said Martha.

'At this very moment, the *Poseidon* is four or five days away from Durban. As soon as she offloads, we will receive thirty-four dollars a barrel, in cash, in Switzerland. And of course there's no Ahmed to take a slice off the top.'

Ricky stood back and shook his head.

'You're an effin' miracle, Sime!'

Simon looked across at Martha.

'It was Martha's brilliant criminal brain that did it,' he said with an ironic smile. 'Back red *and* black, she said. So I did.'

'Don't involve me in your swindle,' she said coldly.

'Come on, Martha . . .'

'Leave her,' said Ricky. 'She don't appreciate big business. OK, Sime, what's the final figure? And we ain't cuttin' that Mo in, either.'

'After Costas' whack, I reckon we'll end up with about nine hundred grand each.'

'Christ Al-bleedin'-mighty!'

There was a ring on the doorbell.

'That'll be Billy,' said Simon.

'Or Winston with a headache,' said Martha.

Ricky grabbed Simon's sleeve.

'What about Billy's whack?' he hissed.

'Nine hundred each, I said. That's for the three of us.'

17

£905,240.67p to be exact.

Simon picked up twenty-five grand in cash at a branch of the Union Bank of Switzerland in the City. He took a taxi straight to the property agents in Mayfair and paid the balance on the farmhouse in Tuscany.

His dream had actually and finally come true.

He sat over a watery expresso in a cafe opposite, still numb with disbelief.

He was a rich man. He'd won the prize. He could do anything he wanted. Travel on scheduled airlines at full price, not on charter flights through bucket shops. Go to any restaurant and not even glance at the price column. Buy any paints and canvases, go to any shows or clubs, swim and sunbathe on any beach he fancied. He need never see a final demand again, never grovel to his bank manager or lie awake at night worrying if he'd displeased his boss or how to get rid of forty thousand pairs of shrinking jeans. He'd never go cold or hungry, never get drenched in a bus queue, never gaze into a car showroom and turn sadly away. Overnight, all life's anxieties and frustrations had evaporated.

But suddenly he felt very lonely.

What was all this worth, without the person you loved to share it with?

It had all come out that night, after Ricky and Billy left.

Martha had been gentle but aloof. She'd kept her distance, as if afraid of some violation of her body space.

She'd told him she cared about him and his happiness. Yes, she loved him.

'How?' he'd demanded. 'As a friend or a lover?'

'As a close and dear friend.'

'You don't fancy me any more, you mean.'

'Simon, it goes deeper than that.'

'But we were wonderful lovers!'

'The physical is just one component. It's not enough if the rest isn't right.'

'I'll *make* it right! I have all the time and money anyone could dream of. In Italy, there'll be none of the aggro and hassles. I'll be a different person.'

'Simon, you couldn't be, even if you tried. I realised that tonight. I couldn't live with a man like you. You're entirely amoral.'

He'd launched into a tirade of self-justification, but the words fell emptily like spent cartridges around him.

It was hopeless. The mould was broken, the spark dead. The will and the energy to try even just once again were simply no longer present. In her mind, Martha had moved on.

And in deed, too.

She'd then told him about Roger. How she'd left the squat before the siege and had been living with him in Islington since then. How he was everything she wanted. Not as exciting, perhaps, nor as good a lover. But their views meshed, their interests coincided and they shared the same set of values and ambitions. Roger was definitely not amoral.

In the early hours, she'd rung for a taxi and left. He'd sat on the bed, looking at the photographs of her smiling at him from every shelf and top, and wept.

He'd lost the girl who gave his life its meaning. The television set had turned from colour back to monotone.

Ricky had fifty grand cabled across.

He went on a round of settling debts. He gave Morris ten, getting him to swear on his mother's life to pass it

231

on to Lucy. He slipped Bert, the caretaker at the club, a couple of grand as a thank-you for looking after him when times were bad. He could forget Billy's ten grand: doubling his nine hundred in under three weeks, Billy wasn't going to be petty. Ricky paid nine to William Hill's, six to a private bookie, a couple here and a couple there, and the fifty grand was soon gone.

For the first time in his life, Ricky Stone owed no man a penny.

That was not to say he didn't owe certain companies. He was, after all, still an undischarged bankrupt. But he wasn't going to lose sleep over that. He'd never be coming back, whatever the boys down the club predicted, and where he was going he wouldn't be needing tick.

He ordered a new Merc, left-hand drive. He bought a new set of golf clubs and golfing gear. Over a massage at Billy's, he discussed the merits of Spain versus the South of France, and the next day he paid the deposit on an apartment in a brand new de-luxe development overlooking the bay of St Tropez.

It was going to be sunshine and feet up all the way.

No more aggro. No more ducking and diving, screaming and shouting. No more charleying Melvyn into taking gear he didn't want, no more blanks from Eli and Abby, no more rucks with Chapati Joe and Spaghetti Jim, no more haggling with Chris the Crisp and Walter and Terry, no more broken biscuits and broken watches, no more dodgy jeans and dicky shoes . . .

Wasn't life going to be just a little empty?

Not if you had company.

Sonia looked like Miss World, 1966. Her hair was bouffed up in a beehive and she wore a low-cut woollen dress with a string of pearls that traced the line of her bolstered breasts and disappeared down her cleavage. She drank her tea with her little finger stuck daintily out and held her angel cake so as not to get crumbs under her long painted fingernails. All of this she did with her right hand. Her left lay on the tablecloth between them. Not for touching, as Ricky quickly discovered, more somehow for *show*.

He stabbed a blunt finger at the brochure spread out on the table.

'Lift, porter, underground parkin',' he recited. 'All new chandeliers and antique dinin' table. Balcony over the harbour, what did I tell you? And do me a favour, just look at that view! Beautiful!'

The hand on the table waggled at him.

'Our bedroom,' he went on. 'King size double! We'll have a few right good scenes there, doll.'

'Ssh!' she hissed. 'People can hear.'

'They shouldn't be listenin',' he responded.

He looked around the hushed tearoom. Heads turned quickly back to their timid, whispered conversations.

'Ricky . . .'

'They can mind their own business,' he went on more loudly.

'*Ricky!*' This time she held her left hand under his nose. 'Can't you see something? Do I have to say it?'

'I like your perfume, doll.'

'Not that. The *ring*.'

He leaned back and squinted. There, on the fourth finger, was a bleedin' great Koh-i-noor. Suddenly it all made sense.

He swallowed hard.

'Who's the lucky geezer?'

'His name's Bernard.'

'What happened to Charles?'

'He's Bernard Charles. He has a chain of hairdressing salons.' Her eyes softened. 'I'm sorry, Ricky.'

He looked hard at her. She was a decent sort, really. But maybe she wasn't for him. She deserved better. He'd treated her rough. After all that carry-on with Beryl, he couldn't blame her. The geezer would probably make her very happy.

233

When he took her hand this time, she didn't withdraw it.

'I wish you well, doll,' he said. 'A kiss for the bride?'

He leant forward and gave her a noisy smacker that echoed around the walls of the tea room.

She blushed and looked down at the tablecloth.

'I'll never forget you, Ricky,' she said quietly. 'Other men won't ever quite . . . measure up.'

Alfie settled into one of the dimly lit, plush cubicles at the Lamplighter Club and beckoned over a topless waitress.

'Now *this* place has the right idea,' he said. 'All girls, and every one a goer.'

Ricky pulled a long face as the waitress left with their order.

'Can't afford your tastes, Alf. I'm potless.'

'The whole Bigwood's deal was a fiasco,' agreed Alfie. 'And then the tanker gets blown up. That's too unlucky. I suppose there's always the insurance.'

Ricky made his face even longer and shook his head.

'An act of war, Alf me old china. I hope you've got somethin' up your sleeve for me, 'cos we're right back to square one, you and me.'

Alfie leaned forward.

'Suppose I was to get you discharged.'

'From bankrupt? How can you do that?'

'Let's say, I have some influence with the creditors. They might be persuaded. On humanitarian grounds.'

'I have paid my debt to society,' said Ricky piously. 'So what's the deal?'

'That, in return for the you-know-whats.'

Ricky affected to ponder.

'You're a right hard nut, Alf,' he said grudgingly. 'But all right. You get me discharged, *then* you get the snaps.'

Alfie hesitated, then stretched out his hand.

'Done.'

Simon went with the small removals van up to Islington. Inside was everything out of the flat, from the kelims to the cats. It felt like travelling to hospital with a terminally ill friend, a sad, one-way journey.

Martha was alone when he arrived. The house was semi-derelict and she and Roger were rebuilding it with their own hands, a room at a time as they found the money. She was glad of the stuff but insisted on paying for it.

'Please,' he implored. 'It's really nothing.'

'It's the principle, Simon.'

He flared up.

'Sod principles! Can't I give you a present?'

'Gifts imply obligations.'

'A present *without strings*! All right, then, give me fifty quid.'

Whoops, down a snake again.

She was right. Their value-patterns just didn't match. How could he put it without sounding patronising? Goodness knew what she'd say when she found out about the money he'd lodged in her account and learned that the deeds to Poonah Mansions had been transferred into her name. At least he'd be in Italy and he wouldn't have to face the kangaroo court. Couldn't he simply *share* his good fortune with her without committing a political crime? How would Moral Roger do it? Simon looked around at the chipped plaster and peeling wallpaper. Of course, that situation would never arise. There was no money or possessions to be divisive about. Their poverty ensured their ideological purity. Skint equals good, rich equals bad: the same old dreary equation, born of resentment.

'Have it your own way,' he said with pique.

She laid a hand on his arm.

'Try and see it from the other side. You arrive with a lorry-load of charity . . .'

He opened the front door.

'Martha,' he said wearily, 'give the bloody stuff away. What about all those people they've kicked out of the squat? They could use a few sticks of furniture.'

'Forgive me,' she said more gently. 'I was over-reacting. It's kind and thoughtful of you, and we'll both be really grateful. But are you sure you won't miss it in Italy?'

'There's only one thing I'll miss in Italy.' He looked into her dark eyes and felt the familiar lump rising in his throat. His hand faltered on the door jamb. 'We had a good time together, you and I, huh?'

'A fine time. Better than I make it sound.'

'Don't only think of the rows. Remember the good times too. Think well of us. In our own funny way, we were quite wonderful.'

'I'll forget nothing, Simon. Some things will never be quite the same.'

He fought down the welling pain.

'Well, come and stay in Italy one day. Both of you.'

'Goodbye, Simon. And good luck.'

Ricky looked at his watch. The car would be there at any moment. He felt in his inside pocket to check his passport. Three large suitcases were lined up in the hallway, looking like three hundred in the mirrors.

Beryl came down the hall with a parcel wrapped in silver foil.

'Tuck this in your bag, pet. They don't feed you properly on them planes.'

'Beryl, how am I goin' to pack that lot in?'

'They won't know how you have to have your nosh either,' she said.

She took back the parcel, knelt down and began opening a suitcase. Ricky caught her by the arm and lifted her to her feet. Her eyes were filled with tears, smudging the mascara. She tried to look away.

'Change your mind, doll,' he coaxed.

She shook her head.

'No, Rick. You got a life out there. You need your freedom. I'd only be in your way.'

'But we're a team, right?'

'We was a team once. That was with the Ricky Stone I knew.'

She fumbled for a handkerchief in her sleeve. He put out a hand but she avoided his touch.

'We've been through a rough patch, that's all, doll. Plenty of people do, then they get together again. A few weeks in the sun and I'd be the same old Ricky you ever knew, ruckin' and shoutin' . . .'

She managed a laugh through her sobs.

'And leavin' the place like a hurricane's hit it.' She sniffed. 'No, pet. This is my home. I'll stay put. You go. Enjoy yourself. You're young enough. Have who you want, and no rucks from me.'

Footsteps came up the path.

'There's the cab,' she said, pushing him towards the door.

'I'll miss you, doll,' he said.

'Hurry up or you'll be late for your plane.'

Ricky and Simon met at the bar in the Departures lounge at Terminal 2. A harvest sun was setting behind the distant hangars, spreading a bluish evening haze over the runways.

Simon ordered champagne while Ricky went to the duty free shop for booze and fags. Simon gave him his boarding card and asked him to get a bottle of brandy at the same time.

Simon handed him a glass of champagne when he returned.

'Here's to us,' he said.

'We did it!' grinned Ricky.

They drank. The bottle grew emptier. Ricky insisted on buying another. The flights were called. Nice from Gate 14, Pisa from Gate 30. Plenty of time, said Ricky, refilling their glasses.

'What a team!' toasted Simon.

. 'They couldn't see us comin'!' agreed Ricky.

They chinked glasses again.

'So, when are you coming over to see me?' asked Simon. 'We'll go to Florence and Sienna and have a really good time. I'm picking up my Merc at the airport tonight. We can cruise around in convoy. Just make sure you don't lose the address.'

Ricky slipped a card out of his top pocket.

'Somethin' or other, Poggibonsi,' he read. 'What kind of a hole is that? 'Ere, you slip over to San Tropay. They have whole beaches they go topless! You won't do no good for crumpet in Poggibonsi.'

'Oh, I dunno. A painter must have his models.'

A puzzled frown passed over Ricky's face, then suddenly cleared.

'You mean, paintin' *pictures*, like in museums?'

Final calls were announced.

Ricky poured more champagne.

'Paint me one, Sime,' he said. 'To go over the mantelpiece in the livin' room. Somethin' romantic.'

'An English landscape?'

'Nah! I don't want to be reminded of that poxy weather. No, a silver beach with palm trees and blue sea . . .'

'But in St Tropez . . .'

'Would the last remaining passenger for Nice go immediately to Gate 14 . . .'

'That's it, Sime,' he said, standing up.

Simon held out his hand.

'So long, Ricky. It was really great!'

'See you, kid. Don't forget that picture.'

Simon watched as he stepped jauntily towards the departure gates. Slowly he picked up his briefcase.

'Would the last remaining passenger for Pisa . . .'

Suddenly he realised Ricky had still got his boarding card.

He caught up with him at a junction in the corridors. Ricky was squinting at the gate number on his own card. Simon read it for him.

'Thirty,' he said. He grabbed the other card and looked

238

at the number on it. 'I'm down the other way. Better run! Take care, Ricky.'

'You too, kid,' Ricky called back.

And the two men separated and hurried to their planes.

Ricky sat in the first class cabin, wondering how long the stewardess was stopping in Nice for. Her name was Valerie, she came from Newcastle and she'd given up a beautician's job to travel.

'*On your left,*' the captain was saying, '*you can see Mont Blanc. We are on schedule to land at Pisa at eight-fifty, local time . . .*'

But Ricky had eyes and ears for Valerie alone.

'Val,' he began, 'know San Tropay, do you?'

Simon sat in the economy cabin, staring out at the moonlit Alps and wondering why no-one had ever painted aerial landscapes. He looked in his briefcase for pencil and paper and found only some felt-tips and an accountant's analysis pad. First thing he'd do in the morning would be to stock up on materials. Poggibonsi would be sure to have an art shop.

The stewardess came by with the duty free trolley. She quickly lost interest when she saw he'd bought his duty frees already.

He delved again in his briefcase. Calculator, business school address book, company notepaper . . . What did he need all this crap for now?

He began ripping it up, tearing it into ever-smaller pieces and jamming them into the net pouch on the back of the seat in front. The man next to him, with whom he'd had a primitive conversation in his school French, began chattering loudly as if humouring a child with a contagious insanity.

And so it was that Simon missed the captain's announcement that they were flying at 31,000 feet, the weather *en route* was good and the temperature in Nice was a pleasant twenty-two degrees.

239

It was all Frog to Ricky.

He took his first exploratory steps into his new native language. *Dogana* said *Customs* underneath. *Controllo di passaporti*, well, that was easy, and *riclama di bagagli* was obviously something to do with baggage. The porters had *portieri* written on their caps and *Taxi* meant taxi. It wasn't going to be so hard to master the lingo.

As he was following the porter to the limo that would be waiting, he stopped dead in his tracks. Through the blur of champagne, beer, wine, brandy and sweet Martini, he saw a man holding up a sign-board with the name *Mr S. Brotherton* on it.

Had Sime sneaked aboard the flight too? He looked about him, but there was no sign of the young kid.

Puzzled, he approached the man. The man's face lit up.

'Signor Brotherton? I have your Mercedes outside.'

Through a haze of champagne and red wine, Simon pieced together what the man next to him was saying. The food in London was *affreux* and he couldn't wait to get a *salade niçoise* inside him. The poor chap was going to have a devil of a time in Pisa. Perhaps he should let him have his Italian For Beginners tapes, but then they were half in English.

There seemed to be quite a colony of French in Pisa, he thought as he stood waiting for his luggage in the arrivals hall. Probably something to do with the Crusades, or perhaps Caesar conquering Gaul.

He was standing in the public concourse, looking for a man with a sign-board, when his eye fell upon the signs for the airport buses.

Autocars vers centre ville, he read.

He looked around.

Tabac. Départs. Location de voitures.

It was the definitive *Bienvenue à Nice* that finally did it.

The Merc had to be signed for. Ricky signed. He took the keys. What was he to do? The airport was closing down for the night.

He felt in his top pocket.

Where the hell was Poggibonsi?

Lights were going out all over the airport. Simon stood alone among his suitcases. Algerian cleaners wandered by, sweeping up cigarette butts and luggage tags. The departure indicator board whirred and flipped and finally went blank.

He was stranded.

A man in a blue suit and a chauffeur's cap had been eyeing him for a while. He now came forward.

'Monsieur Stone?' he enquired. 'St Tropez?'

Simon broke into an idiotic grin. And where was Ricky? Off to Poggibonsi?

He turned to the driver.

'*Allons-y*,' he said.

241

18

Ricky woke with a violent start to find a wrinkled face staring at him, just inches away. The mouth was moving but he couldn't hear the words.

Where was he? He sat up sharply and banged his head. He was in a car. What was he doing in a *car*? Who was this man? What was that pile of ruins behind him? Gradually it all came back.

He lowered the window. An incomprehensible gabble greeted him.

'Bonjour, Jim,' he began.

The walnut-faced peasant stopped abruptly, then broke into a gold-toothed grin.

'*SprechenSie Italiano?*'

'Not a bleedin' word, mate.'

Ricky got out slowly and stretched. His golf-swing muscles howled with pain. His neck wouldn't straighten. His mouth felt like last night's fish and chip paper. The harsh dawn sunlight hurt his eyes. Squinting, he looked about him.

Ahead lay a derelict farmhouse. Plants grew from the crumbling stone walls and hens picked and pecked among the fallen tiles that littered the courtyard. Here and there a rusty corrugated iron sheet was tacked up across bare rafters, and on the far side a door swung in the breeze on a solitary hinge.

Was *this* what the wet-eared ponce had been raving on about?

He turned back to the walnut face.

'You look a bright sort. Tell me, where can I get a nice cuppa?'

The man's face went blank. Ricky spoke more loudly, more slowly.

'A cup of tea. Tea. Stuff you have with milk and sugar. Never heard of tea? No wonder you mob lost the war.' He tried again. '*Tea*. Like coffee. Café.'

'Café? Si, signor . . . !'

A whole lot more gobbledegook poured out. Then the little old man pincered Ricky by the elbow and pointed back down the track.

'*Ein kilometer*,' he shouted.

'Ein kilometer,' repeated Ricky. 'Danke shon, me old china.'

He got back into the Merc and reversed down the dusty path.

What was going on? You woke up in the middle of Italy and there was some old geezer spouting Yiddish at you. Thank God for the English Channel. Anyone who went south of Dover needed his loaf examined.

Simon was woken by a pneumatic drill hammering immediately above his head. In a chink of sunlight through the curtainless windows he watched a small flake of plaster float down from the ceiling. The juddering grew louder. He fancied a crack was appearing. He rolled off the bed and hobbled stiffly to the bathroom. He'd been sleeping fully dressed, wrapped in a cashmere coat he'd found in one of Ricky's suitcases, for there were no sheets or blankets in the place.

A cockroach scuttled away among the builders' dust. The lavatory wouldn't flush. There was no water to wash with, either. He picked up the phone to find out about flights to Pisa but it wasn't connected. Desolate, he looked about him.

The window panes still bore their whitewashed crosses. Peering out beyond the scaffolding, masked by the walls of the apartments on either side, he could see a tiny sliver of blue sea, so narrow that only the yachts on the horizon were visible complete from stem to stern.

So this was Ricky's fabulous pad with its views over St Tropez harbour.

Shivering and aching, he rooted about in the suitcase for something fresh to wear. In one case he came across a pair of thick golfing socks bulging with banknotes like Christmas stockings. In the other, a small silver-foil parcel had burst open and bits of pickled cucumber lay stuck to a silk dressing gown. He tried on a sweatshirt but it came below his knees.

He sat down on the bed, his head thumping painfully as the drilling upstairs grew still louder. This wasn't what he'd had in mind at all.

'*Mille,*' said the barman.

He wrote the figure on a paper napkin.

'A *thousand*?' exclaimed Ricky. 'Some bleedin' rip-off joint, this!'

He peeled off a thousand franc note. The barman looked at it oddly. He seemed about to hand it back, then put it swiftly in the till. He put two short glasses on the zinc bar and pulled out a bottle of some clear yellowish liquid. It turned milky when he added water.

Ricky sniffed it and nearly threw up. What kind of dump was this where they drank aniseed balls for breakfast? He looked in a glass cabinet at a plate of dry bread rolls filled with leathery ham, then saw the price. Five hundred! There must be a big market for wheelbarrows here, to carry money around in. Flies were copulating on the ham. He looked away. Right now, he'd give a wheelbarrowful for Beryl's little parcel of salt beef and cucumber sandwiches.

First he'd pay his morning visit, then get to the nearest decent town, find a Hilton and book a flight to Nice. He crossed the bar, already full of old men drinking and smoking, to a door marked with the Gents symbol.

Three seconds later he was out and on his way to the

car. Call *that* a khazi? Typical of them Eyeties: build the hole and then stop.

She was giving him the eye. Simon glanced behind him to check it wasn't someone else she meant. No, it was him. She had long blonde hair, a Brigitte Bardot mouth and the best legs he'd ever seen. He was going to enjoy himself in St Tropez, waiting for Ricky to turn up. Maybe he could repay him the favour. *Wait till you see the bird I've got sorted out for you, Ricky! A real peach. Right up your alley.*

He called a waiter to offer her a drink. The man went off with a barely concealed smile.

The blonde acknowledged the drink with a long, sultry glance from beneath her eyelashes and let her tongue play suggestively around the rim of the glass. Simon felt the heat rise a degree. He'd have a leak, pay the bill and take her back to Ricky's pad for a siesta. With any luck the pneumatic driller would be having one too.

He was standing at the urinal when he heard the door open. An exotic scent wafted in. A moment later he felt a hand on his bum. He turned to protest: they couldn't do it there! As she pressed her lips to his, his hand brushed the front of her tight skirt. He touched something strange, lumpy . . . not a handbag . . .

He sprang back, choking. He looked down and saw the unmistakable bulge.

This was no woman.

He stumbled out into the daylight and, brushing past the tables, made for the open street. There, heedless of the waiter's yells, he broke into a panic-stricken run. Dodging the traffic and knocking over postcard stands, he bolted through the crowds as though the Devil himself were at his heels.

There was no Hilton at Pisa, and the only thing grand about the Grand Hotel was the prices. You could tell the

Mafia ran the gaff. It was one price for the locals, another for the tourists. They didn't even try and hide the fact: you saw *menu turistico* written up everywhere. Seven hundred for a coffee! A fiver for a thimbleful of tar? Bleedin' daylight robbery! He'd pay a fiver not to drink the crap.

Ricky looked about him in the dingy hotel lounge. In a corner sat several short, fat women dressed in black, all jabbering at once. At another table was a pair of girls, one thin and the other spotty. Anyone who took two looks at the draks in this country was greedy! The place had gone right downhill since Gina Lollobrigida. His Beryl could knock spots off any of 'em, corset or no corset. She had class, too, in her way. Take her anywhere and she'd do you proud.

'But jealousy's a terrible thing, Beryl,' he said aloud to himself. 'It's a disease. Eats people up. If you weren't the jealous sort, doll, you'd be the best woman in the world.'

He went back to the car. The sooner he got to St Tropez the better. A few topless beaches would cure his homesickness.

Simon wasn't going to stay another minute in that city. Too bad if Ricky turned up with his new Merc after he'd left. The question was how to get to the farmhouse. Should he hire a car and drive, or fly?

He'd fly. He stopped a taxi and asked the fare to the airport, but decided to take the bus. Count the pennies and the pounds take care of themselves. Getty had a payphone in his house.

It was already late afternoon and there was no connecting flight. Rome, Milan, Turin, yes; Pisa, no.

Flights arrived and departed. Beautiful people greeted and waved off other beautiful people, but Simon had no appetite for them. As he sat in the cafeteria, he was swamped by a desperate feeling of loneliness. He was an exile, and all alone. This new life had made sense when planning to share it with Martha. But what was it really going to be like? Eating supper every night in some romantic trattoria deep in the Tuscan hills with only *Teach Yourself Italian* for company . . . ?

He looked about him. People, people everywhere but not a face he knew. He began to yearn to see someone familiar. Anyone. Even if Julian Wetherby were to walk through the arrivals gate at that moment, he'd have embraced him. In his mind he went through the girls back home. Louise. Francesca. Marian. Charlotte. Susanne. Carol.

Carol, the promotions girl. Now *she* was a sport. And unfinished business too.

Ricky left the Merc in the airport car park with Simon's luggage in the boot. Inside, he stood for a while beneath the Departures board. He couldn't get his eye off the word LONDRA. As he watched, it seemed to transform itself into BERYL.

He'd hardly been away twenty-four hours, yet he missed the old girl. Think what she must be feeling right now. How could he do it to her? She'd played fair, she hadn't cheated on him, she'd been true to her word. Of course she was jealous, but hadn't he given her cause? Things just didn't seem right without her. No-one else knew how he liked his nosh, no-one else made him feel a man the way she did. He even missed the rucks. She was still a peach, too. But most of all, she was his woman – always had been and always would be. It was no fun going off on your own, leaving your woman behind with the heartache.

He bought a ticket to London. He paid from his roll of currency. It came to about twenty cups of coffee.

'Carol? Simon Brotherton. Remember me?'

''Ullo, Simon!' she squealed. 'Thought you wasn't talkin' to me since that time. T'riffic to hear you, Simon. You at home?'

'I'm in Nice.'

The line crackled.

'Neasden? What you doin' there? Listen, fancy comin' over? My girlfriend's out tonight. Promise I won't pass out on you.'

Simon bit his lip.

Just then, the public address system began an announcement. *Depart destination Londres . . .*

He looked at his watch.

'I'll be there around eight.'

He put the phone down with a silent whoop. Carol, topless, would knock spots off any of the beautiful people down here. And anyway, it was far easier to get to Pisa from London.

Alitalia #807 from Pisa landed at Terminal 2 at 7.15 p.m. Air France #550 from Nice landed five minutes later.

Due to building work to the piers, the Alitalia flight drew up on the tarmac. The passengers were to be bussed to the terminal building.

The Air France flight was packed with Brits and the queue at the UK passports counter moved slowly.

Steps were in short supply, and the Alitalia passengers had to wait five minutes before they could disembark.

Simon went smoothly through passport control and headed for the exit. He looked at his watch. Sod it, it would have to be a taxi.

Ricky lit a cigarette in the bus as they waited for it to fill and was told off by the driver. He stamped it out irritably. You were a first class citizen in the air but a prole on the ground.

Simon's taxi queue inched forward, under the bossy eye of a female parking warden.

Ricky watched, fuming, as a geriatric on sticks refused a wheelchair and struggled painfully to board the bus. The one behind was already driving off. He found some Italian chewing gum which had cost him an arm and a leg. It tasted of aniseed and he spat it out.

Simon coughed in the taxi diesel fumes. A dispute had arisen ahead among a group of white-robed Arabs. The queue ground to a standstill.

Ricky pushed his way to the head of the passport control line. The officer scrutinised his face, checked a black book, checked it a second time, then reluctantly waved him past. He strode off towards the exit.

It was a dapper businessman first, a sun-tanned holiday couple next, and then it was Simon's turn.

Effin' queues! stormed Ricky. That's the trouble with this bleedin' country. They're all sheep. Got no initiative. Skirting the queue, he slipped quickly down the far side of the line of waiting taxis and picked the one three from the front. He flashed the driver a twenty pound note.

'Norwood, mate,' he said.

The driver looked at the note, then at the warden, then back at the note.

'Hop in, guv.'

Ricky got in. Just as the taxi began to pull away, the warden stepped out in its path and opened the door.

'Next,' she called.

A young man began climbing in.

'Sorry, pal,' said Ricky brusquely. 'It's taken.'

'But it's my *turn*,' protested the man.

'Christ Almighty . . . *Sime!*'

'*Ricky!* What on earth . . . ?'

The warden had her book out and was about to intervene. Ricky grabbed Simon and pulled him in.

'Get goin', driver,' he shouted.

'You berk!' cried Ricky. 'Giving me the wrong ticket.'

'*You* gave *me* the wrong one!' protested Simon.

'And where's my luggage?'

'You expect me to have brought it back? It's safe in your pad. Anyway, where's my car?'

Ricky pulled out a car-park ticket.

'At that poxy airport. Christ, Sime, you ain't serious about that gaff you bought? I wouldn't put my dog in it.'

'You actually got there? I know it needs restoration.'

'Demolition, more like.'

'I think that's what they're doing on yours. The ceiling's falling down and there's scaffolding all over it . . .'

'I don't give a cobblers!' snorted Ricky. He scuffed the mat. 'Tell you the truth, Sime, I don't go on all this foreign lark. A couple of weeks' golf down Torremolinos, all right, but that Italy – do me a favour! The nosh, the coffee, them *prices* . . . !'

'The girls in France aren't always what they seem, either.'

'There ain't nothin' wrong with this country, boy, except the weather.'

'And the taxes.'

'And queues.'

'Too many people.'

'Too many lefties and not enough grafters.'

Simon looked out of the window and sighed.

'Still, the girls are the best in the world.'

'Job out them Eyeties, Sime. Not a good-looker among 'em.'

'Besides, it's one's roots.'

'It's home, boy, that's what it is. You know, meetin' you like this don't really surprise me. Some things are meant.' A misty look had come over Ricky's eyes. Then he clapped Simon abruptly on the knee. ''Ere, what you doin' tonight? I'm starvin'. We'll all have a spot of nosh at the Pekin' Duck, eh?'

'Actually, I've got a date.'

'You've gone beetroot, boy. Who's the doll?'

'It's, um, Carol.'

'Carol? That's why you come back home! Bring her with!'

Simon thought for a second, then smiled.

'Sure. I will.'

The cab drew up outside Carol's block in Streatham. Simon took out his wallet.

'Let me pay.'

'Nah! What's a measly twenty?'

'Twenty quid?' gulped Simon. 'Then I must. At least go halves.'

'Put it away, boy.'

Simon's tenner hovered half in and half out of the wallet.

'I insist.'

'All right, then.'

Ricky took the note. Simon started. He hadn't expected to be taken seriously. Who would pay for the dinner?

'Down the middle, all the way, right?' he said, getting out.

'Sime, you'll never change. Ten nicker is about one second's interest on your dough. Why be rich and think skint? Don't worry, dinner's on me.'

'No, no, I can't allow that.'

'Careful.'

Simon smiled.

'See you at the restaurant.'

Ricky paid the cab off and stepped out onto the pavement. The trees in Millionaire's Road, Norwood, were already half bare and on the chilly, damp air hung the smell of burning leaves.

He stood at the gate for a long moment, looking at the house as though for the first time. A modest new Metro stood in the concrete car-port, the front door was being repainted, the roses had been dead-headed and the Michaelmas daisies tied back.

In a downstairs window, the curtain stirred.

He could see the outline of Beryl's head but couldn't make out her expression. She was watching him steadily.

What if she wouldn't have him back? Why hadn't he thought to buy flowers, or some perfume at the duty free? He was returning with empty arms, asking her to take him back just as he was.

Drawing a deep breath, he went up the path. He rang on the bell.

For a long time there was no other sign of life than the barking of the Alsatian from the kitchen. Then he heard footsteps and a rattle of locks. The door opened on the chain.

Beryl's dark eyes glowed with suspicion.

'Yeah?' she said. 'Forgotten somethin'?'

He nodded.

'Forgotten you, doll. Let me in, Beryl. Please.'

Her eyes narrowed and she scanned him up and down. For a moment she seemed undecided, then her face imperceptibly softened.

'All right, Ricky Stone,' she said. 'I'll hear you.'

And she unchained the door.

JAMIE REID

EASY MONEY

'Lex can do anything he wants. That's why he's Lex Parlane. A few years ago he even fixed the results of the Grand National.'

'But the Grand National's unique. It's a legend.'

'Lex fixed it just the same.'

That's not all that Lex Parlane fixed . . .

Self-made hard-nosed Glaswegian millionaire Lex sets out on the craziest racing war of all – against the class-ridden antiquated racing establishment. Forming an uneasy alliance with the playboy son of the Senior Steward of the Jockey Club, Lex steers a path through and over crooked jockeys, thuggish gamblers, hapless punters and enticing women in Glasgow, London and Dublin. It's a path few begin and many falter on. But Lex knows only the scent and smell of success . . .

Post·A·Book

A Royal Mail service in association with the Book Marketing Council & The Booksellers Association.

Post-A-Book is a Post Office trademark.

JAMES McCLURE

THE ARTFUL EGG

Someone out there is crazy. Crazy enough to kill a world-famous novelist and then strew her naked body with flower petals and herbs. Or is there method in this madness?

That's the question which tantalises Tromp Kramer and Mickey Zondi, his Zulu partner in the Trekkersburg Murder and Robbery Squad, as they begin an investigation that leads them into an alien world of painters and poets, sculptors and ballet dancers.

Then, to compound the pressure they're under, Kramer is ordered to drop everything until he's cleared up a fatal accident with very embarrassing implications for the police. And then he discovers that this death was no accident . . .

'Mr McClure is an exceedingly skilful writer'
New York Times Book Review

'Kramer and Zondi are two of the most attractive policemen in modern fiction. They are funny, human and vigorous . . . An enjoyable murder mystery and a wry picture of South African life'
The Mail on Sunday

'Sharply observed glimpses of apartheid . . . plus red herrings by the shoal'
Guardian

'A rattling good detective story'
London Standard

CORONET BOOKS

BRYAN FORBES

THE REWRITE MAN

Harvey Burgess is a Hollywood scriptwriter suffering a bad case of professional burn-up. Hoping to rekindle the spark, he answers the SOS of a director stranded in the South of France with a stalled film about the French Revolution. It should have been child's play for a pro like Harvey, but then he hadn't budgeted for his obsession with the mysterious protégée of the director, the very young, very beautiful Laura . . .

'Bryan Forbes has written a very good book indeed, based on all his experience of the film business . . . it's been a long time since I felt such enthusiasm for my bedside reading'

The Mail on Sunday

'A marvellously readable, funny and poignant story . . . Bryan Forbes has created some splendidly living characters, sparkling dialogue and a truly touching novel of obsession and jealousy'

Sunday Express

CORONET BOOKS

ALSO AVAILABLE FROM
HODDER AND STOUGHTON PAPERBACKS